"I appreciate your concern, Sergeant," Lee said. "But it isn't your problem. Really."

That was when she realized that Rock O'Connor hadn't accepted her dinner invitation simply because he wanted to gaze into her eyes over wine and French bread. Standing one step above her, he watched her, his eyes suddenly wary. Before he said a word, she knew she didn't want to hear it.

"I'm afraid it is my problem," he told her in an infuriatingly calm voice.

Lee faced off with him, arms crossed, posture rigid. "And why is that?"

He was at least gentleman enough to step down to her level before facing her. "I wanted to talk to you alone, because I need to find out all I can about the people you know."

Suddenly she couldn't breathe. "Why?"

He didn't even flinch. "Because I think one of them is trying to kill you."

Dear Reader,

Hot weather, hot books. What could be better? This month, Intimate Moments starts off with an American Hero to remember in Kathleen Korbel's *Simple Gifts*. This award-winning author has—as usual!—created a book that you won't be able to put down. You also might have noticed that the cover of this particular book looks a little bit different from our usual. We'll be doing some different things with some of our covers from time to time, and I hope you'll keep your eye out for that. Whenever you see one of our out-of-the-ordinary covers, you can bet the book will be out of the ordinary, too.

The month keeps going in fine form, with *Flynn*, the next installment of Linda Turner's tremendously popular miniseries, "The Wild West." Then check out *Knight's Corner*, by Sibylle Garrett, and *Jake's Touch*, by Mary Anne Wilson, two authors whose appearances in the line are always greeted with acclaim. Finally, look for two authors new to the line. Suzanne Brockmann offers *Hero Under Cover*, while Kate Stevenson gives you *A Piece of Tomorrow*.

I'd also like to take this chance to thank those of you who've written to me, sharing your opinions of the line. Your letters are one of my best resources as I plan for the future, so please feel free to keep letting me know what you think about the line and what you'd like to see more of in the months to come.

As always—enjoy!

Leslie Wainger
Senior Editor and Editorial Coordinator

Please address questions and book requests to:
Reader Service
U.S.: P.O. Box 1325, Buffalo, NY 14269
Canadian: P.O. Box 1050, Niagara Falls, Ont. L2E 7G7

AMERICAN HERO

KATHLEEN KORBEL

SIMPLE GIFTS

Silhouette®

INTIMATE MOMENTS®

Published by Silhouette Books

America's Publisher of Contemporary Romance

SILHOUETTE BOOKS

ISBN 0-373-07571-5

SIMPLE GIFTS

Copyright © 1994 by Eileen Dreyer

This edition published by arrangement with Harlequin Enterprises B. V.

® and TM are trademarks of Harlequin Enterprises B. V., used under
license. Trademarks indicated with ® are registered in the United States
Patent and Trademark Office, the Canadian Trade Marks Office and in
other countries.

Printed in U.S.A.

Books by Kathleen Korbel

Silhouette Intimate Moments

A Stranger's Smile #163
Worth Any Risk #191
Edge of the World #222
Perchance To Dream #276
The Ice Cream Man #309
Lightning Strikes #351
A Rose for Maggie #396
Jake's Way #413
A Walk on the Wild Side #457
Simple Gifts #571

Silhouette Desire

Playing the Game #286
A Prince of a Guy #389
The Princess and the Pea #455
Hotshot #582
A Fine Madness #668
Isn't It Romantic? #703

Silhouette Books

Silhouette Summer Sizzlers 1989
"The Road to Mandalay"
Silhouette Shadows Collection 1993
"Timeless"

KATHLEEN KORBEL

lives in St. Louis with her husband and two children. She devotes her time to enjoying her family, writing, avoiding anyone who tries to explain the intricacies of the computer and searching for the fabled house-cleaning fairies. She's had her best luck with her writing—for which she's garnered a *Romantic Times* award for Best New Category Author of 1987, the 1990 Romance Writers of America Rita award for Best Romantic Suspense and the 1990 and 1992 Rita awards for Best Long Category Romance—and with her family, without whom she couldn't have managed any of the rest. She hasn't given up on those fairies, though.

For Diana, who always gets the really important information for me. Because I'm too cheap to spring for a good lunch.

And for Joyce and Al, who opened their home to me.

Prologue

If Lee tried really hard, she could almost pretend that the skyline of Chicago was a range of mountains. Abrupt, angular, powerful, the buildings reared from the shores of Lake Michigan like a great geologic upheaval at the edge of the plains. Metal and glass instead of rock and dirt, cars instead of cattle. The battering cacophony of humanity instead of the susurrous silence of firs.

Okay, so it wasn't Wyoming. Nothing was. But there were days like today, when Lee could *almost* like Chicago. The sun was so bright it hurt Lee's eyes as it winked off a million windows like shards of a broken mirror. The wind scurried among the buildings and tangled in Lee's hair to send it flying. And the people! Lee could just sit right down here on the sidewalk and watch the—

"Lee, damn it! Stop!"

Lee stopped, just in time. She hadn't even seen the traffic. With a chagrined smile for her companion, who had yanked her to a stop within inches of disaster, she pulled her foot back onto the sidewalk and let the BMW that had blared at her scoot on past.

It even took Lee a minute to remember exactly where they were. She'd been so wrapped up in the beautiful day that she'd let almost twenty blocks go by unnoticed.

"I'm not so sure I should go home," Sierra groused from alongside, her fingers still firmly wound around the strap of Lee's shoulder purse. "The play isn't for three more weeks, and already you're in the ozone."

Lee gave her friend a reassuring grin. "It's not the play," she admitted. "I'm just enjoying the day. I'm pretending I'm home."

Sierra made it a point to look around to include the movement, the noise, the neon and traffic on this bright, warm afternoon. When she turned back to Lee, her soft green eyes were as dry as dust. "Uh-huh. Home. Sure looks like a horse farm to me."

Lee laughed. Sierra was part of the magic of the city. Variety, sass. Color and life. Sierra had skin like chocolate and eyes the color of pale Depression glass. Except for Lee's big sister, Gen, Sierra was Lee's best friend in a place spilling over with new people to meet. After the isolation of a mountain meadow in Wyoming, it was quite a feast. "Imagination, Sierra. You should try it sometime."

"Thanks, girl. It's all I can do to keep track of yours."

Alongside them, the light turned and the Walk sign came on. Neither paid attention. This was where Sierra turned off, walking on to the El stop that would take her home. Lee just needed to head right up LaSalle to Oak and the Memorial Medical Center where she was going to meet her sister, who was due to get off from her shift as senior pediatric resident.

"You do remember where you're going, don't you?" Sierra asked.

Lee gave her a three-point scowl. "I was caught up in the moment, Sierra. Not missing in action. I'll be fine. And thanks for coming along today."

Her friend gave a little wave of her hand, part impatience, part affection. "Shoot, girl. Nobody from my neighborhood gets to go sailin' with the rich folk. I don' mind walkin' you home, if that's the price."

"Thanks," Lee complained. "Now I feel like a six-year-old on a field trip."

"Some field trip. Sequins and champagne last night and sailcloth and gin today." Sierra flashed a sudden grin. "Who says a girl should starve for her art, anyway?"

"A highly overrated notion, to be sure."

Both lifted pinkies in identical salute to the patrons who supported not only their burgeoning careers, but their waistlines as well.

They said their goodbyes. Sierra watched the light, waited with the crowd and headed across, her thick hair shifting with the movement, her grunge jeans and boots making the short woman look more like a boot-camp attendee than an up-and-coming theatrical director.

Lee watched her go. She watched the people on this waning afternoon, locals on the move with heads down and arms full, dodging the tourists with heads back to marvel at the tallest buildings that clustered together in a tight forest just south of the Chicago River. A block away an ambulance wove its way through traffic toward Gen's hospital, its lights strobing, its siren an indignant howl of protest. To the south, clouds piled up in soft white rows that dappled the streets with shade.

Lee remembered how this had all looked like a cubist painting when she'd photographed it from the deck of the sailboat she and Sierra had walked off about twenty blocks earlier. A multichromatic work of art. *Life Descending the Street.*

It was a perfect day. Lee smiled and stepped off the sidewalk.

Someone cried out a warning.

Lee's first thought was that she'd missed the light. For some reason, that was what she checked first.

Nope, it said Walk. She was okay. So she turned, just to be sure. She checked the traffic that was heading toward her on the one-way street. It was safely tucked behind a red light across LaSalle. She didn't see the problem.

She didn't see the problem, because the car that hit her struck from the opposite direction.

Chapter 1

The sky was so blue it hurt her eyes. It hurt everything.

Lee felt so stupid, just lying there in the street in a tangle. She had to let Gen know she was all right. But first, she had to let this crowd know.

"You just lie still now, honey," some woman in a muu-muu was saying as she patted Lee on the arm. "Help's coming."

No, Lee thought inconsequentially. Help was headed the other way. To the hospital. To Gen's hospital. The hospital only five blocks away, and here she was lying in the street with the concrete poking at her back through the gauze of her blouse and a sledgehammer bumping at her head. It hurt.

She hurt all over.

"I'm fine," she said in a voice calm enough to surprise even her. "I get thrown by horses all the time. I'm used to this."

It had felt a little like it, that kaleidoscopic somersault through the air, with faces and buildings and signs all tumbling past her until she'd landed with the kind of thump that knocked the air right out of her.

"Don't call Jake," she said automatically.

"Jake?" somebody retorted from the first row of the growing ring of disaster spectators. Lee wondered if they'd like to pass the time with a little dramatic reading from the Eugene O'Neill play she'd been rehearsing for the last two weeks over at Fandango. "He your husband?"

Her husband.

Oh, Jake. Right.

"No," she said without moving her head. "He's in Wyoming."

He was her brother. Her big brother. The request had been automatic, a holdover from the days she'd really needed to be careful. Every time she'd gone tail over end off a horse. When she'd flunked English that semester in high school. When she'd gotten stranded on a date and had to beg a ride home from one of the neighbors.

Don't call Jake. I don't want him to worry.

She still didn't want him to worry. Jake had worried enough for three lifetimes. Lee was a big girl now. She should handle this all by herself. And if he caught a whiff of this, he'd show up all the way from Wyoming, worrying with that tight little crease right between his eyes that always made her feel so guilty. Besides, this wasn't anything worth worrying about.

Whatever "this" was. Suddenly, lying in the warm afternoon sun with the smell of exhaust and asphalt in her nose and her view limited to belt buckles, bent arms and reflecting sun, Lee wasn't so sure.

"What happened?" she inevitably asked.

"My God," a very nice male voice answered. "Lee? Lee Kendall?"

For a minute Lee was afraid Jake had heard her all the way from Wyoming. But the face that broke through the crowd and hovered up there in her vision wasn't Jake's. This one smiled. At least it did a little.

She knew it. Even upside down, she wouldn't forget a cleft chin like that.

"Dr. LaPierre?" Lee asked, overcoming the absurd impulse to check and see whether her hair was messed up.

His face pivoted until he was pointed the right way, and he smiled again. "My God, I was just headed over to the hospital," he said, crouching down next to her. "What happened?"

"I was going to meet Gen for dinner. I told her this morning when I dropped her at the hospital that I'd be there, and..." Lee looked over to the lady in the muu-muu who still held her hand. "What happened?"

Every one of the woman's chins quivered with indignation. "A hit and run," she pronounced, patting away at Lee's hand as if that would take away some of the outrage. "And driving the wrong way. I think he was drunk."

Dr. LaPierre gently prized Lee's hand away from the woman and surreptitiously began checking for injury. "Did you see him?" he asked.

Lee frowned. "I saw sky and pavement."

"Too bad. Don't move at all until the paramedics get here, okay?"

Lee thought of the picture she must present. She dearly hoped Sierra was already on that train. She didn't want her friend to come running up to find her sprawled in the street, her best pair of khaki twills torn and her tank top shoved half way up her stomach to expose the scrapes Lee was beginning to feel more and more acutely by the minute.

No, she thought. She had no intention of moving. She knew better. And even if she didn't, she wasn't feeling much like jumping back to her feet and dancing off, anyway.

LaPierre's fingers moved gently over Lee's arms and legs as she listened to the approaching wail of help.

"Can you feel my hands?" he asked.

Lee almost giggled. "Under different circumstances, I'd be telling you that you're no gentleman," she informed him.

He had the good grace to smile. "Wiggle your toes."

"Only if you wiggle yours."

She did, anyway. Gen was going to be so jealous. Gen had been the one doing the surreptitious mirror check the last time Dr. Timothy LaPierre, orthopedist extraordinaire, had been called in to set the bones of one of the young patients at the hospital. Gen and every other staff member with readable levels of estrogen in her system. Dr. LaPierre was old family, old money, old manners. Good looks and better bedside manner. Lee had seen him in action once or twice when she'd been hanging around waiting for Gen, who could never seem to leave her shifts on time.

"Gen's gonna kill me," Lee admitted ruefully.

Dr. LaPierre shook his head. "Nah. She'll be relieved that it's not worse."

"I'm one giant scrape, aren't I?"

"You have a few. Nothing serious. Your wrist is broken, though."

"I was afraid of that."

"Are you left-handed or right-handed?"

Lee winced as he probed the bones in her right wrist. "Left-handed this week, I guess. Damn, that's the fourth time. I should be getting a discount by now."

Dr. LaPierre gave her quite a look from his very nice cool blue eyes. "Four?" he demanded. "What do you do for a living, play football?"

Lee grinned. "It's not my job. It's my hobby. Horses."

He nodded. "Say no more."

"Gen's still gonna kill me. I'll put five dollars on it."

"I'm gonna kill you," Gen blurted out in exasperation.

Sitting back against the raised cart, her right arm cushioned by splint and pillow, Lee grinned over at Tim. "See? I win."

Her eyes still tight with anxiety, Gen took in the man leaning against the far counter, arms crossed and eyes smiling, and instinctively ran a smoothing hand over her already smooth French braid. "Hi, Tim."

Lee wanted to tell her sister she didn't have to worry about her looks. She looked just fine with her thick chestnut hair and sweet brown eyes. Lee wanted to tell Dr. LaPierre that her sister worried too much. He did it for her.

"She's fine," he assured Gen, pushing himself upright and approaching. "I've gone over all the X rays twice, just to make sure. She asked me to wait until they could get you down here before I set her arm."

Gen scowled. "Why? She could set it herself by now. She's sure had enough practice."

Tim seemed delighted by Gen's outrage. "Well, she sure must have learned how to land right. She took it like a tumbler. I've seen people with shattered legs and pelvises from something like this."

From her place on the cart, Lee decided that it was time to intercept her sister before things got out of hand. "He's right," she said. "I'm fine. Really."

Gen still wasn't ready to accept that. She stood like a miner's wife at the side of a shaft, waiting for the bad news, her posture stiff, her big eyes full of bad memories and instinctive fears. It made Lee feel guilty all over again. She could tell from the state of Gen's lab coat just what kind of day she'd already put in. Her sister didn't need this on top of it.

"Really," she insisted one more time, trying to negate those memories.

"The last time we went through this," Gen said to Tim, her eyes still firmly on Lee's, "she lost a spleen, part of a liver, and about twenty-four hours up in an ICU with a head injury."

More memories, too easily accessible in Gen's eyes, of that night when Lee had killed her brother's favorite horse trying to save Jake's life. A long time ago by any other clock but the one calibrated by a family's memory.

In the end, there was nothing Lee could do but shrug and smile for the surprise in the physician's eyes. "They don't call me the klutz for nothing."

He smiled back. "Might be worthwhile investing in a football helmet."

When the door opened into the treatment room this time, a nurse Lee didn't know poked her head in. "Dr. La-Pierre?"

His attention was immediately hers. It gave Gen the chance to close in for the kill. Lee figured she'd just have to live through it.

"You owe me twenty," Gen said with a tired grin, a hand instinctively up to pat Lee's cheek as if she were still falling from bikes in kindergarten.

"Twenty?"

Gen pointed at the various bandages and ice packs adorning the sorer parts of Lee's body. "I bet you wouldn't go a year without something happening."

"You bet me it would be on a horse," Lee protested.

But Gen was shaking her head. "Nope. All I bet was that you'd end up prone. Nice job. Just what am I supposed to tell Jake?"

That got frowns out of both of them. "Don't tell him anything," Lee protested. "He doesn't need to know about this."

Gen was not amused. "And if he and Amanda happen to pop in unexpectedly and find you this way?"

"You make it sound like I'm pregnant."

Lee was sure she was supposed to keep her mind on the conversation. After all, it would not be a pretty sight if Jake found out about this before she told him. She was the baby of the family, and everybody still tended to treat her as if she were twelve and climbing trees. Of course, since she did have an unfortunate habit of ending up in emergency rooms, Lee supposed the worry was at least a little justified. On the other hand...

On the other hand, she'd just noticed that Dr. LaPierre suddenly looked upset. He and the nurse were still standing over at the opened door, she with a chart in her hands and a gentle frown of distress on her features. Tim looked even more upset. Those classic features looked as if they'd been chiseled by a grieving man.

"Lee?" Gen goaded.

"Keep Jake out of this," Lee instructed her, even as she tried to hear the murmured conversation.

"...Not supposed to happen, damn it. It was just his leg."

The nurse shrugged in that way that denotes things being beyond our control, accepted his signature and backed out the door.

"What happened?" Lee asked. Alongside her Gen made her own face reminding Lee of the value of discretion, but that had been one thing Lee had never been long on. If she wanted an answer, she usually just asked the question.

Tim looked up with a slight shrug. "One of my patients. He, uh, died unexpectedly early this morning while I was out of town and out of touch with the hospital. That's what I was headed here for, to sign off his paperwork and talk to the staff, when I came across you."

"I'm sorry." Both Lee and Gen responded simultaneously.

Tim smiled and gave his hand a little wave as if to say he wasn't the one who deserved their concern. Even so, he didn't look a lot happier. Lee felt for him. She knew just what Gen went through every time one of her kids died, and Gen had someone to share it with. So far, according to hospital gossip, Tim LaPierre had no real relationship.

"Dinner," she blurted out ungracefully.

Gen and Tim looked over, one more puzzled than the other.

"At our house," Lee clarified. "Tomorrow night. I'm not a bad cook, and I'm obviously going to be stuck there for a few days."

Tim shot Gen a look. Gen just bunched her shoulders up and shoved her hands in her lab coat pockets, a sure sign that Lee was in for more than her share of trouble. Lee had always said that Gen resembled nothing more than a stubborn mare when she got her mind to it, literally digging herself into position.

Lee didn't give her the chance.

"To say thanks," she insisted to Tim. "Come on, Dr. LaPierre. You can't turn down an offer like that."

Evidently, Dr. LaPierre couldn't. With a sudden, bright grin that showed off cute crow's feet and a cuter dimple, he nodded. "Let me set your arm first. After that, the offer might not still be open."

It was. An hour later as Lee sat again on the cart, her arm, still numb from the local anesthetic, now sporting a new cast that felt comfortably warm and light, she found herself more focused on what she was going to fix for dinner the next night than on what places on her body were still sore.

Of course, the pain medicine they'd given her might have had something to do with her good spirits. All her experience with the inside of hospitals had taught Lee one thing. She was a cheap date where medication was concerned. But just as much credit had to go to Dr. LaPierre, who had gentle and patient hands. So when the emergency room physician who had initially evaluated her popped her head back in the door, it was to find Lee leaning back, gazing at the very dull white ceiling, humming the tune to "Streets of Laredo."

Lee knew she'd been caught when she heard the giggle.

"I hate it when the party starts without me," the doctor objected, walking in far enough to betray the fact that she was at least seven months pregnant. A little taller than Lee, she had burnished mahogany hair, freckles and dancing blue eyes. She also had that special glow people talk about during pregnancy, because even with thick ankles and a rolling gait, she was beautiful.

Lee knew Abbie Viviano from Gen's rotations through the emergency room. A top-notch ER doc, she lived for three things: Häagen-Dazs, rock and roll and the family she'd started with her husband Michael, a lieutenant in the Chicago police force. From what Lee had heard, the story of their meeting was quite a classic. Some day when Abbie wasn't so distressingly pregnant and Lee so preoccupied, she was going to have to ask her all about it.

"No problems here," Lee said with a grin. "Aren't you off duty yet?"

Abbie scowled. "You sound like Michael. I don't know how anybody's safe in this city with him spending all his time here making sure I'm okay." She stood a second, rubbing her belly as if making a wish. "Where's Gen? I thought she was in here."

"She and Dr. LaPierre went off to look at the post-reduction films of my arm. Then maybe they'll have dinner." Lee giggled again, probably the only one who appreciated how funny her joke was.

Abbie was polite enough to at least smile. "Well, you sure had the right doc stop at the scene. Tim does more accident cases here than Triple A. You up for company?"

"I've had company. Gen's been in my hair for three hours now."

The doctor smiled. "She worries about you. Try and have five brothers. It makes her look like long distance."

"I have two, and it's plenty. What company? Is it anything like Dr. LaPierre?"

Abbie rolled her eyes in some distress. "Nobody is like Dr. LaPierre. Every time he walks through I find myself trying to hide my stomach. As if that would make a difference. No, this one's definitely not Dr. LaPierre. But he needs to talk to you, anyway."

"About what?"

"About the fact that somebody almost killed you."

"Oh," Lee said, dismissing her with a blithe wave of the hand. "That."

"Yes," a very impatient male voice echoed tersely. "That."

Lee took one look at the man who had appeared in the doorway behind Abbie and decided that she didn't care if somebody *had* tried to kill her. It wasn't enough to make her talk to this guy.

He was as dark as Tim was light. Angry. It was the only word that came to Lee's mind through the pleasant haze his presence was threatening to dispel. Glowering dark eyes beneath heavy dark brows. Features broken from granite and wind instead of crafted from marble and care. A jaw that bore no weakness, cheeks furrowed instead of dimpled, and a mouth set in a grimace of displeasure.

And those eyes. Hard eyes. Hot eyes. Eyes that smoldered with enough energy to light up Chicago for a week, none of it good.

Standing there in a suit and white shirt, he still somehow looked not so much informal as insolent. His pockets drooped from constant abuse, his collar was frayed from neglect and his posture was wary and defiant.

Lee didn't like him. What's more, she didn't trust him. What was even more than that, for some reason, she felt sorry for him.

"If you're here to apologize," Lee said anyway, "I accept."

And then she simply closed her eyes, figuring he'd just go away again.

Chapter 2

He didn't need this. It had been damn near thirty hours since he'd seen a bed, the last eighteen hours spent humping the streets, looking for answers to the murder of a little girl they'd found two days before along the Turning Basin of the Chicago River. He was new to the area, just having been transferred from Area Six two weeks earlier, so that he didn't even know whom he could trust yet. And then, when he'd walked back into the station to try and get some reports written, he'd been handed a call for a hit and run. This hit and run. A pampered little fresh-faced blond type who'd scraped herself up when she'd looked the wrong way.

Rock was just not in the mood for this.

If Abbie Viviano hadn't had hold of his arm, he would have walked out and let the girl fend for herself.

"I'd like you to meet Sergeant Rock O'Connor, Lee," Abbie was saying as she edged him in the door. "He's going to be investigating the accident."

Rock shoved his hands back in his jacket pockets where they wouldn't get him into any trouble. Old habit from when it had really been a necessity.

The girl on the bed opened her eyes again to smile at him, and Rock saw something there that looked suspiciously like challenge.

Some other day, he thought blackly. I'm all out of challenges today. They weren't going to find out who it was who killed that little girl, and they all knew it. So they took it out on the new guy, handing him off the pain-in-the-butt calls that would just get in the way.

Rock wanted to be out on the street trying to track down that little girl's other shoe. The shoe she hadn't still had on when they'd found her, the one no one could find. The one that called him like a seer who saw fortunes in smoke. Instead, he was here investigating something that was going to end up having nothing to do with anything, and it made him furious.

"Your name's really Rock?" the blonde asked abruptly, as if she'd lost the fight to be polite.

"You got a problem with that?" he demanded.

Abbie laughed. But then, Abbie knew his name. If she had any sense of self-preservation, she'd leave things alone.

The victim on the bed bobbed her head, smiled and lifted her hand as if expecting it to be kissed. "Nice to meet you, Sergeant O'Connor."

Rock couldn't help it. He stared. "I'm not real sure you want to shake my hand," he told her, lifting his gaze to get snagged by a set of the clearest blue eyes he'd ever seen on a human. "I've had it in garbage all day."

It was when she giggled that Rock realized that all those smiles were because she was dosed with something for the arm she'd broken and the nasty scrapes on her face. He cut her a little more slack for that. Not much, though. He was sure he didn't like perky, fresh-faced blond types.

"Garbage?" she echoed. "Business or pleasure?"

He sighed. Her hair was such a light blond, almost white where the sun had gotten to it. Short and simple, with a cut that made it look like the wind was always tossing it around. Rock noticed that. But only in passing.

"I was trying to find out why somebody would kidnap and murder an eleven-year-old girl," he said baldly, as if that would protect him from her.

It didn't. Especially when the animation on her clear young face crumbled into real distress. It made Rock feel like he was a hundred, and he bet he hadn't outlived her by ten years.

"That little girl they found in the river," she said, eyes wide with real pain. "Please tell me you found whoever did it."

"No." Rock shoved his hands down further. Stiffened his posture against her concern. "We didn't."

She shifted on the bed and winced. "Then you shouldn't have to waste your time with me. I probably just wasn't paying attention."

"Not according to the witnesses," Abbie insisted. "That guy hit you heading the wrong way. He could have killed you, Lee."

The girl on the bed waved off Abbie's insistence as if it were inconsequential. "I'm fine. A few scrapes and bruises. A cast. Big deal. Let him go, Abbie. He has better things to do. Sleeping, for one, if what I've been hearing about that case is true."

Rock didn't like being referred to in the third person—especially by somebody who had just offered him his fondest wish. So he pulled out the battered little notebook he carried with him and turned over one of the crinkled, stained pages.

"Since I'm here anyway," he said, pulling his fountain pen apart like a statement, "we might as well get the paperwork done. What's your full name?"

That got the kind of grimace that made her freckled nose crinkle up. Cute. Terminally cute, in the mood Rock was in.

He sighed again. "Is that too tough a question?" he demanded.

"Is this going to take a while?" she countered.

"Probably."

She nodded. "In that case, don't you think Abbie should get off her feet?"

She'd done it again. Damn, this was gonna be a long call.

"No, really," Abbie insisted. "I'm fine."

"Explain that to Viviano," Rock retorted.

Viviano. The doctor's husband. Rock's lieutenant and ruler of his life for however long he lasted at Area One.

"You wouldn't want Sergeant O'Connor in trouble, would you Abbie?" the girl asked with a mischievous grin.

Abbie gave in without much grace and hobbled out the door, making Rock feel worse for keeping her behind.

"Thanks," he said to the patient on the bed. "I should have thought of that."

"You're distracted," she assured him. "I would be too if I'd been through what you had."

Rock found he couldn't do much more than stare at her. *If she'd been through what he had.* He'd been through a week's worth of TV dinners and used diapers. She'd been through a first-degree assault by a Buick.

"Your name," he repeated, rubbing at his eyes in weariness.

"Amaryllis Jane Kendall."

He stopped rubbing. He went back to staring.

She was already scowling in anticipation. "Why do you think I sent her out of the room?" she demanded. "Because I was worried about her ankles? You say a word of this to anyone and I'll tell Lieutenant Viviano that you called his wife a water buffalo."

"It has to go in the report" was all Rock could think of to say.

"You couldn't just refer to me as Lee?" she asked. "Or maybe 'the victim?'"

"Amaryllis?"

She was losing that perky smile real fast.

Rock damn near laughed. "Is that with one *L* or two?"

She spelled it for him. "Now, then," she said. "Fair's fair. Is your real name Rock?"

Rock flinched. There probably wasn't any way he was going to get around this. He glared at her with full intent of injury if she reacted. "Francis Xavier Aloysius."

Her face lit up. Rock waited for the inevitable, but it simply didn't happen. She was probably waiting to blind-side him. God knows, he would have.

"All right," he said, bending to the paper that held the single word she'd so carefully enunciated for him. "Exactly what happened today?"

She was dabbing at the scrape on her cheek with careful fingers. Sore, he bet. Parallel lines of strain had appeared between her eyebrows. "Well, I was on Creighton's boat."

"The university?"

"The architect. Creighton Holliwell."

Rock nodded. Looked away. Looked down when he caught himself picturing her with some rich, damn, gray-haired, paunchy architect with a bass boat.

"His sailboat," she amended absently.

Rock put them beneath sails and felt worse.

"We'd had a wonderful fund-raiser last night," she said, "and he was treating the staff today with an afternoon of sailing."

"Fund-raising? For architects?"

"For theater. Fandango. It's on Halsted just south of Armitage."

No paunch. Culture. Rock wasn't sure whether he felt better or worse. At least there was a staff on the boat. Not just Amaryllis Jane Kendall with her sparkling blue eyes and impish giggle.

He rubbed again, harder, as if he could wear away the surprising images.

"So, you were sailing."

She nodded, sending her hair adrift so that Rock had to watch it. "When we docked, Sierra and I—she's one of our directors—decided it was a great day to walk, so we headed across Grant Park from the harbor and up Michigan. We parted at LaSalle so she could catch the El and I could catch my sister here at work. I admit that I was a little distracted. It was a beautiful day, I was feeling really great because we're probably going to be able to run a wonderful program for schoolkids on the money we made last night, and I was people watching. But I did think I was paying attention at the crosswalk. I just never saw a car coming at me from the wrong way."

"So you didn't see what it looked like."

She shook her head again. Rock wondered just how many questions he could ask that would make her do that again, just so he could watch.

"Nothing," she said. "Did anybody else see it?"

"Oh, yeah. The police on the scene got descriptions that range from a dark green Range Rover to a metallic-blue Mustang."

To Rock's surprise, Lee yanked back the sheet that was covering her legs. He looked. They were long, lean, with shape and style, and ankles as delicate as a thoroughbred's. He was too tired for this. Much too tired.

"I'd lean more toward the Mustang," she said, and looked up at him.

He couldn't decide quite what to say.

She smiled and pointed at the abrasions on the sides of her lower legs. "Wouldn't a Range Rover have hit me higher?"

Rock held on to that notebook as if it were the last handhold on his sanity. "Uh-huh."

There was this odd little silence in the room there for a minute as Rock reeled his brain back into some kind of working order. He wanted to touch those legs, and that was the most idiotic thing he'd ever thought. And Francis Xavier Aloysius O'Connor had thought of some pretty idiotic things in his long and sorry life.

"You have some ID I could get?" he asked abruptly, when he realized his palms were damp.

She stared at him for a minute, as if catching up. "ID."

Rock sighed. This was getting tougher by the minute. "Driver's license. With your current address."

She looked around, as if expecting to find it on the bed with her. "I . . . my purse . . ."

"It might be a help," he said.

She looked around again. "Maybe Gen has it."

"Gen."

"My sister. She's a doctor here. Maybe they gave it to her."

"You don't have it?"

She looked back at him, those bright blue eyes just a little distracted, just a little softer. She was picking at the blanket with her free hand, and the patient gown was threatening to slip down over her shoulder. Rock couldn't quite take his eyes from it.

"Would you ask?" she asked. "Gen. My sister. She's probably out with Dr. LaPierre. I don't remember where it is. I don't think they told me."

Rock asked. He couldn't find the sister, so he asked the nurse. He asked Abbie, who was sitting in the lounge with her feet up, and he asked the paramedics who had brought his victim in. But no purse had ever been recorded as having come in with the patient.

"You're sure you had it," he said when he'd returned to find that the patient gown had made good its threat to expose just enough tanned expanse of shoulder to make Rock's throat go dry.

Lee Kendall didn't even seem to notice. "I had it. I don't suppose the police on the scene have it."

"Not likely."

She nodded absently, eyes unfocused, fingers picking again at the blanket. She sighed, and Rock was furious to see tears in her eyes. She smiled almost ruefully. "Oh well, I guess it could have been a lot worse. Whoever walked off with it is going to be disappointed. They're gonna get a lot of useless junk, my driver's license and a bunch of family pictures."

Rock couldn't figure it. He'd spent the last two damn days hip-deep in misery. He'd spent the last ten years of his career wading around in it like a lifeguard in an undertow, and one set of suspiciously damp eyes was threatening to make him come undone.

He wanted to get her damn pictures back. He wanted to make her smile again. He wanted to put his mouth on that perfect expanse of tanned shoulder and have her put her arms around him.

He didn't even notice that the stiff little silence fell again. That the noise from the hallway outside filtered in like static from a broken radio. He didn't see the spreading ink stain on his notebook from where his pen had stopped.

"Dinner," Amaryllis Jane Kendall suddenly said.

Rock started to attention. "What?"

She gave a funny little shrug, as if she'd been caught, her color high. "Well, I'm having Dr. LaPierre over to dinner tomorrow night," she said. "Maybe you'd like to come, too. If you're not busy."

Dinner. Rock wasn't computing at all. Except for that part about Dr. LaPierre. The Dudley Do-Right with the stethoscope he'd met out in the hall.

"No," he said, flipping his book closed. "Thanks."

She pulled the sheet back over her legs. "You're busy," she said with a nod.

"I need to get the report filed."

Rock barely got out of that room alive.

"You asked who where?" Gen demanded the next afternoon as she and Lee stood in the kitchen of the apartment they shared.

Lee looked up from the cast-iron skillet in which she was stirring tomato sauce. "He couldn't make it."

Gen shook her head. "I swear, Lee. If they'd found the guy who was driving the car, you'd ask him to dinner, too."

Lee concentrated on her cooking. "He just looked so tired. Like he needed a good dinner."

"The driver?"

"The policeman. I felt sorry for him."

Gen was back to shaking her head again. "You felt sorry for him. The man looked like he gnawed on iron filings for dessert, and you felt sorry for him."

This time Lee did look up. "Is it a crime?" she demanded.

Gen's smile carried a wealth of memories. "No, honey. It's not. But one of these days you're gonna invite one too many stray puppies home, and you're gonna have problems."

"It's only dinner, Gen."

"And we already have Tim LaPierre coming over."

As if in punctuation, the doorbell rang. Gen lifted a hand when she saw Lee react.

"No. Let me answer it. Otherwise we could have two traveling salesman and a team of Mormon missionaries to dinner, too."

Lee knew better than to argue. She simply went back to her sauce and thought about how she was going to get Dr. LaPierre to notice her big sister tonight over dinner. It was certainly better than thinking about the policeman. Because she'd been doing that since he'd stalked out of the room almost twenty-four hours ago.

He'd stared, he'd scowled, he'd frowned. Not once had he smiled. Lee didn't like men who didn't smile. She bet he didn't even like her that much, either. Then why did the thought of this man wake her up in the middle of the night?

Why did she want to take some of that weight off his shoulders when she didn't even know what had put it all there?

"You're only allowed to be dramatic on my stage," a melodious male voice announced behind her.

Lee turned around to find Creighton Holliwell III standing in the doorway. Tanned and silver-haired with sloping forehead and patrician features, Creighton was the very latest in urbane and witty theater gurus. Creighton was also the driving force behind the theater company into which Lee had managed to insinuate herself. Creighton, with his perennial blue blazers and gray flannel slacks, his tasseled loafers and convertible Rolls, was every fundraiser's dream and a playwright's best guardian angel. Lee should know. In the last year Creighton had become her personal guardian angel, and she couldn't be happier.

He lifted a suspiciously familiar backpack her way. "Left it on the boat. Need it?"

"Oh, thanks, yeah. My extra jeans are in there. Just dump it on the floor." She flashed him a smile and a wave of her wooden spoon. "You're just in time for dinner."

He cast a suspicious eye at the slinged arm she held carefully to her side. "Just what would slow you up?" he demanded, walking on in to bestow a kiss on her forehead. "Open heart surgery?"

"Heck, no," Gen offered before Lee got a chance. "She'd write a three-act musical about it while she was in recovery. And then invite the surgery team to dinner the next night."

Lee ignored them both. "I'm fine," she insisted. "Just like I keep telling everybody."

"When the police called to tell me what had happened," Creighton said softly, "it sounded as if you were in intensive care."

That definitely got Lee's attention. "The police called you?"

He was in the process of accepting a glass of white wine from Gen as he answered. "They wanted to ask a little about the afternoon on the boat—mostly, I think, whether there was any alcohol involved. A rather unpleasant gentleman named after an igneous landform or something."

Lee scowled. "Stop being a snot, Creighton. His name's Rock, and you know it. He was the policeman who talked to me in the emergency room."

"She wanted to adopt him, too," Gen offered, lifting her own glass.

Lee decided the kitchen was getting far too crowded. She liked to cook alone, especially when her sister was in this kind of mood.

"I'm sorry they bothered you, Creighton," she said, shepherding him and Gen toward the door into the living room. "It wasn't necessary. Now, why don't you two sit down and visit while I finish my pasta?"

"Of course it was necessary," he protested, stopping right in the middle of the doorway. "I have a show to recast now."

That brought Lee to a dead stop. "Oh, no you don't."

The three of them ended up wedged in the doorway as if there wasn't another square inch of room to stand in.

"What are you talking about?" Creighton demanded. "You can't do *Long Day's Journey* like this. That's a demanding play, and we premiere in less than three weeks. And you still have a third act to finish on the play you're writing, to close the season, which, if you remember, was the premier reason we got such good money from the patrons yesterday."

Lee waved him off. "Write the broken wrist in. Eugene O'Neill won't mind. And as for my play, it's almost finished. So stop worrying."

Creighton turned to Gen with a mischievous grin. "She says that a lot, doesn't she?"

Gen scowled. "Usually when all hell's about to break loose."

All hell did break loose that evening. Only in the best way, of course. Friends heard about the accident and came over to commiserate. Tim LaPierre showed up for dinner sporting chinos, a cool blue cotton shirt and a bottle of very nice red wine. Sierra stormed in the door with a mighty frown and some vitamin E salve her mother swore prevented scars, and Creighton stayed. Even Marlyse White, the woman who had lost the part of Mary Tyrone to Lee, showed up with flowers in hand and hesitant good luck. They ended up with six for dinner and another seven or eight afterward, until the apartment resembled a dorm lounge with people everywhere and conversation peppered with laughter.

Along about ten o'clock, Lee found herself standing in the kitchen door, ubiquitous glass of lemonade in hand, considering the scene before her.

She really loved this place. She and Gen had stumbled across it during Lee's second foray to Chicago to test theatrical waters. She'd meant all along to return to Wyoming after college, where she could pursue fiction writing like her sister-in-law, Amanda. Keeper of old tales, spinner of dreams. But somewhere in her sophomore year, Lee had fallen in with a bad crowd and ended up spouting Shakespeare instead of Larry McMurtry.

Her master's thesis had been a play based on her own family called *Some Men's Dreams,* which had ended up garnering her an award and a career. But Lee wasn't an East Coast kind of girl, and few fledgling playwrights got their chance in Lost Ridge, Wyoming. So she'd come to Chicago looking for some kind of compromise and, at least for now, found it.

She missed the Wind River Mountains of home like a refugee, but there was still time to deal with that. She could get to see her brothers when she really needed to, and had Gen right here where she could reach her. She also had her friends, the ones she'd made at her theater and at Gen's hospital. Bright, energetic, interesting people who almost made her forget how much she missed the wind whistling through the tall grass in the pastures where horses ran.

The apartment had been the cement that kept her comfortable. The owner, a very lovely older woman with grown children, offered her house to people she liked. She let them pay what she thought they could afford, which in the Lincoln Park West area of town was a godsend. Lee and Gen had ended up with five big rooms on the third floor of a renovated old Gothic Victorian with glossy hardwood floors, high ceilings and bay windows in the living room and Gen's bedroom. It all sat on a tree-lined street of brownstones where baby carriages ruled the sidewalks and gardeners transformed tiny plots of land into color and birdsong.

Inside, the decorating was eclectic. Gen had hung posters of museum exhibits—Gauguin, Hopper, O'Keeffe, van Gogh. Lee had countered with posters of plays she'd done and plays she'd wished she'd done, so that the bright lithographs marched across the high white walls like vivid panels. Gen had managed to get her piano up here, and Lee had brought her saddle. They'd found a chintz couch from a nearby estate sale and had brought their mother's favorite rocking chair, a moth-eaten old thing that creaked like a horror flick every time it moved. There were cast-off chairs and bright pillows, a vivid red silk piano scarf that trailed fringe to the floor, and across the mahogany mantle, a

chorus line of old dolls Gen had collected over the years. A
stereo, an old hand-painted lamp and a livid green-and-
purple papier-mâché gremlin on the windowsill. Wind
chimes for the breeze and books for the silence.

There wasn't any silence now. The room bubbled and
spilled with conversation and laughter. With people and
ideas. With friends. With Gen. Lee had spent too much
time in the company of strangers. She'd done her time at
Harvard where she'd been fortunate enough to attend
school. She'd lasted to pose for the picture she carried in
her purse of her in cap and gown with her arms around the
man who'd sacrificed everything to be able to give it to her.

The picture that was gone now. God, she hated losing it.
It was such a special picture for her, a symbol of what her
family had been, what it had become. What Jake had given
all of them.

It could have been a lot worse. She could have lost her
family instead of her pictures. Lee looked over at where
Gen sat in intense discussion with Creighton about the
current native American exhibit at the Art Institute, and
thought about what life would have been like without this.
She couldn't imagine it. She couldn't imagine being alone,
having tables not crowded with framed photos of nieces and
nephews and holidays spent laughing and playing. Of
friends and memories that ended up finding their way into
her living room with more regularity than they did the plays
she tried to write.

"What's this about growing up in a house without running water?" Tim demanded from his place on the couch
alongside Marlyse, who was making cow eyes at him.

Lee laughed. "We had water. We even had a john.
Wanna see pictures?"

Everybody else groaned, all too used to her pictures of
home. "I'd love to," Tim encouraged her and called down
the gods of consequence. "It sounds wonderful."

Lee was already pulling out her album. "Oh, it is. I have
maps...."

A purse was a small thing. Lee Kendall folded herself up
on the arm of the couch, thought about what a lucky girl

she was and smiled. She wished this for everyone. She wondered, in an offhand way, whether Sergeant O'Connor, with his glowering looks and terse questions, was nearly as lucky.

Half a city away, Rock O'Connor stood in front of his open refrigerator and waited for inspiration. He thought he was hungry, but he couldn't quite work himself up to making something. It didn't matter, anyway. There wasn't anything to make. The refrigerator was as empty as the house. He had a choice of three beers and a frozen pizza, which didn't appeal to him in the least. Besides, he was just too damn tired to cook the pizza.

He should have been in bed. He had exactly ten hours until he was due back up at the Area One Violent Crimes Detective Bureau to start a new shift working on hopeless cases. He'd already downed three beers in an effort to feel sleepy. It hadn't worked. He was too exhausted to lie down, too frustrated to relax.

Most nights he didn't notice the silence when he walked into the house his parents had bought after the Korean war. He didn't notice the layer of dust or the books and magazines that had collected on the coffee table. Most nights he ate his dinner down at the bar with the other cops and saved walking in that door until he was too tired to care that nothing waited for him but an empty bed in an empty house.

Tonight he hadn't lasted down at the bar. Tonight he'd missed most of the conversation and all the jokes, until more than one of his buddies had suggested that he needed a good lay. Tonight he'd ignored them and ignored the police groupies who tended to hang around cop bars hoping to get lucky. Tonight he'd gone home instead and found himself standing in his gym shorts and bare feet at an empty refrigerator thinking what an idiot he was for wishing that when he walked into that bedroom a girl with wild blond hair would be waiting for him.

Tonight he found himself caught in the trap of wishing
he could be more than he was, and it made him hate the girl
with the blond hair all over again for making him remember it.

Chapter 3

"Are you sure you're up for this?" Sierra demanded from where she sat in the dark three rows up.

Lee didn't want to admit that she was sore and tired. She didn't want them taking the role away from her at the last minute. Mary Tyrone was a role actresses bit and scratched to get. The vague, tormented Irish mother in the classic Eugene O'Neill family. A tour de force in a play that was a marathon of tours de force. It was going to be a great play. The actors who were going to portray the rest of the Tyrone family were the best Lee had seen since first walking into a theater, and even Marlyse, who would play Cathleen, the maid, added depth and range to the role. Sierra was a genius, and Lee had bitten and scratched as hard as any actress who had vied to work with her.

So she didn't want to admit that she might just not have the energy to do Mary's big soliloquy, because that meant they might take the entire four-hour play away from her—and it opened in less than three weeks.

"I'm fine," she insisted into the gloom beyond the lights, her arm aching and her shins aching and her head aching as they headed into the third hour of rehearsal.

It had only been three days since the accident, and Lee knew perfectly well that things always got worse before they got better. Besides, she'd done too much the day after the accident, which meant she was paying for it now. But she didn't want to give up just yet. So she lifted her hands, one of them wrapped in the newest in polymer-hardened material to protect her grating bones, and tried to remember the words that would take the audience back into Mary's lost past.

"I could run lines with the rest of the cast," a thin, plaintive voice offered from the darkness of the wings.

"No, thanks, Marlyse," Sierra answered easily. "It's Lee who needs the work. Not Tom or Barry."

Lee offered her friend a particularly charming grimace, even though she knew Sierra was just fending off Marlyse as best she could.

"Isn't it lunchtime yet, dears?" Creighton suddenly asked from the back of the theater.

Everybody stopped where they were and stared. Especially Lee. Creighton never interrupted his players. And he certainly never did it at eleven in the morning.

"What are you doing here?" Sierra demanded over her shoulder.

Creighton appeared from the back, casually elegant as usual, smiling. "I'm on my way to acquire grant money, dear. Power lunches with the rich and generous."

Considering the fact that it was Sergeant O'Connor who followed Creighton down the center aisle, Lee wondered just what kind of grant it was Creighton was looking for.

"Besides," he said as if reading her mind, "there's somebody here to see Lee."

Lee was, after all, an actress. It was why she was able to remain impassive where she stood. She wanted to smile. She wanted to jump off the stage and meet him halfway, and considering how unhappy he looked, that was a very silly idea.

Sierra took one look at the rumpled, unhappy man who faltered to a stop about ten rows up, large paper bag in hand, and she got to her feet. "This is a closed rehearsal," she announced, obviously torn between protection and curiosity.

"Trust me," Lee told her as she walked to the end of the stage and sat down on the edge. "He doesn't want to join the cast."

"I'd run lines with *him,*" Marlyse offered in that same wishful voice.

Normally, Lee just would have jumped down. Today she slid off on her bottom and eased onto her sore legs.

"What can I do for you, Sergeant O'Connor?"

He didn't move forward. "I need to talk to you."

Lee saw his surreptitious looks around, saw the way he'd jammed his free hand in his pocket. She saw that he would rather have been caught in a crossfire than here among people he didn't understand. She saw it and thought of her brother Jake, whom she'd caught looking just like that a time or two, and knew she had to rescue him.

"Can I have a few minutes, Sierra?" she asked, already knowing the answer.

Sierra didn't move. "Lunch!" she yelled, her gaze glued to the interloper.

There was a certain amount of rustling backstage, and not a few questions. Lee ignored them all. She ignored Creighton, who was standing there wearing that cat-in-the-cream smile of his, and she ignored Sierra who watched with silent suspicion.

Before Sergeant O'Connor could move, Lee grabbed him by the arm and turned him toward the back of the theater. They made it into the scaffold-and-poster-decorated lobby before he made any move to comment.

"Holiwell said you write plays," he said as if she'd betrayed him somehow.

"I do."

"You didn't write that play."

Lee brightened. "You know O'Neill?"

Sergeant O'Connor did not brighten. "Only under protest. We had to read him during detention in high school."

For some reason that really disappointed her. Lee had never been the type to believe that all the earth should love and understand theater. Taste was taste, and everyone was entitled to his or her own. But Lee realized with an odd start that she'd somehow hoped the sergeant would be one of the ones who had chosen her tastes to share.

"What would make you risk unpleasant memories on a nice day like today?" she asked, sliding her own hand into the pocket of the wheat-colored jeans she wore with a matching oversize sweater.

For some reason, that seemed to make him even more uncomfortable. He couldn't seem to take his gaze from the vicinity of her left earring. And while Lee admitted it was quite something to see, with three different levels of silver bangles that sounded like wind chimes when she moved, she didn't think it warranted a close inspection.

"I, uh, needed to check and see if you recognized this," he finally said, and handed over the brown shopping bag.

She accepted the offering and was surprised to realize that it was heavy. When she opened it, she realized why.

"Oh..." For one of the few times in her life, Lee was at a complete loss for words. She wanted to thank him. She wanted to cry. She wanted to laugh and dance and drop to the floor right then to make sure the important things were still there. She didn't manage much of any of that.

Her purse. He'd found her purse. For a minute all Lee could manage was another "Oh..." as she stared at it, as if it were the Holy Grail itself. But she couldn't help it. She'd told herself she could live without her pictures, her mementos of her family. But she'd spent all of last evening scrabbling through her things trying in vain to find the negatives to her graduation pictures.

"You might check and see what's missing," he suggested.

Lee didn't even answer. She just reached up and hugged him, bag and all.

"Thank you."

She was making things worse for him. She knew it. Sergeant O'Connor evidently wasn't the kind to accept random displays of affection. He stiffened in surprise. Lee pulled away and tried to smile for him.

"I'm sorry," she apologized, surprised herself at the realization that beneath all that rumpled attire there was a very well-built man. A tall man who made her stretch to match his height. "Gen says I get out of hand."

The sergeant shoved his hands back into his pockets. "You might want to check and make sure there's anything left worth getting excited over," he suggested diffidently, his color just a little higher.

Handsome.

Somehow Lee hadn't noticed before. Beneath all that thunder and threat was also a handsome man. A man with strength and determination. A man with intelligence and sensitivity.

A man with sad eyes.

Lee fought the urge to invite him over to dinner again and retreated to one of the red plush benches that lined the walls, figuring the policeman would follow.

She dug into the brightly woven purse and found her stash of pictures and didn't have to go any further. "They're here," she marveled, flipping through them to make sure they truly were all there, as if the thief would really walk off with her purse just to take one picture of her brother.

"Credit cards?" Sergeant O'Connor asked. "Money?"

Lee was still focused on the pair of windswept faces smiling back at her from her small picture album. She and Jake arm in arm at the edge of the quadrangle. Hers had been the first graduation Jake had arrived at on his own. The first graduation he'd been able to really enjoy. This picture was more important to Lee than all the credit cards in the world. Lucky for her, she guessed.

She looked up. "Oh, I don't carry any."

O'Connor's features darkened considerably. "You don't have any credit cards?"

"One. I keep it in my sock drawer, just in case I need to fly somewhere. Other than that, it's Cash-and-Carry Kendall."

"Is anything missing?" he asked carefully.

She dug back into the bag and pulled out the various books, receipts, notes, combs and tools that littered the bottom of the carpetbag.

"Why not just pack a suitcase?" O'Connor asked dryly when he saw her pull out the screwdriver and pliers.

Lee probably should have been insulted. She knew better, though. "I'm the proud owner of a car that is always having its spark plugs pop free," she explained, digging deeper and coming up with a pair of glasses, three pairs of brightly colored plastic earrings and one very moth-eaten pair of panty hose.

"You have a car here?" he asked.

"Nope. In Wyoming. But I don't change purses that often."

"Uh-huh."

"My driver's license is missing," she admitted, digging through again. "Twelve dollars and change. My passport." She looked up, still too relieved at getting her pictures back to be upset. "That's all."

"It's enough," he assured her, pulling out his own notebook. "You should report those right away."

Lee grinned. "Yes, sir."

O'Connor didn't seem to think she was particularly funny.

She stood up. "I can get a new driver's license. What I thought I'd lost was my pictures. My family, see?"

He had no choice but to see the group shot of the four Kendalls mugging for the camera at the last Christmas get-together. Jake, Gen, Lee and Zeke, who was at the moment hunting Indian artifacts in Arizona.

The policeman looked. Looked away, as if he'd just been shown the picture of a disaster, instead of one of celebration. Lee found herself standing there in front of him, the picture still extended, feeling as if he'd refused a gift. She wanted to know why. She wanted to know why that pair of deep creases had just appeared between his eyes.

She wanted to know what made him back away so quickly.

Stray puppies, Gen would have warned. Lee tried to think of excuses to get him to talk to her.

"Thank you," she said, pulling her minialbum back. "You really don't know what it meant."

His answer was a grunt as he finished making some note with his old-fashioned fountain pen.

"How did you find it?" she asked.

He didn't even look at her. "A fluke," he said. "Whoever grabbed it dropped it not more than ten blocks away, and nobody else was interested in your pictures enough to grab the bag again."

"You just stumbled over it?"

"Something like that."

She nodded, holding it against her as if that could better protect it now that she had it back. "Thank you."

"You already said that."

"I know." She wanted him to smile. That shouldn't be so hard. Just a little smile. "But some things are worth two thank yous."

He closed his book. Stuffed it in his coat. Glared at her, as if she were the one who'd stolen the purse in the first place.

"I'll let you know if we find out anything else," he said. "But the truth is, I wouldn't hold my breath. Get on with your life."

He'd already turned away and opened the door when Lee found her voice again. As usual, she spoke on an impulse that would have had Gen running for a whip and chair.

"What did I do?"

He stopped, the door halfway open so that the sunlight and traffic noise spilled into the dim foyer. "What?"

"If it's something I've done that's made you so upset," she said, "I'd like to know. Maybe I can at least explain or something."

He turned back to her, but Lee couldn't see his features. The sun haloed him like a dark angel bent on retribution. Lee felt his gaze, though. It skittered along her nerve endings like the touch of a live wire. It stole her breath just as surely.

"What makes you think you've done something wrong?"

Even his voice was harsh. A growl of danger, of challenge. Of strain. Lee heard things there she thought maybe Sergeant O'Connor didn't know had escaped. Things that intrigued her too much.

"You're so angry" was all she could say, her voice small, her determination wavering with his electric silences.

Another enfolded them both. Outside a car honked. Another answered, and voices punctuated the exchange. Somewhere a church bell chimed the quarter hour, the sound frail music against the rumble of the traffic. Inside, there was silence. Even the noise of the people beyond the doors into the theater auditorium was hushed, as if only Lee and the sergeant stood in this building.

Lee waited. She thought she saw something flicker on that dark face. She held her breath, not knowing what for. Feeling the sudden, suffocating stillness that seemed to compel her closer to him.

His eyes. She wanted to see his eyes. She wanted to know what it was that was setting off that odd dance in her, even as he tried to intimidate her.

My God, she realized suddenly. He isn't just handsome. He's magnetic. Provocative. Even with his angry eyes and his ramrod-stiff posture, he radiated a raw sexuality Lee had never known before.

"I'm not angry" was all he finally said, although again Lee heard more. She heard Jake again, denying problems it had taken her eighteen years to discover. She heard her own blithe acceptance, and remembered what it had ended up costing. Still, this wasn't her brother. He wasn't her friend or her lover, so she had no rights to press. She didn't know what else to do.

"Can I call you if I have questions?" she asked.

When he shrugged, all Lee could think of was resignation. "If you want."

She tried again, the pressure swelling in her chest. Stay, she wanted to say. Talk to me. Touch me. She saw his fingers move, as if in answer, and all but felt them on her skin.

She flushed and knew that this was a dangerous man. Not because he would hurt her. Because he wouldn't let her near enough to hurt at all.

"Thank you again for finding my purse," she said, feeling stupid and ungainly. "Especially when you were so busy with the other case and all."

"I told you," he snapped, turning away again. "I didn't do anything."

Lee tried her darnedest, but she couldn't think of anything else to make him stay. He walked out the front door without so much as a goodbye, and she was left holding on to the gift he'd given her without the satisfaction of knowing that he understood what it meant to her. She watched the door close behind him and realized that she hadn't been given half a chance to know him. And she wanted to. She wanted to understand what it was about him that made him so angry at her, because no matter what he'd said, she didn't believe him.

She wanted to dip her fingers in that field of sensuality once again. Just once, so she could know that what she'd felt hadn't been a fluke.

She wanted to know that beyond all that power and fury, there was a satisfying silence.

Instead, she turned away herself and walked back into the theater to pick Sierra up for lunch. But all along, all she could think about was how she could keep track of the dangerous policeman with the sad eyes who wanted nothing to do with her.

"Can't I give you a case that doesn't turn into the crusades?" Lieutenant Michael Viviano was saying as Rock paced before his desk. "It was a simple hit and run, Rock. Something to give you a breather from the Havlacjek case."

"I figured I could get something on it," Rock defended himself, knowing perfectly well that the lieutenant was right. "Nothing else was panning out."

"You spent four hours of your shift and ten you were off looking for that damn purse. Was it really that important?"

Rock wasn't about to tell his lieutenant just what it had done to him to see the tears in Lee Kendall's eyes when she'd reached into that purse and come up with those pictures. It hadn't been why he'd rummaged through every Dumpster on the north side, not really. After spending hours talking to sobbing parents and grandparents and neighbors who looked out their windows with the numbed confusion of survivors, he'd just wanted something good. A little closure, a check mark against his name in his own private scorecard.

"My little girl," Lisa Havlacjek's mother had moaned over and over again, her daughter's jacket clutched to her chest. "My little girl."

And Rock had hoped that just this once it would be different. He'd prayed, deep in a place that had forgotten what prayers were. And then he'd cleansed himself in a search through trash Dumpsters and sewer grates.

If he'd been honest with himself, he'd probably admit that he wouldn't mind Lee Kendall feeling grateful to him. It had been so long since anybody had been grateful to him. But he hadn't gone in anticipating what effect her reaction would have had on him. He hadn't realized that he'd have to run like hell from her and than spend the next hour driving Lake Shore Drive from one end to the other, just to clear her out of his head.

But that wasn't something a lieutenant wanted to know about his newest transfer. It wasn't something Rock ever thought to share with anybody, even somebody as good as Viviano. Rock and the lieutenant were old acquaintances, having served together on the force at one time or another. He liked the lieutenant. What was more, he had a real respect for him, a good supervisor who had earned his degree on the street like all the best cops. But if Rock had learned one thing in his life, it was to be careful. So he was careful now.

"Nothing to worry about now," he said simply, his gaze carefully focused on the front of the battered old Formica-and-metal desk the lieutenant used. "I got her purse back, the rest of the case is a wash, and my time is all yours again.''

"And after all, it was my idea for you to take that call in the first place," Viviano retorted. "Right?"

Rock was surprised to look up and find Viviano smiling. Yeah, he could have drawn a much worse hand than this. His own grin was grudging. "Something like that."

"You needed a little break from the streets," Viviano said, his relaxed posture belying the meaning behind his words. "And you didn't get it by getting transferred up here. So I think you'll probably be getting more cases like Lee Kendall's and fewer like Lisa Havlacjek. At least for a while."

Rock stiffened, not sure whether he was more outraged or afraid. Viviano better not be telling him he was taking him off the streets. Rock couldn't survive off the streets. But nobody really knew that but him.

"I'm already on the Havlacjek case," he retorted instinctively. "You want me to just blow it off?"

"You're on the case because you threatened O'Banyon's life if he didn't let you on the team. O'Banyon thought that might be a little gung ho, even for somebody trying to make points in a new area."

"It's my job."

Viviano didn't move. "You racked up more homicide clears than any copper in Area One this last year. You got your transfer because you got caught taking files home when you were supposed to be on vacation."

"I didn't—"

The steel flashed in his lieutenant's eyes. "Everybody has to take time off, Rock. Even you. Even if the victim is an eleven-year-old girl on her way home from school. You just can't get them all."

Rock damn near snarled. "I can try."

Viviano all but sighed. "Listen. I don't know what sin you're trying to atone for, but this isn't the way to do it. Go to confession like the rest of us. I need you too badly to let you explode like an overripe tomato. So take some easy cases, and let them be easy. All right?"

Rock fought the fury, fought the terror those simple words produced. Don't give me time off, he damn near pleaded. Don't make me spend time with nothing but myself to buffer the emptiness.

Rock knew the system. He knew just how to answer so he could skate clear for a few more days. He straightened. He nodded. He acquiesced, even as he figured out how he was going to do more. "Yes, sir."

And Viviano knew exactly what he was doing. Rock could see it in the almost bleak disappointment in his eyes. "Well, above and beyond anything else, I really appreciate your taking the case," he said anyway, as if the conversation were really comfortably back on track. "Abbie's really taken a liking to Gen Kendall and her sister, and I knew you'd make things easy for them."

Rock didn't bother to disagree with him. "Well, if the sister doesn't start paying attention to what she's doing, Abbie's going to spend more time treating the Kendalls than visiting with them."

"Just bad luck?"

"Just bad luck. She was looking the wrong way, just like everybody said. The witnesses figured on a drunk driver who couldn't read the one-way signs. He did not hang around to apologize."

"All right. Well, go ahead and get the paperwork done." Viviano paused, obviously uncomfortable with his need to change the subject again. "Then you can get back to the Havlacjek case where you really want to be. You got any ideas on it?"

Where he really wanted to be. Rock almost laughed. The lieutenant had no idea. He really didn't.

Rock gave a careful shrug. "Once I find that shoe, I'll let you know."

"O'Banyon thinks it's a serial thing. Guy's already scopin' out playgrounds in Indiana or something."

Rock shrugged again. "I'll let ya know, Lieu."

Back to business as usual. Rock felt it begin to build all over again, like a tightening band around his head. Frustration, desperation. Fury. She had asked him why he was so angry at her. He was angry at her because she didn't know what waited beyond the beautiful day she'd been enjoying. She didn't know what people like him paid for it.

And God, he hoped he could keep her from ever finding out.

"This is your last chance, sweets."

Lee stretched the weariness out of her shoulders as she stepped through the door and flipped on the lights in the apartment. "I thought you wanted me to finish the second act," she said, her attention already on the cool emptiness of the rooms.

"I thought the second act was already in the can."

Lee turned to find Creighton lounging in the open doorway, cashmere coat thrown casually over shoulders, ankles crossed. All he needed was an ascot and a hat, and they could do a scene from just about any Fred Astaire movie ever made. He got her grinning. "It's only going to be in the can if I can have a few evenings to finish it, dear. Now go play and leave me be."

He gave her a handsome pout. "But the De Havens always cough up twice as much money if they get a chance to dine with our rising new star."

Lee patted his cheek. "Feed them twice. I'm beat."

"You're going to be here alone?" he demanded. "All night?"

"Alone," she assured him, thinking how nice it would be to have the apartment to herself. There was a storm brewing, and she always wrote better in the rain. "All night."

Creighton straightened and dropped a kiss on Lee's forehead. "I'll tell them you're recovering from your injuries."

"You do that. Good night, Creighton. And thanks for the ride home."

"Always a pleasure, my dear. Always a pleasure."

With Creighton safely on his way, Lee turned to the next order of business. Maybe she wasn't letting anybody else feed her, but she was hungry. She kicked off her flats on the way through the shadowy living room just to feel the cool wood against her feet. Right after food, she was ditching the jeans and T-shirt she'd worn to the theater for her real work clothes, a set of short purple cotton pj's and terry-cloth robe. Gen was pulling a twenty-four-hour shift to-night, and Lee could count on peace and quiet. Now, if she could only stay awake long enough to do it, she had to whip some dialogue into shape between her two lead characters.

She'd barely made it through the kitchen door when the phone rang. It didn't occur to her to stop her progress just because she picked it up. The light from the refrigerator she opened provided enough illumination for both tasks.

"Hello?"

"Lee? Is that you?"

For just a moment, Lee forgot the contents of the open refrigerator. It was Tim LaPierre's voice on her phone.

"Tim?"

"How are you doing?" he asked, his voice soft and deep. Just the sound conjured up his image, crinkly blue eyes and dimpled smile. The smell of Aramis and the touch of skilled hands.

Lee couldn't help but smile. "I'm just fine. How are you?"

"Waiting on some films on a trauma patient. I just saw Abbie Viviano here, and it made me think of you. Thought I'd check and see how my patient was doing."

"You checked on your patient two days ago," she protested.

"I never discuss business over wine and pasta. How's the arm?"

Sore, Lee thought. But she doubted seriously that it was news that would surprise an orthopedist. "It's doing great," she said instead. The chill from the refrigerator finally got her attention. Pulling out a piece of cold chicken, she shut the door, which left her in the shadows again.

"I had a great time the other night," Tim was saying. "Thanks again for the invitation."

Lee laughed. "I didn't mean for it to turn into a melee."

"No problem. I like your friends. I'm even considering buying season tickets to Fandango."

"You'd love it," Lee assured him, brightening. "Gen comes all the time. You could sit with her."

"Or I could wait at the stage door for you."

Lee stopped cold, her food forgotten. She hadn't anticipated this. Gen was the one who should find a nice doctor to date, not Lee. Lee didn't have a schedule. She didn't have any kind of stability in her life, anything worth talking to a doctor about. She didn't really want a doctor, and she'd just realized it.

But it would only make sense that if Tim LaPierre hung around a little, he'd surely see the benefits of choosing Gen over Lee. Besides, who was Lee to turn down a potential season ticket holder? Creighton would never forgive her.

"The season starts in three weeks," she replied, hoping she was ambiguous enough.

"And you have a date to see me in the office in ten days," he said. "Until then, I expect you to take good care of that arm. No wild parties or late nights on the town."

Lee laughed again. "The only assignation I have planned for tonight is with my computer. I'm crawling into my jammies and working a play I'm writing."

"Your jammies, huh?"

Lightning flickered outside. Standing there in the darkened kitchen, Lee saw its faint shudder along the wall. "Alone," she repeated, just like she had with Creighton.

Good heavens, she thought impatiently. All this time without so much as an offer to go for a beer, and in one night I have two men making suggestive proposals. And of course that one night had to be the one she'd reserved for work. Story of her life.

This time it was Tim who laughed. "It was just wishful thinking, anyway," he said. "I'm not going anywhere but surgery for the next eight hours or so. But I'll tell you what. To say thank you for the other night, the next dinner's on me. You and Gen both, all right?"

"That would be wonderful. I'll tell her."

"Nah," he said. "I will. I saw her around here somewhere a while ago. That little Italian place around the corner on Ohio, okay? I'll tell Gen to pick the time."

"Sounds great."

"Till then?"

"I hope surgery turns out well for you."

"And your play. Good night."

"Good night."

For a long few moments after she hung up, Lee stood there in the darkened kitchen staring at the phone. She could hear the wind begin to tune up and the syncopated rumble of thunder, which meant that she should be curled up on her bed with her notebook computer propped on pillows and her radio turned to alternative rock. But for just that moment, she studied her own surprise.

She should have been weak-kneed with excitement. God knows she would have been a week ago. Dr. Timothy Michael LaPierre was making courting noises. He wanted to take her out. He wanted, evidently, to see her in her jammies. Any woman in her right mind would have unlocked the door and told him to appear any time surgery was finished.

She guessed she wasn't in her right mind.

It wasn't that Tim wasn't good-looking. He was. No, he was beautiful. Classy and funny and strong-shouldered, with long, graceful hands and a shy, little-boy smile that made women moan. When he'd been over for dinner, he'd traded sailing stories with Creighton and blues opinions with Sierra. He was solvent and popular and he smelled good. And yet, for some reason Lee couldn't comprehend, she didn't find him compelling anymore.

When she closed her eyes these last few days, she hadn't been looking for him. She'd seen instead features that had taken some abuse. A nose slightly out of kilter, a chin marred by scars. Eyes that couldn't seem to relent, and the balance of a fighter. She saw contrasts and wondered. She remembered small kindnesses and angry silences and wished she understood.

She had been protected by Tim LaPierre and pushed away by Rock O'Connor, and it was Rock O'Connor whom she wanted to wait for her by the stage door.

Oh, well, she thought, finally pulling the wrap off the chicken. She certainly wasn't going to figure out the sergeant in a week. She might as well concentrate on the people she was supposed to understand. One sandwich and a glass of fruit punch, and it was off to her bedroom to see what happened when the man and woman caught on their mountain in Kentucky were confronted by the voracious appetites of progress. Maybe she'd write a play about angry cops next.

She must have fallen asleep. The light was on by her bed, and the computer blinked unattended on its nest of bright pillows in front of her. Outside, the thunder had passed to leave behind it the wash of rain and the whisper of a cooling breeze. The glass chimes Lee had bought at the Gold Coast Art Fair spun and tinkled against the bright aqua-and-royal-blue, fabric-draped windows. Whimsical fish leapt and dove across similar seas on Lee's bed. Over on her wicker chair, the three-foot stuffed bear Zeke had won for her at the Wyoming State Fair last year sat lounging in a pair of Gen's pajamas and Jake's oldest, rattiest cowboy hat.

Lee wasn't sure what time it was, but she knew it was late. The traffic had diminished to a low hum, and there weren't any lights on in the houses that backed up to theirs. She couldn't figure out what had woken her up.

And just when is it right to fight for something? she read from the screen in front of her. The beginning of Jimmy Ray's last, impassioned speech. The theme of the play about values and greed. The cohesion of everything her big brother had taught her about honor and the reputation of men.

Sitting up, she ran a hand through her hair and rubbed her eyes. She could still finish this tonight, she thought. Right after she got a little something more to eat. Right after she took care of other business.

She was swinging her feet over the side of the bed when she heard it.

Scraping. Movement.

There was somebody at her door.

Instinctively, Lee sought a clock. Maybe Gen was home early. Maybe it was later than Lee thought.

But Lee didn't keep clocks in her room. It was a little challenge with her, a private discipline that woke her without help every morning just when she needed to be awake. Unfortunately, that internal clock was a little confused right now.

She thought to call out. She didn't. Suddenly her voice wasn't working any better than her lungs. She slid the rest of the way off the bed and got to her feet. Crept to the door. Looked into the living room, where the light was off. Heard the scraping again.

The door, which she had carefully locked before retiring to her room, was trembling. The knob turned. Someone was trying to get in.

"I don't need this," she protested instinctively, as if her casual words could warn the intruder that she was composed.

Right. All he had to do was hear her heart. See her hands. Someone was breaking into her house and she couldn't move.

Lee looked around the apartment for help. There wasn't any, of course. She was alone in her short pajamas and bare feet with not so much as a fire extinguisher close enough to help. She wasn't afraid now. She was terrified. Acid ate at her throat, and her stomach was cartwheeling in place. She wanted to cry. She wanted to call out to Jake for help, but she knew this time Jake was too far away. And even when she did whisper a small, desolate call for help, it wasn't Jake's name she uttered. It was Rock's.

There was a curse. Low. Vehement. A snap. Lee stood frozen in place as the knob turned and stopped. Then the door eased open, and a hand wearing surgical gloves snaked through holding a pair of bolt cutters. Lee had run out of time.

Chapter 4

Rock wasn't sure how he heard the call. He'd been pulling a little overtime trolling video arcades and comic shops for information about the kind of guy who might like to hang around kids. He hadn't been having any luck. Even with the juvy sex officer along, they hadn't come up with anything but the usual list of culprits, all of whom had alibis for the afternoon the Havlacjek girl disappeared.

Rock had treated the officer to some late food and seen her off for home. And than he'd just driven, the way he always did when he had to think. He was one of the primaries on the Havlacjek case, but they weren't going to get any miracles there. The further away from the crime they got, the more apparent that became to everybody. If something big didn't fall in their laps in the next few days, it would be left to the FBI and reruns of "America's Most Wanted."

At least, that was what Rock hoped. He hoped it bad, even as he looked for that damn shoe and a Mr. Stranger Danger who didn't even know that little girl.

Rock had tried stopping in at the Harp and Shamrock on Fullerton to have a round with the regulars, but the frustration wouldn't ease. He wasn't accomplishing anything.

None of them were. So he left in an even worse mood than when he'd walked in, and turned his battered old pickup truck for home. He'd just reached Clark and Division when he heard the call on the radio he kept even in his off-duty vehicle. There'd been a B and E on Barton.

Barton.

If he hadn't been so preoccupied, he would have picked up on it right away. If he hadn't deliberately relegated Lee Kendall to a closed case file in his memory.

Lee Kendall was out of his league. Out of his reach.

Out of his jurisdiction, as of two days earlier.

Lee Kendall lived at 1225 C Barton, and somebody was trying to break into an apartment on the third floor there.

"Be advised," the dispatcher drawled in response to some question Rock had missed. "I have just lost voice contact with the complainant. Before breaking off, she did state that the intruder was armed with a handgun."

"Son of a—"

It wasn't his case. He was technically off duty. He should be heading home. Instead, he pulled a U-turn on Division and headed back the other way.

Barton was one of those back streets over by De Paul University in the upscale Lincoln Park West area. Tree-and-BMW-lined, it boasted trendy brownstones where Yuppies had gone to raise their babies. Not anywhere near the kind of place Rock was familiar with. Sure as hell not someplace he'd catch himself dead if he weren't on a call of some kind. He had no time for people who wasted their time on cappuccino and homemade damn pasta. He counted streets and prayed, not even realizing he was doing it.

Then he saw the shudder of other strobes and swung in behind the two black-and-whites that had already responded.

One of the uniforms was already turning his way with a warning when Rock jumped out of his car. Rock showed his gun in one hand and his badge in the other. The officer, a pimply kid named Marconi, visibly relaxed and signaled him to follow.

"You heard?"

Rock was busy scanning the scene. The houses were dark and silent, the one they approached a three story brownstone with turrets at either corner. Nice. Real nice. Two other uniforms were edging around either side toward the back, their sight blocked by trees. Bad setup. Rock felt the adrenaline kick in. Felt the hollow taste of fear and realized with a surprise that it was Lee he was afraid for.

"I heard. Might have something to do with a case I'm working on."

Blue eyes. Rock could see them, wide and hurt when he'd told her about that little girl. More upset for a kid she'd never known than herself, when she'd just been tossed twenty feet by a car. Rock felt the silence twist in him and stepped into the two-man pattern with the rookie, trying like hell to concentrate on procedure instead of the idea that he might get up those stairs to find those wide blue eyes lifeless and staring.

The name on the mailbox for apartment C read Kendall. The stairs rose to the right. Rock climbed all three flights without breathing. He reached the gaping door to her apartment and had to bite back an oath. Let her be safe. Just one thing in my life, he thought, briefly squeezing his eyes shut as he set up to go in.

The lights were all off, so that the only illumination came from the streetlights that shone through the big windows across the front. Rock could see the rooms, though. High, quiet rooms with comfortable furniture. Rock scanned them, eased in, covered as his partner followed suit. Fought the staccato of his heart as he waited for the perpetrator to suddenly appear with his gun up. With his gun at Lee's throat.

The rooms had been tossed. There was debris everywhere. Pillows, stuffed animals, drawers. Rock could see it all, scattered as if there'd been a windstorm. He crept in, back to the walls, gun up in both hands because his palms were suddenly sweating.

He wanted to call out to her, to make sure she was okay. He wanted to beat the guy senseless who had done this to her.

He motioned the rookie to the kitchen. It was empty. He edged toward the front bedroom. Nudged the door all the way open to find it in the same condition. Light flooded in to find nothing.

His heart was beating faster. He didn't want to know. He didn't want to be too late. Not this time. God, not this time.

The other bedroom. The rookie stood just behind him, quivering like a dog on point. Rock was sweating bad.

He caught the door with his toe, pushed it open. Checked behind it for a lurking shadow.

Nothing.

He saw the computer lying on its side on the tumbled bedspread and crouched into position.

There was no one here. He could feel it, right there where his cop instincts lived. Nothing was breathing in this place but the two of them. He straightened, looked around. Saw something to his right and damn near shot a big stuffed bear wearing a cowboy hat.

"Son of a . . ."

"He's not here," Marconi muttered.

Rock saw the phone cord and followed it across the floor to where it disappeared under the bed. He let the weight of his gun drag it down. He held his breath. He didn't want to look, because even if she was under there, she still wasn't breathing. Which meant only one thing.

He looked, anyway.

Nothing. The phone lay there, the receiver on its side, as if dropped in a hurry. Rock reached for it, informed the dispatcher, who still waited on the other end, that he'd arrived. That he hadn't found anyone there. She sounded upset.

She had no idea.

Rock couldn't seem to get back to his feet, even when the rookie's radio stuttered to life to announce that the search outside had been similarly fruitless. He just sat there on the floor where he could see the jumble of clothes and books that had ended up on the floor. A lacy bra and jeans. Cowboy boots and the complete works of Dylan Thomas.

Yellow fish jumping and diving all over the hot aqua-and-blue sheets. A kid's sheets on a woman's bed.

"Go ahead and turn on the lights," he said, unable to look away from the bright serendipity of her room. "And call for evidence. We might as well get started."

The rookie had just turned for the door when Rock heard it. A funny little scraping noise against the back wall. A soft mutter.

He turned that way. Saw the window cracked open just a little. Battled the twin assaults of hope and caution.

"Hold on," he said in his calmest voice, bringing the rookie to a dead stop.

The rookie hadn't heard what Rock had. It didn't matter. Rock lifted his gun and crept for the window. It was absurd. He was praying that he'd find white-blond hair there.

"Lee?" he called quietly. "Lee, answer me. Are you there?"

Nothing. Not a thing. His hold tightened; his throat burned.

"Amaryllis Jane Kendall," he snapped, "are you out there?"

Fingers. He saw them the minute he pulled up the window. They were clutching the sill, white-knuckled and trembling. Then he caught sight of the cast and shoved the window right up with a slam.

He never remembered reholstering his gun. He caught her by the wrists just as her grip gave way. She gave a little cry of pain, but instinctively wrapped her fingers around his arms.

"What the hell are you doing here?" he demanded, his head out the window, his knee on the sill.

If he'd been expecting gratitude, he was sorely mistaken.

"What do you think I'm doing here, you jerk?" she demanded, her white-blond hair soaked and dripping, her wide blue eyes dark with terror as she hung two-and-a-half stories above the ground in nothing but a short nightie and her cast. "I'm pretending I'm a wind sock!"

Rock wanted to laugh. He wanted to hurt her for scaring him like that. He held on to her with all his strength. "Well, at least you're all right."

She wasn't appeased. "And did you have to mortify me on top of it? All you had to do was call me by my other name. I would have answered. After all, I haven't been doing anything but hanging around waiting for you guys to show up."

"I *did* call you! You didn't answer me, damn it. What did you want me to do? Wait till I heard the thump and go scrape you up? And what the hell made you decide to do something as stupid as hang out a window, anyway?"

That actually made her sigh and close her eyes for a second. "It seemed like a good idea at the time."

Rock tested her weight and realized that she wasn't as heavy as he'd thought. Her bones were small enough that her wrist fit easily in his grip. Her bare feet dangled aimlessly, those sleek legs stark white against the dark building.

"Marconi!" Rock yelled without turning away. "Get those two under her to catch her!"

Marconi repeated the instructions into his mike. Rock never took his eyes from his catch. "Hold on," he said uselessly. "We'll get you down."

"I am not going down," she grated. "I tried that and it didn't work."

"Why didn't you just stay where you were, damn it? You were perfectly safe under the bed."

He got another glare. "Could we please discuss this when I'm inside? I'm freezing out here. And you're hurting my arm."

"You want me to let go?"

"No! Get me in," she begged, her voice suddenly small and unsure, her eyes wet with more than the rain that steadily beat down on her upturned face. "Please. I'm terrified of heights."

"Don't start crying on me," he threatened, more afraid of that than any intruder with a gun.

"Crying?" she countered on a strangled little sob. "Don't be stupid. I don't cry." The tears she denied slid down her cheeks with the rain.

Rock heard the siren of the approaching rescue crew. He knew he wasn't going to last much longer. Her hands were too slippery, that cast too fat to get a good purchase. And those damn blue eyes were turned his way pleading for help.

"I should have stayed in the bar," he muttered.

"You and me both," she retorted.

The uniforms had reached the backyard. Rock could see them down there, their faces nothing more than pale globes in the dimness. He didn't want to think what would happen if he let Lee go.

"Can you hold on until we get something under you just in case you slip?" he asked.

She was reduced to nodding by now. Rock saw that tumble of blond hair rest against her arm, heard the stridor of her breathing, felt the trembling in her limbs and sought something that would keep them both calm.

"I'm sorry about the name."

She didn't move. Rock was glad. His own arms were beginning to tremble. His back was screaming in protest, and his hands were cramping.

"Sarge?" Marconi spoke up behind him. "Backup's on the way. Can I help?"

"Yeah," he said. "As soon as rescue's in place, you're gonna help me pull her in."

Marconi helped, but it was Rock who steadied her, Rock who reached over and slipped his hands underneath her arms as Marconi levered her into the window. Rock who caught her as she tumbled to the floor.

Rock who shooed everybody else out of the bedroom and closed the door on them for a minute so she could recover.

Neither of them seemed to notice that she was still in his arms.

"I didn't know what else to do," she said, as if she'd been waiting to tell him. "He was coming into my bedroom, and I knew he'd find me. He had a gun. He just kept tearing through things and getting madder and madder." She laughed, her wet, dripping head just below Rock's chin, her feet curled up under her and her arms tight around her chest. "I think he got my purse again."

"Where did he go?" Rock asked.

He got another laugh, this one less composed, as if the terror were finally bubbling free. "That's what's so funny. He crawled out the dining room window. It's just on the other side of the house from where I was. I saw him drop all the way to the ground. If I'd done that, I'd have broken both ankles."

Rock stayed where he was, his arms around her shivering body, his hand in her hair. "You did great," he said, trying to calm his own dying shakes. "I'm sorry for yelling at you. You scared me."

"I *terrified* me," she retorted, never moving to get free. "I thought . . . I thought . . ."

It was as far as she got. Rock pulled the bright blue comforter off the bed and wrapped them both in it and held her as she sobbed. He rocked her, this beautiful, fresh-faced woman who was wearing nothing but cotton pajamas soaked into near transparency by the rain. Her skin was cold and her legs were folded against his, and her eyes were wide. Her eyes were the color of rivers, and Rock wished he could always look down to find them waiting for him.

He sat there on the floor as she cried and wished with all his heart he could think of some way to keep her there. He wished it even though he knew better.

Lee couldn't seem to hold still. Rock had set a mug of steaming coffee in her hands, but she couldn't drink it. She wanted to pace and she wanted to throw up and she wanted to cry all over again, which wouldn't do her a whole lot of good. Rock's shirt was still damp from the last time she'd tried that out.

"I'm sorry," she said for the twentieth time. "I can't seem to . . . concentrate."

"You're doing fine," Rock assured her from where he was standing with the team of evidence technicians who had just sprinkled powder all over her house and poured plaster of paris in her garden to get shoe prints.

"It was dark, Sarge," one of the policemen was saying, all but wringing his police cap in his hands as he stood before Rock's withering gaze. "I was concentrating on hiding places."

"It didn't occur to you that our perp might be hiding a couple of stories over your head?" he demanded, his fingers white around the coffee cup he was holding.

They were all milling around the living room. What was left of the living room, anyway. Lee was glad little Mrs. Moffitt was gone for the weekend. All the excitement at three in the morning would have been hard on her. Lee knew. It was hard on her, and she was only twenty-five, not seventy-two.

Calluses. He had calluses on his hands. She'd felt them as he'd stroked her hair, as he'd held her close to warm her. And then, after she'd apologized for the tenth time for dissolving on him, he'd smiled, and Lee had known what he'd been hiding behind those terrible scowls.

"I was trying to hold still," she said on the officer's behalf, still shivering, still distracted by the feel of roughened hands, the sight of surprising dimples. "I wasn't sure who was making what noise by then."

"Don't defend him," Rock snapped, making Lee flinch. "That mistake could have cost lives."

Lee didn't know about that. She just knew she was tired and shaking and her arm hurt all over again, worse than it had the day she'd broken it. She held it carefully against her chest as she sat curled on the corner of the couch, wrapped in Gen's big velour robe and her blanket, waiting for the shakes to ease. Wondering why Rock always reacted with anger, when his smile had been so very sweet.

"It won't happen again, Sarge."

For some reason, that made him even angrier. Lee could see it in his eyes. They seemed to darken even more, until they were fathomless black in that battered, tired face. Gen had won a lot of money in cards from Lee because she simply did not possess a poker face. Neither did Sergeant

O'Connor. The difference was that the only emotions Lee had ever surprised on his face had been dark ones. She wanted to see him smile again. Just once. Really smile, as if he meant it.

"You need to check for any missing items," he said, bending to replace the cushion that had been pulled from the couch. The chintz looked ridiculous in his hands, hopelessly frivolous. Then he looked up at Lee and she lost even that thought.

Close. Suddenly Lee had images of those fierce brown eyes when they'd been soft. When those taut, impatient hands had been infinitely gentle. When he'd wrapped her against him and just held her until she'd calmed down. She saw these things and wondered for the first time whether Sergeant O'Connor had a wife, whether he had a little girl he rocked that way until her nightmares eased.

"Lee?"

His voice, softening imperceptibly, yanked her back to the present.

She tried to smile. She had to admit that it wasn't a huge success. "I'm sorry. What?"

He nodded, settling onto the couch across from her. "Do you have any valuables here you want to check on? Something he might have taken with him. Marconi here needs it for his report."

Again, it took Lee a minute to comprehend. She'd found herself looking at his legs and realizing for the first time that he was in jeans. She'd never seen him in jeans. They were old and scuffed and frayed. And they fit him far better than the suits he'd worn before.

"Jeans," she said.

He looked up, surprised. "What?"

"You're wearing jeans." It conjured pictures of him on a horse, but Lee didn't see him as rancher or a drover. She saw him as a circuit rider, dark and furious. The sheriff of a town that only he kept from corruption. She saw him in the Old West, not the new one. She wondered what her sister-in-law Amanda would say about him. How she would cast him in her historical novels.

Rock looked down at his jeans, at the blue police T-shirt he wore with them that had molded to his chest from the rain, and looked back up, bemused. "I'm off duty. My suit's in the truck. Got a problem?"

She shook her head, not sure how to tell him that he'd just gone from father image to sexual threat.

It was the jeans. They revealed more than those formless suits. They betrayed the sensuality of him, the long, lean lines that went with the hawklike nose and fierce eyes. They put him right in the league of all her teen fantasies, which had been populated with swaggering men in jeans and boots and little else.

Those fantasies had nothing on the form of Sergeant Rock O'Connor, and now wasn't the time to bring it up.

"No," she finally managed to say, her voice a little strangled. "No problem. It was just a surprise. Do I have to give you the list now?"

The sergeant didn't seem to be having any better luck than she at holding a train of thought. For a minute there, he just stared at her, those earth-brown eyes unreadable. Lee shivered under their scrutiny, suddenly remembering how little she had on beneath the robe and comforter. How very vulnerable she'd been in his arms. How, suddenly, the chills of fright were metamorphosing into something far more disturbing.

"Uh, it would help. Once we get you out of here, I don't want you coming back for a little while. And the place will be vulnerable until I can get the locks fixed."

"Leave?" she echoed immediately. "I can't leave."

His face immediately clouded over. She could almost hear him count to ten. "Where's your sister?" he asked.

"She's on call tonight. She'll be back by five tomorrow...no, this afternoon."

With a brisk nod, Rock reached for the phone where it had fallen near the pillow. "Good. That'll give me enough time to get a locksmith over here. Until then, you can't be here alone."

It was his tone of voice. Suddenly imperious, as if she were nothing more than a kid who'd broken the corral gate.

It set off every button Lee had. "It's almost two in the morning," she protested. "Just where am I supposed to go?"

He didn't even look up from where he was dialing. "Well, the first place you're going is to the hospital to get checked over."

"Hospital?" Hackles again, the same ones he'd raised when she'd been hanging out on the ledge. Silly responses she hadn't been able to help since she was six and all three of her siblings had ganged up on her. "I'm not going to any hospital. I'm fine."

He didn't say a word. He just reached over and gently rested a hand on her casted arm. Lee almost passed out on the spot.

The phone went back on the cradle. His brow lowered. "Lee?"

She couldn't quite answer. It felt as if he'd just rearranged the bones in her wrist with the benefit of a sledgehammer. Fine, she wanted to say. You're right. It does hurt. I must have done something to my wrist hanging out on that ledge. She couldn't quite say any of those things. She couldn't get her breath past the stabbing pain, the nausea, the sudden, surrounding darkness.

"Oh, damn..." was the only thing she could say, because she knew that after all this, she was about to pass out. And that made her furious.

Chapter 5

If Lee was the kind of person who swooned for effect, she would have loved the one she got. By the time she opened her eyes again, there were no fewer than five policemen hovering over her, every one of them holding a magazine or placemat to fan in her face. Unfortunately, contrary to what her career choice might have implied, Lee was not the dramatic type. So the first thing she did when she managed to focus on all those terrified faces was to laugh.

"'I have always depended on the kindness of strangers,'" she quoted in her best southern belle accent as she struggled to get up.

Rock did everything but plant the palm of his hand in the middle of her chest to push her back down where they'd settled her on the couch. "You're not going anywhere until the ambulance gets here," he informed her, his face betraying the most emotion of all. But only in a flash, as if that weren't allowed. Then he was back to just being angry.

"There will be no ambulance," Lee informed him eye to eye, even though hers were horizontal. "I mean it."

"Don't be stupid," he retorted. "You just passed out."

"So would you if a cop with hands like a yak had just punched you in your broken wrist."

"I did not—" He got that far before he saw that she was teasing. It didn't help any. In fact, it seemed to make things worse. "Marconi!" he barked. "Go down and wait for them. The rest of you—"

"Marconi," Lee interrupted handily. "Tell them to go home. If you don't, I will refuse when they get here. I am not wasting their time with this. It's just my wrist."

"You fainted!" Rock insisted as if she hadn't been there.

"I know. I overreacted, and I'm so embarrassed I want to die. Now, let me up and call off the paramedics, or I'll really get ugly."

"You want me to put you under protective custody?" Rock demanded. "Then we'd have to do it my way."

Lee glared with every bit of energy in her. "I already have a big brother, Sergeant O'Connor. In fact I have two. I'm not in the market for any more, thanks."

Lee caught the reactions of the other officers in the room. She decided it was a good thing Rock didn't. He darkened enough as it was.

"Marconi!"

"I'll radio them, Sarge."

That broke things up, leaving Lee a couple of minutes to pull herself together before she had to make good on her threat to move on her own. By then, Rock had dispatched the rest of the men, which left only the two of them occupying the tumbled room.

"I'm sorry," he immediately said, standing stiffly by the front door.

Lee had just made it into a sitting position where she was praying the pain in her arm would ease up just a little before she had to make that big leap to her feet. She didn't want to end up on her face again, because that would just guarantee her a place on the gurney. And if she was going to have to show up at Gen's hospital again, she wasn't going to do it in quite so dramatic a fashion.

Rock's apology got her attention.

"I didn't mean to yell at you," she apologized back with a rueful shake of her head. "It's just that I really am fine. I guess this just shook me up a little more than I thought."

He edged his way closer, as if nervous she'd bolt or something. "Don't be silly. Of course it was going to shake you up."

Lee shrugged. "No. I've been through worse in my life. Heck, I ended up in an ICU for two weeks once when I fell down a ravine on a horse. But..." She shook her head, trying to understand. "I guess I never really had the time to think about what was going to happen before it did. No one has ever threatened me in person before. And certainly not with a gun."

She looked up at Rock, thankful that he was the only one there. Uncertain how she knew he'd keep her secrets safe. "It was a long time out on that ledge," she admitted, her voice very small.

She wanted him to come back to her. She wanted to have his arms around her, just for a minute, just to shore up this uncertain place in her. For the first time in her life, she'd felt the real threat of violence, and it unnerved her.

But it seemed that now that he'd separated himself from her, Rock O'Connor wouldn't come back. Instead, he busied himself picking up some of the knickknacks that had fallen to the floor. Geodes from Zeke's treks into the wilderness, a papier-mâché dragon from Lee's nephew Micky. Picture frames filled with laughing faces and friendly eyes. Rock seemed to pause over those.

"I can look for you," he offered, musing over a picture of the entire family crowded around the Christmas table the year before. "To see if anything's missing."

Lee couldn't take her eyes from the pensive look on his face, the tight angles of sudden discomfort. "No hiding places," she tentatively acknowledged. "No valuables. Gen's a resident and I'm an aspiring writer. We're not exactly living the high life here."

That at least got Rock's attention away from the picture. He took a look around the room instead, and his opinion was all in his eyes.

"Mrs. Moffitt likes us," Lee acknowledged without being asked, giving her arm a test wiggle for the next stage of the trip. "She gives us a great break on the rent. I also have a sneaking suspicion that my brother Jake is supplementing things a little so that Gen and I don't have to go far to work. He worries."

Understatement of the year. And this time, Lee didn't think she was going to be as lucky keeping the news from him.

"What about your purse?"

Lee shrugged, edging closer to the edge of the couch. "I thought I saw it over his shoulder as he went down. I'll tell you what, a lot of people have gone to a lot of effort to get a lot of nothing."

"What about your pictures?" he asked.

It was a small thing. A question that might not have meant anything from another person. Lee had a feeling Rock didn't betray his compassion lightly, though. It made her smile.

"I had 'em on my bed when I was working," she assured him. "That purse is his with my blessings. Why did you come over if you were off duty?"

That caught him up short. His shrug was just a little too stiff as he settled the red-fringed scarf back on the piano. "I was still in the neighborhood."

"Any luck with that little girl?"

He just shook his head. Lee saw what it cost him, though. She could almost feel the weight of that victim's name on him. She wanted to tell him it was going to be okay. That they'd catch the man responsible. That this was a horrific aberration that couldn't possibly happen again. Even though she wanted to believe that with her whole heart, Lee kept her silence. She saw the reality there in Rock's stiff, unyielding posture.

"Are you married, Sergeant?"

That got a surprised look from him. "Married?"

She smiled. He sounded as if she'd asked if he were an Elvis impersonator. "Married. Wife, kids, white picket fence."

"No."

As simple as that. As bald. For some reason, Lee hurt for him much more than she did for herself. Especially since she had no idea how to ease the bleak finality of that word.

"Well, I'll tell you what," she offered, lurching all the way to her feet and saying a silent prayer of thanks that she didn't go right over on her nose. Everything held its place, though. "If you feel the need to stay till I'm safely dispatched to the hospital to get my wrist checked, get the cab while I'm in getting some clothes on. Then you can go home and get some sleep."

She seemed to have insulted him again. "I'm not calling any cab. I'll take you over."

Lee came to a stop, no more than five feet from him. Again she thought of how tall he was. How, except for her brothers, she'd never felt so small around a man before. "No, really. I'm—"

"Fine," he finished for her. "Yeah, I know. I don't care. I don't trust you to get there without interrupting a bank holdup. Now, go ahead and get your clothes on. I'll call the locksmith while I wait."

She sighed. "Sergeant..."

He did smile then, but it wasn't the kind meant to reassure. "I'm a public servant, Miss Kendall. I'm serving."

She hated the way that sounded on him, especially since she could still so easily imagine the hesitant comfort of his hand in her hair. "Lee," she said simply, the only concession she could give, and turned for her room.

"How well do you know Sergeant O'Connor, Abbie?" she asked forty minutes later as she sat back on the emergency room cart having her wrist looked at.

Her attention on the electrical cast saw that whined in her hand, Abbie Viviano offered up a vague kind of smile. "About as well as any of the guys on the force."

"What's he really like?"

Abbie concentrated on getting Lee's cast off as she talked. "I like him," she said.

The problem was that Lee heard instinctive defense in the doctor's voice, as if she'd had to make the assertion once too often.

"But?"

Abbie looked up, surprised. The saw whirred to a halt. "I need to get this done, Lee," she admonished gently. "Whatever you were doing tonight really screwed this up. You're so swollen again that your circulation's being compromised."

"You can't talk and saw at the same time?"

Abbie's grin was brief and telling. "You know that Rock isn't his real name."

Lee just nodded.

Abbie went back to sawing, the high-pitched whine grating as it bit into the hard material. "It's a nickname he earned on the street. Kind of a variation of *cojones,* if you get my drift. He'd do things nobody else would do. Had no fear. Some of the guys also call him the Terminator, because he's relentless. He's a hell of a cop."

"But?"

"But..."

For a minute the saw grated on, Abbie's movements gentle and competent, her eyes introspective. Lee waited as patiently as she knew how, not even sure why she was so anxious for Abbie's answer.

"He's only a cop," Abbie finally finished.

Lee wasn't sure what she'd been expecting, maybe an admission that Rock hit people, that he didn't get along with anyone, that he was suspected of being a vampire. This one didn't compute at all.

"Abbie," Lee protested. "I'm not married to a policeman. I don't even know any, except for the sheriff back home. If that's supposed to be some kind of code, I don't get it."

Abbie faced her this time, her eyes level, her concern clear. "Rock lives, eats and breathes being a cop," she said. "He doesn't have any friends outside the force. He doesn't have any hobbies anybody knows about except target practice down at the range and an occasional Cubs game with the other detectives. I've seen him with a woman only three or four times since I married Michael, and I didn't see any of those women again."

"Are you saying he's gay?"

That got a laugh. "No. He's not gay. But he is—"

She never got the chance to finish. With all the panache of a jilted leading lady, Gen slammed through the door, Tim hot on her heels.

"Good God!" she protested, eyes wild. "Can't I leave you alone for a minute?"

"Think of it this way," Lee countered. "You're up another five on me."

That didn't seem to help any. "Boy, if you didn't have bad luck, you'd have no luck at all, ya know it?"

Lee knew it far better than Gen did.

Tim forwent the introductions for a look at Lee's swollen, purple fingers. While Abbie sawed, he used the spreaders to facilitate cast removal. The minute the cast eased open, Lee could feel the terrible pressure ease.

"Another car?" he asked.

"A windowsill," Lee told him, trying not to wince as they moved her limb, ever so gently.

"You slammed a window on your arm?" Gen demanded.

Lee was going to have to thank Sergeant O'Connor, wherever he was, for not filling Gen in on all the news before Lee could defuse it a little. She knew just what would have happened if he had said that she'd been the victim of a break-in before Gen could see for herself that Lee was all right.

"Not exactly," she admitted, exchanging meaningful glances with Abbie. "I, uh, was hanging from my bedroom window so the guy who broke into the apartment wouldn't see me."

That brought both Gen and Tim to a dead stop.

"What?" they both demanded.

"As you can see," Lee intercepted, "I'm just fine...well, mostly fine. Although my purse is missing in action again."

Gen was reduced to complete silence. Tim, on the other hand, straightened in outrage, his eyes flashing. "Your apartment was broken into?" he demanded. "How? What happened? Where the hell were the police?"

"Right on the scene, after I phoned," Lee admitted. "That 911 is a real handy number."

"The policeman just said that he saw you back down here again," Gen objected, as if that made all the difference.

"He did," Lee assured her. "He brought me. Matter of fact, he hauled me up out of the rain in my nightgown. It was quite dramatic."

Gen did react then, her eyes widening. "You were hanging three stories above the ground by one hand?"

Lee just nodded, not particularly interested in reliving the moment.

"Oh, honey," Gen breathed, knowing perfectly well what it meant. She'd been the one who had inadvertently created that phobia about twenty years ago when she'd talked Lee into climbing far too high into the backyard elm and then been unable to catch her when Lee plummeted to the ground for her first round of casts and rehab at the ripe old age of four.

"Well, you were lucky," Tim admitted after his cursory examination. "I think you probably pulled the bones out of alignment, but considering what could have happened, I'm pretty happy."

"I'm thrilled," Lee assured him, and was relieved to see him smile in return.

He nodded, all business behind those nice blue eyes. "Okay, well, we'll get it taken care of and have you back home in..." He looked up, upset all over again. "Where are you going to stay tonight?" he demanded.

"I think your first option was a good one," Lee said.

"You can't do that," Tim protested even before Gen got a chance. "Not after what happened."

"Well, Sergeant O'Connor's probably back at the apartment now," Lee said, not wanting to encourage her sister's distress. "He said he was going to get locksmiths over. I could go home after that."

"No, you can't," Tim said. "I don't want you by yourself."

"Why not? I didn't hit my head or anything."

"She won't go home alone," Gen assured him. "She can stay here tonight."

"She's a big girl," Lee reminded her sister. "She can make her own decisions."

It was Tim who defused the situation with another smile and concerned eyes. "Doctors do tend to take over, don't we?"

Kind of like police sergeants, Lee wanted to say. She didn't.

"I just don't think you'll want to be alone tonight," he said simply. "That arm's going to hurt like a bad tooth."

"Why don't you come on home with me?" Abbie asked. "I'm just about ready to get off."

"Oh, I can't do that," Lee protested. "I have friends I can call."

Abbie's eyebrow rose. "At three in the morning? Come on, Lee. Michael and the kids are already asleep, and we have the room. It's no problem at all. I can bring you back here when I come on."

Gen was already nodding. "I'll just be getting off then," she agreed.

"Shouldn't I tell Sergeant O'Connor?" Lee asked.

Abbie smiled. "Oh, we'll figure something out."

What they figured out involved Michael Viviano, who ended up sitting at the breakfast table in his gym shorts wiping the sleep out of his eyes at four in the morning. He was going to have to do something about his wife's impulsive generosity. It had been six years since they'd met, and he was still trying to catch up with her.

This time, though, he probably agreed with her. Lee Kendall did look a little puny to be going home on her own. Besides, he didn't like what Rock was telling him about the break-in.

"You've only been on my crew for a couple weeks, O'Connor," he groused, taking a gulp of the coffee his wife had brewed him before she'd awakened him from a sound sleep to take care of their latest houseguest. "Tell me you're not going to make life difficult for me."

"Every chance I get, Lieu. I just got a feeling about this."

"Yeah, Swann warned me about your feelings."

Swann, Michael's former partner and best friend, one of the best detectives in all of Chicago. He was also O'Connor's boss before he got his transfer. Even if he hadn't known Rock before, Michael would have taken his suspicions seriously just based on the fact that even after the disciplinary hearing, Swann had fought like a dog against the transfer in the first place.

"I don't believe in coincidences," Rock said.

Michael sighed. "Neither do I. Go ahead and check it out." He asked the next question out of duty rather than conviction. He knew better than to think Rock would take a back seat on the Havlacjek murder. "You want to hand off your stuff on the Havlacjek case?"

"I don't have to. I can do this while Kramer's recanvasing the neighborhood to double-check those time inconsistencies for me. And I can search for a shoe and a purse at the same time."

"All right. But remember what I said before. I think after this, you're due for some vacation time."

"Sure, Lieu."

Which sounded suspiciously like "When pigs fly" to Michael.

Michael hung up the phone, his eye on the clock. It was closing in on 4:00 a.m., and Rock was still wired and ready. He'd probably head right from Lee's apartment to the area headquarters on Belmont to start running down ideas.

Climbing to his feet, Michael carried his coffee cup over to the sink and emptied it, thinking of what it had been like in the years before he'd met Abbie. When he'd come home alone and hurried back out to work just to see friendly faces. Dependent on his job for his life.

Not nearly as dependent as Rock O'Connor. Michael had known a lot of cops like him. He didn't want to see Rock end up the same way, because those cops usually wrote their retirement notice with the action end of a .45.

But that wasn't something he could do anything about at four in the morning. His wife was already curled up in bed, probably already situated halfway onto his side of the bed so she could snuggle right up against him, her back to his chest so he could rub her swollen belly as they fell asleep. Even with the questions about Lee Kendall's suspicious misfortune and Rock O'Connor's obsessions still plaguing him, Michael smiled in anticipation. It was time to turn off the light and tune out the force. So he did.

Left alone in the silence of Lee Kendall's apartment, Rock sat very still and looked around. He'd righted the overturned furniture and picked up the knickknacks, folded away the strewn linen and restocked the kitchen cabinets, and in the process collected an image of Lee Kendall that sharpened with each thing he'd handled.

Amaryllis Jane Kendall. Actress, playwright. He'd seen the depth of her talent in the minutes before he'd interrupted the rehearsal the other day. Sheer metamorphosis as the lithe, agile young blonde had become a wilted, washed-out old woman who couldn't focus on reality or make peace with her lost past. Rock didn't like theater. He'd always thought it was a waste of time. But after seeing Lee Kendall on stage for five minutes, he realized he'd been missing something powerful.

And it wasn't just her acting. It was her writing. Rock had seen it on the computer screen where the cursor still blinked as if patiently waiting for her return. "Just what is worth fighting for?" her character had demanded, and Jake had looked to see.

He'd read her words. Forceful, simple, straightforward words about honor and trust and commitment. Heartfelt words written by a hopeful person. Alien words that belonged in a world Rock didn't recognize.

Lee Kendall, horsewoman and scholar. A saddle, old and well-tooled, bookshelves full of classics and comedies. She kept her degrees in a steamer trunk and her riding boots on a hat rack.

Lee, fanciful child and seductive woman. Helium balloons hovering near the ceiling from her last birthday and red silk chemises spilling out of drawers like dangerous promises.

Rock looked at them, at everything he touched in these bright, whimsical rooms, like a light pouring through the window of a stranger's house on a cold night. Bright fish and plastic dishes. Roller blades and literature. Pictures of people he'd never know laughing with a delight Rock couldn't understand. The music of a party to which Rock had never been invited.

So he stood there, alone with the echoes of Lee's laughter in everything he touched and saw, and he ached in ways he hadn't since the day he'd walked out of his own house for the last time.

He'd meant to stay to get an idea why Lee Kendall had been attacked twice in the same week. He'd ended up pulling open all the old wounds, so that he felt more alone in these rooms than in that house from which he'd been running for twenty years.

He couldn't stay anymore. He couldn't look those old ghosts in the face when they appeared in a place like this. So, once he was certain the new locks were in and working, he turned off the lights and headed for the station so he wouldn't have to go home alone.

Chapter 6

By the time she walked back into her apartment, Lee had been cosseted and pampered and sung to by a pair of three-year-olds in Sesame Street pajamas. She'd been fed as if she were the last victim off the boat from the famine. If she weren't so amazed by Abbie Viviano's energy, even seven months pregnant, Lee would have been depressed. Two kids, another on the way, a police lieutenant for a husband, a career as a trauma surgeon, and Abbie still evidently managed to spend her mornings singing with the kids and baking chocolate chip cookies for the back-to-school party at the preschool.

It wasn't until Lee walked back into the apartment where only she and Gen lived that she realized that she was jealous. She wanted that controlled chaos in her life. She wanted sticky-fingered hugs every morning. She wanted to be so busy she didn't realize how lucky she was.

She missed Jake and Amanda and the kids. She missed Zeke with a passion. She missed the baby sisters and brothers she'd been forever asking her mother and then Jake for as she'd grown up. And she realized it when she walked in to find her own house back in order.

"What disaster?" was Gen's first reaction.

The living room had never been this clean. It even looked as if it had been dusted. Lee didn't know quite how to react. "Good grief," she finally managed. "He must have been here all night."

Gen immediately went on alert. "He who? Your policeman?"

Lee walked on through the room, noticing that Rock had put the pictures back on the end tables at precisely balanced angles, instead of the haphazard herd into which they usually clustered. The trunk was closed and the piano scarf perfectly aligned.

"He's not my policeman," she said absently. "I wonder if he does windows?"

"I wonder if he did ours?"

Lee took a peek in the kitchen. The dishes were washed and dried and lined up on the drainboard. The glasses that had shattered were suspiciously absent. "All he told Abbie was that he waited for the locksmith."

"He can wait any time he wants," Gen assured her. "As long as he brings his vacuum with him."

Lee decided not to pay any attention to her sister. Besides, she was feeling a little unsettled by the idea of Rock going through her things. She took a peek in her bedroom to find her chest of drawers neatly shut and all the stuffings carefully restuffed. That actually made her blush. She remembered those chemises hanging from the open drawer like petals from a forbidden flower, gifts from Amanda with an eye toward giving Jake more gray hairs.

And Rock had handled them. It was almost as if he'd had his hands on her, and just the thought made Lee uncomfortable. Warm. Restless, because she had a sudden image of those hands. Strong hands. Lean, craftsman's hands with calluses and grace.

Hands she could still feel wrapped around her like a father's embrace after he'd pulled her off that ledge, but hands that seemed to possess a restless life of their own when Rock dragged them through his hair in frustration or burrowed them into the back pockets of his jeans to maintain control.

"I really wish you two would reconsider," came a masculine voice from the doorway.

Lee turned around to fend Tim off as he followed them inside. "The worst is over," she assured him as he shut the door on his way in. "I need to get home and get to work."

He shook his head, a finger already wagging at the cast-covered arm he'd personally seen into a sling. "You've had two traumas in a matter of a week. You should be taking it easy."

Lee laughed at his concern. "I'm writing a play, Tim. Not roping cattle."

He still didn't look too happy. "I'm getting a little worried about you," he admitted, his bright blue eyes just a shade darker.

That made Gen laugh. "You're about twenty years too late," she informed him as she got down to the business of getting everybody refreshments. Since it was Tim standing there in the living room as if he had his hat in his hand, Gen pulled out the bottle of red wine somebody had given them for Christmas. Lee wondered what she'd offer if it had been Rock standing there.

"You're not on call tonight, are you?" Gen asked him.

Tim looked from Lee to Gen and back again. It had been Tim who had sat with Lee while she'd waited for the regional anesthetic to take effect, Tim who had returned at the end of Gen's shift to see the two of them safely home. "I shouldn't encourage you to drink after the medication I gave you," he said.

"Red wine?" Lee demanded with a grimace before she considered how impolite it was. "Don't worry. I'm strictly a Kool-Aid and water girl."

It was Gen's turn to wrinkle her nose. "My sister the Philistine."

That was when Tim finally began to relax. He stood in his Dock-Sides and polo shirt as if *he* were the one shoeless at the ball. It amazed Lee. She hadn't ever considered that Tim LaPierre might be uncomfortable in any situation, certainly not being offered a glass of wine in a resident's apartment. But then, even at its cleanest, the place still looked like the tail end of a flea market. Lee figured he probably looked a whole lot more comfortable on a Kharistan rug, sipping from old Baccarat. Instead, he got old hardwood floors and chipped jelly glasses.

Gen handed Lee a glass filled to the brim with a liquid the color of toxic waste. Rhinosoberry, or something like that. Lee sighed with satisfaction. No matter what Tim might have preferred, this was civilization at its finest.

"To friends," Lee toasted.

Gen handed Tim his wine and lifted her own glass. Lee turned to clink glasses with Tim and came to a dead halt, her glass suspended in midair, her gaze locked on his. He was watching her, all right. He even had his glass up in the air, his grace making even the Flintstones look elegant. But there wasn't a "let's be friends" look in his eyes. Not even close. Tim LaPierre had the bewildered expression in his eyes Lee had always dreamed a man would have when he realized that he was falling in love.

"Holy cow," she breathed, stupefied, then clamped her mouth shut before she did something really stupid.

"Holy cow what?" Gen demanded, her attention too taken by the pouring to notice the sudden color in Lee's cheeks and the heat in Tim's eyes.

But it was Lee's day to be saved, because just then the three of them were distracted by the sound of a key being inserted in the front door.

They turned, their expressions identical, their glasses still raised, two deep burgundy and the other a livid green.

"Not again," Lee moaned.

Tim hushed her with a wave of a hand. "Get in the bedroom," he ordered in a hush as he set his wine down. "Call the police."

"What are you going to do?" Gen demanded.

He didn't answer. He just took her wine from her and shooed her away. Lee was having trouble thinking. She could hear the mutters of someone concentrating on the lock—the new lock Rock had just had installed. She could hear the rattle of impotent attacks on the tumblers. Above it all she could hear her own heartbeat as it slammed blood past her ears. She briefly thought of just rebreaking the wrist right here and saving whoever this was the trouble of doing it all over again.

"Lee," Tim urged, grabbing her glass and turning her after her sister. "Go!"

He was already reaching for the baseball bat Gen kept at the kitchen doorway for just such eventualities. Lee wanted to tell him to stop. She wanted to close her eyes and make it all go away.

And then she heard it. Clearly, succinctly, right through the door. A terse expletive that had to do with rodents and bodily functions. And Lee knew only one person who cursed like that.

"Well, hell," she snapped, pulling away from Tim's grip.

He made a grab for her and missed as she stalked past. "Lee, don't!"

"Lee?" Gen countered

But Lee was intent on confronting the person on the other side of that door, the same one who had just cost her at least five years of her young life.

"Sierra!" she snarled, pulling the door open with a flourish.

Sierra squealed like a pig caught under a tire. Standing behind her, Creighton jumped at least a foot.

"What are you doing here?" Sierra demanded, the duplicate key Lee had given her some time ago still poised to attack the door.

"Me?" Lee countered, free hand on hip. "I live here. What are you doing breaking into my apartment?"

"Are you all right?" Creighton demanded, charging in with unaccustomed agitation. "We called all afternoon and didn't get any answer. We thought..."

It was Lee's turn to react, and she did it with dispatch. "Oh, my God!" she gasped, staring at both of them as if they'd just stepped off a spaceship. "Oh, my God, rehearsal. I'm so sorry. I completely forgot!"

That brought the both of them to a complete halt.

"Forgot?" Creighton demanded in that tone of voice that implied that what she'd forgotten was her brain, not her rehearsal. Considering the fact that Lee had never missed a rehearsal in her entire career, especially when it was an Equity production, and one this important, he had every right.

"She was at the hospital most of the night," Tim said, defending her before Lee got a chance to ask him not to. After all, she knew just how her friends would react, and they did.

Before Lee could protect herself, both of them were on her like mothers with an injured child. Lee fended them off with what grace she had left. Gen just pulled out more jelly glasses. The wine they'd received as a Christmas gift disappeared faster than ice on a July sidewalk.

"The play!" Creighton all but howled when Lee admitted that the intruder had been in her bedroom.

"As safe as my virtue," Lee retorted with a wry smile.

Creighton was good enough to look abashed. "It *was* going to be my next question," he said.

"So what did he get?" Sierra demanded, booted feet up on the architect's cabinet that doubled as a coffee table.

Lee, safely ensconced on the old couch, shrugged away the trauma—and the tender surprises—of the night before. "My purse."

"Which isn't much," Sierra supplied for her. "Although it has been a popular item lately."

Lee grinned. "And in return, I had the police personally clean and straighten the apartment. All in all, not a bad exchange."

"But you could have been killed!" Creighton protested with a wave of his glass.

Lee waved back, wishing everybody would let the whole thing drop. She sure wanted to. "And then Marlyse would have had a crack at playing Mary, just like she wanted. Maybe she sent that guy over to scare me off, ya think, Creighton?"

"It's not funny, Lee."

"Of course it is. Can you see Marlyse skulking down an alleyway plotting with some guy named Guido to do me in?"

Considering the fact that Marlyse was as vague and distracted as the character she sought to play, the image was a beaut. Sierra laughed. Lee laughed. Creighton did not. Neither, in fact, did Tim or Gen.

"Come on," Lee demanded, dead serious now. "I had an adventure, just like Winnie the Pooh. It is over, everything's fine, and Creighton will dock me a penalty for missing rehearsal. Now, let's talk about something else, okay?"

It was Gen who understood. Gen who smiled and lifted her glass and finished her wine. Gen who turned to Tim, who still betrayed a rather large amount of outrage, and asked him about a patient they evidently had in common. Sierra took the hint and dropped her feet from the table.

"Got any more of this swill?" she demanded.

"Not a drop," Lee admitted.

She nodded and tugged on Creighton's sleeve. "In that case, we're outta here."

"Only as long as you get some more and come back," Lee said. "I thought we all might go get some dinner a little later."

Creighton almost blew it. His expression clouded over as he got to his feet. "You're sure?"

Lee gave him a bright grin. "The second act is finished. I thought you might like to see it."

Sierra was already at the door, her hand on the knob. "He'll be back," she assured Lee. "Gen, what was that dreck you forced down our throats?"

"Châteauneuf-Du-Pape."

Sierra scowled mightily, which on her soft, round features, made her look like a black troll doll. "That's what I thought. Well, I'll have to drag Creighton along with me to make sure I buy something at least as awful."

"It was a '69," Gen offered, knowing perfectly well that it was Sierra, not Creighton, with the exquisite taste in wines.

Sitting very quietly on her corner of the couch, Lee finished off her punch and waited for her friends to leave. Then she could excuse herself from Gen and Tim and escape back into her room until they got back. She could have a few moments to herself to finish putting what had happened behind her where it belonged.

Sierra and Creighton made it to the door. Sierra opened it, Creighton right on her heels. Lee prepared to sigh and ease her way out of the living room. Then Sierra turned to walk on through and stopped. Stared. Smiled. And Lee realized she wasn't going anywhere.

"Is Lee Kendall here?" a familiar voice asked.

"Maybe," Sierra answered, leaning her weight on one hip and tilting her head way over to give him the once-over. "What'd she do now, hit a police car?"

Biting back a few curses she'd learned from Sierra, Lee launched herself to her feet. "Down, girl," she warned, walking on over to where her director was holding Rock from the door.

The first thing Lee thought when she saw him was that he was the one who needed some time off. He looked so tired. So strained, as if basic civility was already well beyond his allotment of energy. She wondered what he'd think if she wrapped him in the comforter and rocked him, just as he'd done for her the night before.

"Come on in, Sergeant O'Connor," she invited him with a hand past Sierra. "Pay no attention to these two. They were just leaving."

"We're getting wine for dinner," Sierra goaded. "Are you staying, too?"

Rock didn't even flinch. "No."

Sierra threw Lee a look, obviously in search of reaction. Lee gave it, but not the one she wanted. Without a word, Lee threatened her friend with bodily harm if she didn't escape that very minute. And Sierra, who had known Lee since college, understood perfectly. Grabbing Creighton by the arm, she edged by Rock without another word and fled.

"Come on in," Lee invited, hoping he didn't see how worried he made her. "You just missed visiting with the lovely Miss Sierra Worth and Creighton Holliwell III, whom you've met, and you of course remember my sister Gen and my orthopedist Tim LaPierre.''

''We've met.''

Lee managed to get Rock inside and the door closed before any new contestants signed in. Courtesies were summarily exchanged, Tim getting briefly to his feet and Gen waving, as was her wont when Lee introduced another new guest into the fray.

Lee just ignored her like she always did. ''We're out of wine,'' she told Rock, who was still standing there just inside the doorway as if it were the only safe place in the room, ''but I bet there's a beer someplace in here.''

''I'm on duty,'' he demurred with all the ease of a man in a lingerie shop.

''Oh, garbage,'' she retorted. ''You were on duty at two this morning, and I know darned well you didn't go home after dropping me off. Now, have the damn beer or I'll get a hose and pour it down your throat while Gen and Tim hold you down.''

For just a second, he glared. Those hot, deep brown eyes of his flared and darkened, as if he wanted to hurt her. Lee faced him down, knowing that wasn't at all what he wanted to do. Knowing somehow that he needed someone to give him permission to relax, or he wouldn't do it.

Behind her, she heard the sudden silence from Gen and Tim, who were trying their best to be discreet about their curiosity. Lee knew that all attention was on Rock, and wondered what that would do to his answer.

He actually took a fraction of a second to consider the implications. Then he returned his consideration to Lee, who was still waiting for him to smile.

He didn't. He did relax, fractionally. Lee saw it in the set of his shoulders beneath that limp, well-worn suit coat. She saw it in his eyes that backed down from angry to wary. She recognized it in the instinctive lessening of pressure in her own chest, and knew that at least she was going to be able to give him this much.

"Maybe one beer," he relented, his eyes easing all the way to a kind of careful chagrin. "It has been a long day."

Lee backed away from the door and showed him in. "I bet. I'm exhausted, and all I've done is sing ABC songs with Johnnie and Mary Rose Viviano."

"Have you found something out?" Gen asked.

That seemed to stop Rock in his tracks. His features darkened again as he jammed his hands into his sagging pockets. "No," he said without grace. "Nothing new."

Lee wondered if Gen knew that his anger was directed at himself.

The little girl. Lee could almost hear it in his voice by now, a bleak, controlled fury that seemed to spill over everything. She didn't know anything about the case, not really. Nothing more than what was in the papers, which mostly amounted to repeated interviews to find out how the grandparents felt about such a sweet girl dying at a stranger's hands. It didn't matter. Lee wanted it all over. She wanted some kind of closure for Rock, no matter what it was, because this was eating away at him like a bad cancer.

She saw Tim getting to his feet, as if the direction of the conversation demanded a certain formality. She thought of the quiet regret he'd exhibited when his patient had died, and thought how different he was from Rock. She'd been right before. Rock had been broken from the earth, while Tim had been crafted from it, all patience and talent. Rock was drive and determination and primal energy. She thought he took up all the extra room in the apartment, even though Tim moved more comfortably in it.

She realized that Tim lived life, but Rock attacked it like an adversary. It made her wonder how he would approach a woman.

Just the thought sent those odd skitterings of nervous energy through her. Frissons of anticipation, as if she could already feel his hands on her. Commanding, this time, rather than comforting. Compelling . . .

"Lee?"

She started to attention, blushing at her unaccustomed fantasy. She'd known the man a matter of one crime report and a night spent pulling her off the ledge, and already she was fantasizing about his discovering just why she wore those red chemises of hers. And that was before she'd even found out if he'd ever laughed.

"I'm sorry, Gen. What?"

Gen was staring at her as if she'd just stripped down naked in front of them.

"The beer," her sister prodded a bit primly, which meant she knew exactly what Lee was thinking.

"The beer," Lee answered with a brisk nod and whirled around for the kitchen. "What can I do for you besides that, Sergeant?"

She flinched at her own choice of words, especially since her imagination was providing suggestions in quick succession, one of which involved the sergeant's holster and very little else. She cooled herself off in front of the open refrigerator.

"Well," Rock answered from behind her, his voice suddenly hesitant. "I, uh, need to talk to you alone for a few minutes, if I could."

Lee didn't even bother to look up from where she was rooting through Gen's health food and her own junk food to find the beer she knew was lurking in there somewhere. "Fine. Take me to dinner."

She found the beer, tucked away behind a head of frozen lettuce. She was thinking that it probably had ice floes of its own, when Rock startled her with his answer.

"Okay."

Lee straightened so fast she almost gave herself a brand new concussion.

"Pardon?"

Rock shoved a hand through his tumble of thick, dark hair, his attention straying just a second to the living room. "That's fine," he said, not sounding sure at all. "Where would you like to go?"

"The Pump Room," Lee promptly answered, which got her a great double take. She grinned like a pirate. "But I'll be happy to settle for Juan Ton's over on Halsted."

She wanted to demand to know whether he was serious. One look at his taut features deterred that idea. Instead, she shut the door and straightened. "Is it okay if I get changed?" she asked, trying very hard to keep the sudden anticipation from her voice. "I've been in these clothes all night."

"Yeah," he said, his eyes flashing with something hot and close. "I know."

Lee almost didn't move. She almost couldn't. Just that hint of emotion in his eyes resurrected the memory of his arms around her, his hand in her hair, his voice, tender and patient, as he eased her away from her shakes. More, it promised, and that was what scared her, because she'd never heard that kind of promise before. She'd never realized that she'd wanted to. Not like this.

She fled to the safety of her room before he got the chance to answer, just in case he thought to change his mind. And then she deliberately forfeited that safety by slipping on one of those hot red chemises beneath a sweater with a V-neck that slid off her shoulder and a long, pleated cream skirt that whispered around her calves as she walked.

When Lee returned to the living room, it was to find Gen trying her best to engage the sergeant in some kind of conversation with herself and Tim. Tim sat back on his chair, legs elegantly crossed, his glass of wine almost drained. Rock didn't exactly sit. He perched, as if anticipating flight. He faced Gen, his beer can trapped between his hands, his tie yanked just a little to the side, his posture stiff and wary.

Lee wondered why she hadn't grilled Abbie Viviano a little more closely about Rock when she'd had the chance. They'd had the entire day. But every time Lee came up with a question, she thought of something else to say. Something that wouldn't jeopardize her half-formed hopes about a man she barely knew.

"I'd put five on it, " Gen was saying.

"Never take one of her bets," Lee warned Rock, walking on in. "We're trying to break her of the habit before it's too late."

He looked up. He went very still. Lee saw his knuckles go white around that can. She could almost hear his breath catch. He knew what she was wearing, and Lee fought an unholy urge to smile.

"She says I'm going to end up saving you again," he said. "That you're always needing to be saved from something."

Lee forced herself to move. She didn't want to. She wanted to stand where she was for hours and just soak in the heat from Rock's eyes. She wanted to make him sweat, and she'd never felt that way before in her life.

It scared her.

It thrilled her.

For the first time since she'd bought that first red chemise as a kind of personal dare, she realized just how sensual cool silk felt against the skin. How just wearing it, even with only one strap visible, could escalate a confrontation into delicious warfare.

She wanted to wage warfare of the most dangerous kind, and she knew better.

She'd always known better. Lee was not the kind of person to deliberately tempt a man. She'd never really had the time or seen the need to before. She'd always had so much on her plate that men were simply another lovely side dish. Suddenly she saw how wrong she'd been—and it was, of all people, this taciturn, hard-edged man who fit her furniture like a hawk settling into a Fabergé cage whom she wanted to make her main course.

She didn't know what to do about that. Especially now, because she knew that now, more than ever, the last thing Sergeant O'Connor needed was her throwing pheromones into the mix.

She couldn't help it. Suddenly, for the first time in her life, she felt like a woman instead of a little sister trying to break curfew.

"Lee always needs saving," Gen offered dryly, her attention a lot sharper than it seemed. "She doesn't look before she leaps."

Lee faced her sister, understanding perfectly well that she knew exactly what was going on. Needing more than anything to ask her advice. Wishing they were alone instead of standing between two men, so she could ask it.

Instead, she smiled brightly. "I sure did before I dove out that window," she insisted. "Now, if you kids don't mind, I'm going out." Another grin, this one chagrined, as she looked around for the purse she always threw on one of the chairs as she walked in. "I don't guess I'll take my purse, though."

Rock was already on his feet, still holding his beer like an unaccepted ritual offering.

"I guess I'll be going, too," Tim said, setting down his glass and getting to his feet as well.

Lee didn't wait for Gen's reaction. "But I thought you were going to hang around," she objected.

She didn't notice Rock's reaction. She caught Tim's, just a flash of discomfort, and she was furious with herself. She wanted him to stay for Gen. She wanted Gen to have her own company tonight. She almost begged.

Gen forestalled her. "Thanks for everything, Tim," she said in that tone of voice that also reminded her little sister that she didn't need pampering. "You really didn't have to go to all this trouble."

Tim's smile was bright and easy. "Anything for my two favorite ladies." He brandished a finger at Lee. "I do not set the same arm three times," he admonished. "Be careful."

Lee grimaced. "Contrary to whatever Gen says, I do not make a habit of this. Thank you again, Tim. Your invitations back here are purely social."

He nodded and smiled, a brilliant smile that betrayed intelligence and whimsy and music. Everything Lee had always said she wanted in a man. "In that case, you have a deal."

Finally he turned to Rock. "Sergeant," he said, extending his hand, "hopefully the next time we won't see each other in an official capacity."

Rock shook hands. "Doctor."

Lee showed Tim out, and then turned to her sister. "What are you going to do now?" she asked.

It was Gen's turn to pull a face. "What do you mean, what am I gonna do? I'm gonna catch up on my reading, just like I'd planned all along. And, I guess, I'll wait for Sierra and Creighton to bring me some more wine."

"Oh, God," Lee blurted. "I forgot." She turned to Rock. "I'm supposed to be going out to dinner with my friends."

Gen shooed her like an old mother hen. "Oh, for heaven's sake. Go."

She was going. She really was. And then the phone rang. Lee instinctively picked it up on her way by.

"Lee?" the voice demanded fortissimo from the other end of the line. "Is that you?"

Lee's stomach skidded into her knees. She'd been found out. She did the only thing a raving coward would do in a situation like this. She handed the phone to her big sister. "It's for you," she said, knowing perfectly well that Gen had heard that voice.

Then, before she could do anything about it, Lee literally pushed Sergeant O'Connor out the door to dinner.

"What was that all about?" he demanded halfway down the steps.

"Nothing," she snapped as she clattered down the steps at breakneck speed.

"If it's nothing," he countered, close on her heels, "what's got you so upset?"

She reached the bottom of the steps and turned on him, suddenly angry that she couldn't even evade her own cowardice.

"Sergeant," she said, "I appreciate the concern, but it isn't your problem. Really."

That was when she realized that Rock O'Connor hadn't accepted her invitation simply because he wanted to gaze into her eyes over wine and French bread. Standing one step above her, he watched her, eyes suddenly wary and uncomfortable, stance straightening to professional attention, shoulders lifting in a silent sigh. Before he said a word, she knew she didn't want to hear it.

"I'm afraid it is my problem," he disagreed with her in an infuriatingly calm voice.

Even standing more than a full head shorter than he at the best of times, Lee faced off with him, arms crossed, posture just as rigid. "And why is that?" she asked.

He was at least gentleman enough to step down to her level before facing her. It didn't really help in the end, because it wasn't the messenger that upset her, but the message. "I wanted to talk to you alone, because I need to find out all I can about the people you know."

Suddenly she couldn't breathe. "Why?"

He didn't even flinch. "Because I think one of them is trying to kill you."

Chapter 7

Lee did the only thing Rock expected her to do under the circumstances. She laughed. "Don't be silly," she said, turning back for the door and the dusk-scented street beyond.

Rock followed. "I think you'd better listen," he suggested.

"I have bad luck," she countered, not bothering to look back at him as she stepped out on the sidewalk and started heading west. "You could have asked my oldest brother, Jake. That was him on the phone just now, getting all ready to yell at me about not taking care of myself. Jake's used to doing that, Sergeant. He's had to do it since the day I could first walk."

Rock just kept following her, knowing too well by now how to play this scene out. "I think this is more."

That at least got her to stop. They stood in front of his truck, which sat idling and double-parked in front of her house. She turned around on him so fast that her skirt swirled around her calves. The sweater slid down just a little further so that Rock could see the hot red of that chemise strap just at the edge of her neck. In the dusk, she looked ethereal, as if Rock had made her up from the cloth of his imagination. Clear-eyed, pale, clean and fresh and sensuous beyond the hopes of a man who had given up being clean and innocent a long time ago.

She glared at him in challenge, and Rock wanted to give her what she wanted. He wanted to tell her she was right. He'd only made this up to see her again. To stand close enough to her to smell the whisper of soap on her skin, to stare, mesmerized at the damn near silvery glow of her hair. To lose himself in the clear, sweet water of those impossibly blue eyes.

He wanted to admit that he'd been staying at the station because he was afraid to sleep. Afraid to let the memory of her loose in his subconscious.

But, in the end, the most important thing was that he needed to protect the unspoiled enthusiasm in those beautiful eyes. He needed Lee to believe that there was still honor and beauty and goodness in the world. He needed her to believe it, because he didn't.

And maybe if he kept her from walking headlong into the mess this case was turning out to be, he could somehow do that.

"I don't care," she said, posture as straight and certain as honor. "I'm going to have dinner first. And I'm going to damn well enjoy it."

She turned away again, a swirl of silvered mist in the shadow-strewn street. A brief insinuation of scent in the night air. A temptation worse than Rock had ever had in his long, sorry life. And yet, because of who he was, he didn't move.

"Lee," he said simply. "Where are you going?"

It took her a few more steps to come to a stop. When she did, she didn't immediately turn back to face him, as if that act alone would be too much for her.

"I'm going to dinner," she said, head up.

Head up, Rock thought. The difference between the two of us. She always looks up for her answers, as if she believes there really is something beyond her. Something worth looking for.

Rock hadn't had a reason to look up since he could remember.

"The truck's back here," he said simply.

It still took her a second, but when she turned, she did it with the offer of a chagrined smile at the sight of the double-parked truck no more than fifty feet away.

"Somebody's bound to object if I just leave it there till we get back," Rock said.

That quickly, her anger evaporated. As an act of will, it stunned Rock. As a reflection of her true optimism, it bothered him. She'd decided she really wasn't going to believe him. He could almost hear her say it out loud. Well, he was going to have to make her, because he was suddenly sure that she wouldn't ever be objective enough to recognize danger if it came at her from one of her friends.

"Boy," she admitted, settling into a long, graceful stride that damn near outdistanced his. "Your job has better perks than mine does. I've never been able to double-park just because I was a playwright. Do you pay at restaurants?"

Rock couldn't help it. He wanted to laugh. "Yes, I pay at restaurants," he said, lengthening his stride to match hers. "And if somebody holds up the restaurant, I have to arrest them, even if I'm off duty."

He'd reached the passenger side of the truck, suddenly aware that he hadn't cleaned out the front seat in weeks. He wanted to change his mind. To turn off the engine, leave the thing where it was and walk to the miserable restaurant, just so Lee wouldn't see him as he really was.

"Yeah," she was saying as he opened the door for her. "But you don't have to deal with neurotic directors and method actors. I'd rather be at the wrong end of a restaurant robbery any day."

Rock nodded, a chuckle escaping against his will. "So would I."

"Aha!" she yelled suddenly, a finger pointed at his face, sheer delight on her features. "You *can* do it!"

Rock was immediately suspicious. "What can I do?"

Lee gave him her most audacious grin. "Laugh," she said. "Gen bet me ten that you'd never laughed in your life. I assured her that you must have, at least once." Rock gave her one of his most intimidating scowls, sure to quell even the most obnoxious of inquiries. Lee just pushed merrily along. "Probably when you arrested the guy who had the gall to try and stick up a restaurant while you were trying to eat, right?"

"You're pushing it," he warned blackly.

She laughed, unrepentant. "Well, if I don't get you to do it at least once more, how the heck can I collect my ten? Gen'll never pay out on just my say-so."

That almost earned her another one. As it was, he cocked the corner of his mouth just enough and turned her toward the truck. "In that case, you're just going to have to forfeit the money. It's a bad habit, anyway."

Lee went along without protest. "What? Betting or laughing?"

She came close again. "Both. People should always wonder."

Lee wondered. God, how she wondered, as Rock shut the door. What the heck was she supposed to do? Just how was she supposed to react to this news? If she'd been at all city-hardened, like Gen claimed she herself was, maybe she'd take it all in stride. One of her friends wanted to hurt her, and she had to do something about it.

One of her friends.

Lee didn't want to think about it. Not then. Not ever.

She took a long breath as she waited for Rock to make it around to the other side of the truck. Completely against good judgment, she took a surreptitious look around the truck, and suddenly she forgot about her friends. For just a moment she forgot completely about runaway cars and lost purses. She took one look in Rock's truck and wanted to cry.

It was an old truck, well-used, beaten up like the old teddy bear she used to carry with her everywhere when she was a little girl. Cluttered and comfortable in a way that made Lee ache for home. She took in the frayed seats, the Chicago police baseball cap that was tossed over ball glove and jeans. The truck radio set to old rock and the police radio set to the tinny voice of some dispatcher Lee couldn't understand. The toolbox, the fast-food bags, the dog-eared newspapers and books. Lee could smell oil and leather and old french fries.

If there had been a layer of dust and a couple of good-sized potsherds and a trowel added in, it would have been Zeke's truck she'd entered. If there had been tack and the latest *Quarter Horse Quarterly,* Jake's. The homesickness gathered in her chest like a soreness she couldn't dispel, almost taking her sense of place with it.

"Lee?"

She looked over, not even realizing that while she'd been daydreaming, Rock had climbed into the cab. He stopped there, his features folded into concern.

Lee couldn't help thinking that she'd traveled all the way to Chicago to find a man who looked more at home in Wyoming than he did in Chicago.

He didn't belong in that suit. He didn't deserve the lines of strain between his eyes, the weary cant to his shoulders. He should be bright and sharp and smiling, and he wasn't. Again, Lee thought of Jake. Of Jake who had forfeited so much for her, for all of them. Who had ended up looking so much like this man before they'd seen what was wrong.

"Families" was all she could say, fighting sudden, surprising tears. She wanted to run in and grab the phone back from Gen. She wanted to apologize to her big brother for brushing him off. She wanted to go home where he could protect her, just like he wanted.

Rock looked around the cluttered front seat, a little bemused. "Families?"

Lee smiled. "Your truck," she explained with a small, ineffective wave of her hand. "It's making me homesick."

Rock looked around the truck, bemused. "This?"

Lee giggled, even with the lump of emotion in her throat. "Everybody drives one just like it at home. I'm sure I feel worse because I just blew Jake off, but I couldn't let him talk me into going home right now. Especially when I want to."

"What do you mean?"

She shrugged. "It's instinctive. I want to go home when I'm scared. You scared me."

She wasn't sure how she'd expected him to react to that. She sure didn't expect him to nod and say "Good." But he did.

"You want me to go home?" she retorted.

"I want you to be scared. At least enough so you watch out for yourself. I was serious about what I said."

Lee nodded, miserable, afraid, feeling horribly exposed, even here with this honorable man. "I know. I just don't want to believe you. Besides, if you are right, I'm never going to get them all off my back."

"Your family?"

She nodded. Then she looked over at him. Really looked, to see that somehow he didn't quite understand, as if she'd just been expounding on the symbolism behind *Waiting for Godot*.

"Don't you have any brothers or sisters?" she asked.

He shook his head. She heard something in that silence, something small and hurt. She wondered if Rock realized that he'd betrayed it. She wondered what it meant.

"Sometimes it's wonderful, " she said. "Sometimes, though, your biggest brother makes a call like that one and you want to tip them all off a very high ledge."

"You didn't talk to him. How do you know what he was going to say?"

She looked ahead through the windshield, where she saw rows of well-kept brick homes and tended lawns, well-kept cars beneath well-pruned trees. She imagined a high mountain meadow with long fences and glossy horses, and suddenly the street felt claustrophobic.

"Because I'm the baby," she said. "He'd say, 'You're a big girl, Lee. I trust you to be okay.'"

"What's wrong with that?"

"It's not what he says. It's what I'd hear. I'd hear him really wanting to say, 'Come home where I can watch you. Where you'll be safe.' "

"Does he do that to your sister?"

Lee grimaced. "She's not the baby."

"And?"

She stared at him, amazed. "You really don't have brothers and sisters, do you?"

This time she saw it. That brief, bleak emptiness to his eyes. The kind of pain Lee with her close, protective family had never known.

And this time she knew that it wasn't something she could ask. So she changed the conversation completely.

"I bet you'd be more comfortable in those jeans than that suit," she challenged.

It took Rock only a second, but just as deliberately, he responded. Popping off the emergency flashers, he shoved the truck into gear just as a BMW honked behind them. Rock honked back and took off.

"No bet," he countered.

"Baseball?" she asked, motioning to the glove.

"Softball."

"I thought it was considered sissy in Chicago to play softball with a glove."

He gave her a glare and went back to driving, turning east on Dickens toward Halsted. "I thought you were into theater."

Lee laughed. "Contrary to popular belief, people interested in theater can also participate in sports."

Rock actually looked impressed. "You follow the Cubs?"

Lee grinned, knowing she was going to see that anticipation die. "Well, no. Baseball isn't exactly the sport I follow."

"What?" he asked, briefly looking over so that the streetlights glinted in his eyes on the way by. "Football? Basketball?"

"Cutting horses."

His reaction consisted of total silence, for at least two blocks. "Cutting horses."

"Uh-huh. Ever seen one work a cow?"

"Not unless it was during halftime at the Super Bowl."

It was Lee who ended up laughing. "You don't know what you're missing," she assured him. "There is nothing finer than watching a horse work a steer. My brother Jake raises the finest cutting horses in the world."

He gave her another one of those looks, as if needing some reassurance that she wasn't putting him on. Lee laughed again, by now used to the reaction.

"If you think you're amazed, you can imagine what my friends in theater think."

"Especially that guy with the boat."

"Especially," Lee admitted with delight, "that guy with the boat. Actually, I think he's more worried I'm gonna kill myself before I can write the play that's going to secure his place in the annals of theater history."

"It's that important, huh?"

Lee looked over at him, seeking her own assurances. But he wasn't wasting his time kidding her. He was busy working the truck into a parallel parking spot that shouldn't have fit a motorcycle. He managed it with a fluid dispatch that left Lee impressed.

"Maybe I should think about dating a cop," she said. "You guys never seem to have a problem with parking."

"You don't even have a car here," he accused.

Lee unlatched her door. "For this exact reason. It's much easier to find parking in Lost Ridge, Wyoming."

"I'll bet."

It didn't even occur to Lee to let Rock lead the way into Juan Ton's. It was, after all, her hangout, a little Thai-Southwestern café with an owner named Seamus Schmidt, who happened to like theater and sang the menu when asked. Lee was sure Rock wouldn't ask, so she picked up the laminated variety on the way by as Lia, Seamus's Thai-born wife, seated them in the number one booth.

"I don't suppose they have hamburgers here," Rock griped, sliding into the cracked red Naugahyde. His atten-

tion was more on the decor, which consisted mainly of
Navaho pots, cow skulls and variegated sari silk. Lee was
sure that it didn't help that the couple in the booth next to
them was busy arguing the merits of doing *Oklahoma!* in
the nude.

"Hamburgers?" Lee echoed with a perfectly deadpan
delivery. "Seamus serves great hamburgers. Raw. Sea-
soned with cilantro and balsamic vinegar and then rolled up
in a blue corn tortilla."

Rock glared.

"With truffle garnishes."

He damn near growled. Lee laughed.

"Your prejudices are showing, Sergeant," she accused
gently.

It took Rock a second, but he ended up looking abashed.
"You're right," he admitted. "This isn't my..."

"Thing."

He shrugged. "I thought you might explain it to me."

Lee let her eyebrow rise in surprise. "What?" she demanded. "Non-greasy spoon cuisine? That might take a
minute."

"Theater."

"Oh." Her stomach settled lower with the sour taste of
inevitability. "That."

Rock nodded. "That."

Lee was saved, at least for the moment, when Seamus
himself showed up. A red-haired troll of a man who affected a ponytail and pierced earring, Seamus had a grin
like a pirate and a wardrobe that hadn't changed since he'd
come home from Nam.

"Lee, star of my black night," he greeted her in a
booming baritone as he dropped to one well-padded,
denim-clad knee before her. "Flower of my barren desert.
What inspiration do you bestow on me?"

Lee saw Rock physically flinch. She managed another
grin, until she realized that Seamus was also a friend, and
that, according to Rock, one of her friends might have had
something to do with that man who had chased her out her
window.

"Seamus," she said instead, "this is Rock O'Connor. He is not used to theater people or theater hangouts. Do you think you could accommodate his tastes?"

Seamus had a laugh like a chain saw. He inflicted it on Rock and yanked the menu right out of his hands again. "No problem," he said, regaining his considerable feet. "Cop, huh? You checking on Lee's accident the other day, or just using it as an excuse to sit down to a meal with her?"

Lee was all set to interrupt. She saw that Rock was all set to object. Seamus waved a rather large hand and shushed them both.

"It is precisely what I'd do, my dear sir. Now, I'll fry something wonderful for you. The regular, lass?"

Lee just nodded. "The regular."

With a sweeping bow, Seamus melted back into the woodwork, and Rock was left shaking his head.

"That," Lee said deliberately, "is one of my friends."

Rock seemed impervious to guilt. He just gave his tie another good yank so that it was hanging halfway down his shirt, unbuttoned his top button and leaned back in the booth, an arm thrown over the back, so that his suit jacket hung limp behind him and Lee could just see the gun that peeked out from the back of his waist. Already he was casting surreptitious looks around the restaurant, as if sizing up potential suspects. It made Lee wonder whether he was ever comfortable enough to stop doubting.

"I didn't say it was *necessarily* one of your friends," he said. "Merely somebody you might know."

"Why?" she demanded. "Why somebody I know?"

He shrugged. "It's someplace to start. Since I didn't find anything on you but four outstanding parking violations in Boston, I figured it was safe to assume you weren't working for any delicate government agencies, crime syndicates or street gangs. That leaves out the obvious. Which usually means that we have to consider the next best bet, which is that you overheard something or picked up the wrong something or surprised someone doing something they shouldn't have been doing, which means that it is someone you have met who is doing this, and that you might re-member something about it.''

"You checked me in the computer?'' she asked in a strangled little voice.

He really did look at her then. Hard, as if he needed to remind them both of some basic truths. "The very first thing.''

Lee heard it in his voice. She saw it in the harsh accusation in his eyes. She felt it in the sudden, electric silence that followed his words. He wasn't reminding her of her place in the investigation. He was reminding himself.

He was struggling for distance.

Lee looked away. Suddenly, she was fighting for her own distance. Not from this problem, but from the hot ambivalence caught deep in those dark, dark eyes where he thought nobody would catch it. From the sudden, overwhelming urge to comfort a man who didn't want her comfort.

There was too much pain there. Too many old scars Lee didn't want to expose. She had problems enough of her own right now, she reminded herself, deliberately turning her gaze on the bruised, swollen fingers that peeked out over the edge of her cast. She had a family to pacify, a play that wasn't getting finished, and very possibly somebody who didn't want her to last long enough to get that play written.

But for an eternal, unnerving moment, all she could think of was that Rock O'Connor had no one who cared enough to harass him. Rock O'Connor, who took the death of a little girl as personally as a physical wound, who had wrapped Lee in his arms to protect her from her own terror and then resettled her house as carefully as he'd settled her. Who had then driven to work to try and prove that she was the primary suspect in her own robbery.

Distance.

Look before you leap, Jake had always said, usually after she'd failed to do just that. Lee tried. She really did. But she was afraid it was already too late.

"I think I should have taken Tim's advice and just stayed in bed," she said with a profound sigh. "I don't think I'm ready for this."

Wrong thing to say.

"Do you want to go back?" Rock immediately asked, leaning forward.

Lee looked up from where she'd been unconsciously rubbing at her sore arm. She gave him a grin, right through the fresh guilt. "I meant I wasn't ever going to be up for it," she lied, even as she realized that she really was suddenly tired. Bone-deep tired, as if she'd been pummeled instead of just hung out to dry.

But it wasn't something she could give in to right now. If she did, she'd find herself lost in the dangerous currents of those hot, angry eyes of Rock O'Connor's and never find her way back out again.

"I'm fine," she assured him.

"You're sure," he said, making an ineffectual little move toward her, as if afraid to touch her, but wanting to help.

Vulnerable. Lee saw it in the most fleeting of moments, the whisper of a cloud across the sun. Open, uncertain, as callow as a schoolboy facing his first date. As wary as a virgin in the dark.

It wasn't just that he didn't know what to do for her. It was that he wanted desperately to do something. It was that this dark, hard man who strolled the streets with impunity felt so completely at a loss around a person like Lee. And Lee, who had never felt uneasy with any person in her entire life, suddenly wasn't sure what to tell him.

Somehow Seamus, as perceptive as ever, had deposited one beer and one glass of Thai ice tea on the table without being caught. Lee gratefully reached for hers and drained a good portion. "I'll sleep in tomorrow," she told Rock, retreating behind her glass for safety.

What she wanted right then was to forget her friends, forget herself. She wanted to tap into those different levels of Rock O'Connor. She wanted to mine him for the joy she knew had to be there somewhere, the laughter that had once carved out those crow's feet at the edges of his eyes. She wanted to yank out all that old pain and purge it for him so that he could smile at a woman without reserve.

She didn't. She drank up and she did her best to focus, as if she were involved in an acting exercise.

"Right now I need to understand why you think I'm not just the victim of coincidence," she said instead.

Lee heard his hesitation, but she didn't have the nerve to look for its reason. So she concentrated on her tea. Out of the corner of her eye, she saw him wrap those long, impatient fingers around the neck of the beer bottle and lift.

"Because sometimes coincidences just don't smell right," he finally said, beer still in hand, arm back across the booth.

Lee faced him again, figuring it was safe. "How do you know?"

For a minute he just watched her. Then he, too, leaned forward. "How do you know a play works?"

That brought her up short all over again. "The audience," she said instinctively. "They react at the right moments."

But he shook his head. "No, before. When it's still on that little computer of yours."

For some reason, that made Lee blush. Even his eyes on her underwear hadn't felt this personal. He'd seen her words, still half formed, their power still raw on the page. He'd peeked straight into her soul where those fragile, insubstantial things lived in their purest form.

"You saw it?" she demanded. "You read it?"

He just nodded. "It's very powerful stuff. How do you know?"

She couldn't say. She'd never been able to say, not from the first time she'd put words down on paper as a way to avoid a real paper in class. She was supposed to do a treatise on imagery. Instead, she wrote *Some Men's Dreams*. The premiere had been Jake's first time in a theater, and Lee had seen him cry.

In the end, all she could do was give Rock the truth. She pointed to the place where her plays lived, right in the middle of her chest.

"I feel it," she said. "Here."

And as if he'd known her answer all along, Rock gave her a dark smile. "Exactly."

Lee didn't know what else to say. So she just said, "Oh."

Rock nodded. "Are you ready to hear the particulars yet, or do you need some of that balsamic vinegar first?"

"I need a drink."

"I thought you didn't drink."

"I don't. I'm thinking about it, though. Especially if you're going to try and tell me I can't trust my friends anymore."

"You can't trust anybody right now."

She lifted an eyebrow. "Even you?"

The last thing Lee expected at that moment was honesty. Especially such sudden, raw honesty. The silence alerted her. His eyes warned her. Even so, his words surprised her, because they weren't what she'd wanted.

"Especially me," he said, and they both knew he wasn't talking about the case at all.

Chapter 8

Lee didn't even notice Seamus reappear with ladened plates in hand. "Rose of my desolate winter garden," he greeted her, frowning. "What troubles you?"

Lee startled like a spooked horse. They had been such simple words. Such a bald statement. And it had left her shaking. Again.

Hot. She felt so suddenly feverish, as if someone had just yanked open the door onto a simmering summer street. Anxious. She wanted to move, to give motion to the thousand little shimmers of anticipation and dread that raced through her, to suck in air as if she couldn't get enough. She couldn't quite take her eyes from the raw truth in Rock's, couldn't quite manage coherency.

She'd met incendiary men in her life, explosive sexual energies who had lit an entire theater simply by walking on stage, who had made the women around them giggle and flutter with the flash in their personalities. She'd never met a slow, seething fire like Rock's before, a subtle power that wrapped unexpected tendrils around a woman and hauled her in before she realized it.

She'd never had to struggle so much for balance, the very words of their conversations deadly, shifting currents in waters that should have been clear. They were supposed to be talking about threats and crimes. Instead, they kept stumbling over an attraction so strong it threatened to suck them right under if they weren't very careful.

She had never known such a sudden desperation, because his eyes betrayed what his rigid posture didn't. He wanted her so badly, he was flushed with it. But he had just told her it was the last thing either of them could afford. And he was right.

Lee wanted to give into a case of the shaking hysterics. She couldn't.

"It's nothing, Seamus," she assured him, not able to break Rock's heavy-lidded gaze. "Really."

"Has this lout made unwanted advances?" Seamus demanded, plopping Rock's plate down with unaccustomed force. "Would you like me to handle it?"

That, finally, got her attention. She laughed, even though it grated with anxiety, because, of course, it had been she who had made the unwanted advances. Rock had simply answered.

"Only you would offer to take out a man carrying a gun, just for my honor," she said to her friend. "That's sweet."

Seamus beamed like a boy. "In a heartbeat, turtledove. Besides, I'm far more afraid of your brother Jake than one lousy Chicago cop."

Lee wanted to cry. She laughed instead. Then she motioned to Seamus, for Rock's benefit. "See what I mean? You can't escape the long arm of the family."

Seamus gave them both long looks, hands on hips. Finally, he waved at Rock's plate. "Half-pound hamburger," he said curtly. "Burnt to a crisp. Fries, cole slaw. That okay?"

"That's fine."

He nodded. With one last look at Lee, he left. Lee gave her full attention to her plate of glass noodles and shrimp quesadillas.

"You have a lot of people who watch over you," Rock said quietly.

Lee speared some noodles and twirled as if it were a life-saving device. "I have a lot of friends," she said simply, knowing darn well that the stain of red on her neck and cheeks gave her away.

She'd never reacted like this in her life. She certainly couldn't afford to now. But she couldn't concentrate on anything but the fact that Rock was wiping away the beads of perspiration from his bottle with fingers that trembled ever so slightly. She couldn't seem to hear anything but the sudden rasp of his breathing.

He'd been surprised, too.

She was glad.

So then, she thought. What did she do? How did she handle the fact that in the span of about an hour she realized that not only was someone trying to hurt her, but that instead of wanting to kill the messenger of that particular news, she wanted to...

What did she want to do?

That made her blush even more furiously. She bent her head to consider the contents of her plate as if it were an encoded message. She really needed to talk to somebody about this, sit down with another woman for one of those long, rambling heart to hearts over tea and chocolate. She needed to get herself out to the lake for about an hour's worth of walking in the wind and sun to give herself some room.

But that wasn't going to help now. The only thing she could do now was to handle it just the way she'd handled every other trauma in her life. Full steam ahead and the hell with the consequences.

For a few, long seconds, all she could manage was a blank stare at her food. Finally, though, she managed to lift her head and face Rock, her composure firmly screwed back into place.

"So," she said. "What do you want to know?"

She'd surprised him again. She could tell by the fact that he went very still. Seamus remained poised in the background, as if to evaluate the situation. Lee didn't take her eyes from Rock to notice him. Instead, she gave Rock the biggest smile she had in her at the moment.

"I wasn't raised to succumb to the vapors," she assured her startled detective. "I'd much rather be doing something. Tell me what it is, and we can get on with it."

One corner of his mouth twitched upward, as if he were mightily fighting the urge to smile. Instead, he pulled out that ubiquitous little notebook of his and uncapped the black fountain pen that always rode in his shirt pocket. "You must drive your family nuts" was all he'd admit.

Lee grinned. "Every chance I get."

He nodded, his own composure as well-built as hers. "Okay. This is what I think I need . . ."

Lee was ready. Rock was ready. Seamus had disappeared back into the kitchen to give them some privacy. And then Rock's beeper went off.

"Damn," he snapped, reaching down to shut it off as he shoved his chair back. "I'll be right back."

And Lee, left behind like the last person in an empty theater, picked up her butter knife. There just wasn't anything left to do but impale herself on it.

"Where's my dinner?" Rock asked when he slipped back into his side of the booth some five minutes later.

Lee didn't bother to look up from where she was polishing off the last of her noodles. "I had a feeling" was all she said.

Rock instinctively reached for his beer and emptied the rest in one gulp. "I have to leave."

She smiled that damn, bright, winsome smile of hers. "See? I was right. Seamus is packing it all up to take out."

Rock wasn't very mollified. He'd just spent five minutes on the phone with O'Banyon, who had been trying to intercept him before Viviano found out what he'd done.

"Well, what the hell did you need to take the file home for, anyway?" O'Banyon had demanded.

By then, Rock had been reduced to rubbing at the back of his neck. It didn't ease any of the tension that had settled across his shoulders, or the new headache that was building between his eyes like a bad thunderstorm. "I wanted to go over the interviews with the family and neighbors," he said. "To double-check all those times. What sent up the red flare on it?"

"The feds have a guy they think might be our man. They want all the info."

"Where?"

"Indiana. Nice, huh? He was scopin' another playground, just like I thought."

"It's not him."

"Why?"

Don't ask me, he almost begged out loud. Don't make me tell you what I know. What you should have figured out the minute we pulled that little girl out of the water.

"A gut feeling" was all he finally told the other detective.

O'Banyon never caught the hesitation in Rock's voice. "Yeah, uh-huh. Well, son, all I can say is you'd better have that file back in this office by the time the lieutenant gets back from State Street, or your ass is grass."

Rock sighed, shifted. He didn't have the time right now. He needed to talk to Lee. He needed to just sit there for a second and soak in the sound of her laughter.

"I'm on my way," he said instead and hung up.

And then he'd returned to find that she'd anticipated him.

Damn her. He didn't want her doing that. He didn't want her being kind or considerate or empathetic. It just made it harder to keep his hands off her. It made the rest of it all suddenly so much worse, as if the light from her wide blue eyes made the rest of the world that much darker. That much harder to survive.

"I'll drop you off at home," he said abruptly.

"Where do you need to go?"

Rock couldn't keep his gaze off her eyes. Off those open, trusting eyes that wouldn't survive the world he knew.

"Home," he said as he pulled out his wallet to pay. "I left something there I have to get back to the office."

"Don't bother with money," she said. "Seamus won't hear of it. I'll go with you."

That yanked Rock to a stop. "What?"

She grinned so that her eyes crinkled at the corners. "I'm on the take," she boasted. "I get free food, and I use some of Seamus's song lyrics in my plays." She held out her hands, tilted her head to the side a little. "I'll go quietly, officer."

Rock fought the urge to just touch that smile. To take her hands and then take her. "No offense," he said, scraping his chair in an attempt to get up and get away. "I'll get you home now."

She matched his movements. It made her look as if she floated upward, the white material of her skirt puffing and dying around her. "You need the information," she said. "I've been thinking about it while you were gone. I'll tell you while we're driving to your house. I'll even write it down with that cute pen of yours, if you want."

"You can't—"

She smiled and stopped him dead in his tracks. "Sure I can. I need to do this now while I'm thinking of it. While it's fresh. Besides, if I go home now, I'll just have to face Gen and Jake."

The proprietor appeared behind her with a series of Chinese food cartons in his hand and a massive scowl on his homely face. Rock couldn't quite face him, either.

Lee took one small step closer. "Please," she asked, those guileless blue eyes snagging him and pulling him under.

He actually growled in frustration, which didn't do anything but make that guy in the jeans and apron go on alert.

"You stay in the truck," Rock snapped.

Her hand went up in classic acquiescence. "I love your truck."

Rock growled again, this time to keep from laughing. Damn her from making him want to laugh. There was nothing to laugh about. So he turned on the other guy and accepted the cartons.

"Don't do foam," Seamus said as if it were a judgment against Rock. "The burger's a little stuffed in the box."

"It's fine," Rock managed to say, trying to ignore the whiff of roses he caught as Lee stepped closer. "Thanks."

She kissed the big guy on the beard. The big guy gushed. Rock fled.

Five minutes later, he was gunning the truck to life and swinging it out into traffic. He didn't want to notice the fact that Lee had his old ball glove in her hand, or that she was rubbing her fingers against it as if it were a piece of silk. He didn't want to see that the wind was ruffling at her hair and plucking the sweater off her shoulder again. He should have demanded she go home. He should have never offered to take her to dinner in the first place. She was interfering with his objectivity. She was distracting him. She was breaking his heart.

God, he wanted her. He wanted to touch her and hold her, just as he had when he'd pulled her off the ledge. Had it just been the night before? It seemed like forever. It seemed as if his truck had always smelled of roses. It seemed as if she were so thoroughly intertwined with his life that if she left, he'd simply give up once and for all.

It wasn't that he was old. It was that he was tired. He'd been tired for so long he couldn't even gauge it anymore. He felt like the marathon runner on his last leg who'd just stumbled onto a beautiful woman holding out water. Cold water. Clean water. Water that could save his life if he could get his hands up to grasp it. The problem was, if Rock touched her, he wouldn't be refreshed, she'd be hurt. She'd be changed, and he couldn't bear it.

"Okay," she said in that bright, no-nonsense voice of hers. "Where do we start?"

And for just a moment, Rock dreamed.

It was why he should give this to someone else. He couldn't stay on course with her. He couldn't keep his concentration. When they should have been talking about the danger to her, all he kept thinking of was her hair, her eyes, the sound of her laugh, like wind chimes in a rain. He kept saying things he'd never thought to say to another human.

And every time he'd said those things, she'd understood perfectly.

"Your schedule," he said abruptly, as if that would help focus him.

She nodded, as if she hadn't heard the hesitation. "Simple. Theater and home, and occasionally Seamus's."

"What about the last few days? Anything unusual happen?"

She thought about it a minute, her gaze out front where the traffic ebbed and flowed ahead of them as they headed over to the Dan Ryan and south to the other side of the world. As she thought, she rubbed at his old glove, her thumb moving back and forth, back and forth. Rock focused on the street ahead.

"I've been trying to come up with something," she admitted finally. "Just as you said, something I saw or got or knew. I'm afraid I have to disappoint you. Nobody's given me anything new since my birthday, I see the same people I saw last week, and the only things I know are the lines to *Long Day's Journey into Night* and the bloodlines of every horse Jake's ever raised."

"You said you had a busy weekend. What about that?"

She shrugged, the sweater slipped, and Rock's mouth went dry again. He clutched harder at the wheel, steadying the truck. Steadying himself.

"Friday night we had the fund-raiser, a dinner-dance at the Gold Coast Room at the Drake." She grinned a little in remembrance. "Creighton likes to show off his protégés, so we were all there enjoying the champagne and puff pastries. The next day, like I told you, he took the ten repertory players out on his boat to say thank you for putting on such a nice dog-and-pony show. Except for dropping off Gen's stethoscope at the hospital after she forgot it, that's about all I did."

"Can I get a guest list?"

"Of course you can. But that couldn't be it. Those were…"

"Rich people?" he asked.

She faced him, her expression cautious. "There were some pretty recognizable names on the list," she admitted.

Rock lifted an eyebrow. "Rich people get greedy too, ya know."

For a moment there was just the grumble of traffic, the occasional car horn and syncopated thump of a neighboring radio.

"Poor Creighton."

That got him to look over at her. "Why poor Creighton?"

She shrugged. "He's put his heart and soul into that theater. A cop wading through his most choice supporters isn't going to set well with anybody."

Rock did his best to focus on driving. They'd reached the highway, where the traffic was bunched and clotted, the car lights a thick, sparkling river that swept away from the high rises down toward the old neighborhoods of brick, shingles and clapboard where Rock had grown up.

"I'm going to talk to you about all the theater people," he said. "I'm also checking up on them, and I'll interview them. What I need you to do for me now is to think back over those last two days. The party and the boat. Think if there's anything you remember that struck you as odd. A conversation, an action, something you might have seen that caught your attention."

Lee offered a sorry little smile. "I'm from a one-horse town in Wyoming, Rock. Everything seemed odd. How the heck am I supposed to know if rich people are behaving differently when I've never met one in my life—except Creighton, that is, and he doesn't count."

"Why not?"

She shrugged. "Because Creighton's... Creighton."

He flashed her another scowl, "All right, think about it. Let's go on to other things for a minute. The theater. Tell me about that."

"The whole thing?" she countered. "It's a bit much. Do you want it back to the Hellenistic period, or just the abridged version from Shakespeare?"

"Fandango."

"Oh, that. What do you want to know?"

"It didn't exist three years ago. Now it's the hottest ticket in town. Why?"

Lee shrugged, taking her attention back out to the night. "Genius."

Rock lifted an eyebrow at her.

"Creighton's," she amended wryly. "Fandango is his baby start to finish. He's always been interested in theater, but like a lot of people, went into a career with a stable future. Now that he's made his money, he's able to indulge in his avocations. One of his dreams has always been to find the new plays, like Steppenwolf Theater has always done. I wouldn't have a platform for my work if it hadn't been for Creighton."

"Yes, you would," Rock assured her.

She gave him a funny little smile. "I thought you didn't know anything about theater."

"I never said that."

"What did you say?"

"That I never liked it." He chanced one quick look at her and realized that she'd caught his inadvertent use of the past tense. He saw her hand go still in her lap and knew it was too late to correct himself. "A brand new theater's an expensive proposition. Where does the money come from?"

Lee's relief was carried in her laugh. "You've never seen Creighton work a crowd," she assured him. "He does the best fund-raisers in ten states. Not only that, but he seems to have a gift for grants. We are well funded."

"You ever see the books?"

"Don't be silly. Of course not. I don't need to. Creighton is a—"

Rock looked up, his eyes as hard as his nickname. "Friend. Did you know he was related to the Gianini family?"

"The who?"

"Wise guys," he clarified. "*The* family."

"Creighton Holliwell III?" Lee demanded so loudly that Rock was sure the traffic in the next lane could hear her. Then she just laughed.

"A theater would be a very simple way to launder money."

Lee shook her head. "Uh-huh. Next you're going to be telling me that Sierra's really the last member of the Symbionese Liberation Army."

"She might be. I haven't had a chance to check yet."

That was what finally got her ire up. Not that she was in trouble, but that he might consider impugning the good name of her friends in an effort to protect her. He saw it in the sudden stiffening of her posture, in the way she distractedly yanked that sweater back up over her shoulder to hide away that red strap, as if he no longer had a right to fantasize.

He didn't, but it didn't have anything to do with her friends.

"Tell me about the party," he said, heading off the outrage. Focusing her. Focusing himself. "Everything you can remember, start to finish. Then tell me about the boat. Maybe I can see something you can't, or maybe you'll remember something."

She did. As the city swept by them in the night, she described the rich and powerful hobnobbing over drinks and culture. She drew characters with few words and unnerving precision, and set the stage well enough that Rock could see it all. He could damn near hear the glittery fall of crystal clinking, the purr of cultured voices, the whisper of expensive fabrics. He could see a world he would never be invited to, a world he never would have envied only a few days ago. But his own imagination placed Lee there in that crowd, and suddenly the whole thing changed.

He wanted to be there to see the impish humor in her eyes as she scanned all the people who were so pretentious they didn't know how absurd they were. He wanted to listen to her discourse on her work, on anybody's work. He wanted to soak in the perfume of her vitality.

Instead he drove on down south to the streets of Bridge-
port that encompassed his life. Endless rows of two story-
brick houses and flats ringed by chain-link fences and people sitting out on the stoops on Friday nights. Taverns and
Comiskey Park and double-parked unmarked cop cars. The
muffled shouts of families trapped behind venetian blinds
and blue-collar dreams and alcohol.

Home.

He pulled the car to a stop in front of the old house, another two-story brick with a concrete stoop and sagging
roof, the yard more weeds than grass, the sidewalk cracked
and uneven, the dreams gone out of that house a long time
ago. He shut off the engine and he turned to her and knew
that she had no more business here than he had at the Gold
Coast Room of the Drake Hotel, and it broke his heart just
a little more.

"I'll only be a minute," he said. "Stay here."

"You're double-parked again," she answered with that
mischievous smile.

"So's everybody else. Half the force lives on this block."

That got her head around. She hadn't known. She didn't
know anything about the other side of the city.

"Stay here," he said one more time and climbed out of
the truck.

She'd meant to stay. She really had. But she simply
couldn't imagine what could take the strength out of a
man's posture with nothing more than a walk through the
gate in a front-yard fence. She couldn't help wondering
what secrets Francis Xavier Aloysius O'Connor kept behind that heavy brown front door.

She always ran into her house, anxious for its friendly
smells and comforting noises that greeted her. Baking
bread, horse liniment, coffee. Footsteps, boards creaking
under the weight of remembered feet, laughter of all pitches
and ages. The music of a family, her personal scrapbook of
memories.

Rock trudged up to his porch as if it were a sentence. He
unlocked his door and walked through without even hit-

ting the lights. Lee wondered what could be in that house that would be so bad he wouldn't even want to see it. So before good sense overcame impulse, she climbed out of the truck and headed after him.

It took her a few minutes to maneuver the terrain, since her balance was a little off. Her arm was killing her, and her head was doing its best to sing duet. She'd finally given in back at the restaurant and downed one of the pain pills Tim had given her. But if she told Rock that, he'd take her right home. And she didn't want to go home. She wanted to find out about him. She wanted to follow him home and to work. So here she was, sore and slow and threatening to renew her acquaintance with the dinner she'd just downed, and all so she could enrage the one person who could probably protect her in the next few weeks.

The lights weren't all off. Lee saw that as she nudged the front door further open. There was a light on in the kitchen, which was where Rock seemed to be. It bled over into the dining and living room she could see through the screen door, plain square spaces decorated in hardwood and stark white walls. Dark, thick furniture and the faint, lingering smell of disinfectant and burned popcorn. Books. Piles of them, shelves of them. She saw them when she eased the door open just far enough that it didn't squeak and sidled in. She couldn't see the titles, but there were tomes and there were paperbacks and there were manuals. She absolutely itched to see what they all were, tumbled around the armchair in the corner like favored children. She saw those and forgot the walls, which were as bare as winter.

"I told you to stay in the truck."

Lee damn near jumped a foot.

"Don't do that!" she demanded, free hand to her chest, where her heart was threatening to tumble out onto the rug. "You scared me."

He stood in the dining room, silhouetted by the kitchen light, his shape hard and threatening, his posture rigid. She couldn't see his eyes, but she knew what was in them. Rock O'Connor was furious.

Lee tried smiling her way through it. "I'm sorry. I thought I . . . uh, heard something."

"What you heard," he snapped back, the papers in his hand rustling with his frustration, "was curiosity killing the cat."

"But it's such a cute little cat," she protested lamely.

He didn't answer. Didn't move. Didn't breathe for the longest moment in Lee's life. Then, just as suddenly, he reached out. Hit the switch on the wall and flooded the room with light.

"There," he said, turning away. "Now you can see what you want."

And there he left Lee behind with her view of the stark, empty walls and the mountain of books on psychology and education and mathematics and any subject she'd ever seen in a college catalog. She saw the empty coffee cup and the beer cans in the wastebasket by the end table and the television that had the back taken out and the insides scattered over the floor behind it. She saw brand-new furniture and newer curtains and wondered what it was that felt wrong about this house.

There weren't any pictures. Any. Not of friends or family or Rock himself. On one wall in the dining room, there were ten neatly framed and precisely hung documents. Diplomas, commendations, two medals of honor. She headed for them, seeking explanation.

Her brother Jake had empty walls everywhere in his house but his bedroom. It was there Jake kept his memories, his keepsakes, his family. There where he wouldn't be threatened with sloppy sentimentalism from just anybody who walked into his house. Lee wondered whether Rock had any pictures hidden away in his bedroom. She wondered if it felt any more like a home than the rest of these spare, cold rooms.

"Minimalism," she said out loud, her attention on that wall of commendation. "So few people can get away with it these days. I like it."

Were these his only memories, his only family? Was this all Rock had collected to comfort himself?

"Disinterest," he answered her without looking away from the papers he was gathering together on his kitchen table beyond the arching wall.

Another old room with sparkling new appliances. Another room without personality, as if it had been deliberately stripped and scrubbed of it.

"I like the house. How did you find it?"

"I grew up in it."

She nodded absently. "So you weren't ever married?"

"I didn't say that."

She shut up this time. She wandered a little closer to the kitchen, running a finger over the clean lines of Rock's new oak dining room table. Four chairs, no cloth, no sideboard. Functional.

The kitchen table matched, spare, clean lines and little else. Rock stood before it, his back to her, looking down at the papers in his hands. Lee stepped around so she could see.

She saw.

She saw that what Rock was holding was a color picture of a little girl. Only it wasn't the kind of picture anyone should ever want to see.

"Oh," she breathed in sick surprise.

Rock whipped around on her, and Lee felt even worse. His eyes glittered with emotion. His hands tightened so quickly he almost crumpled the eight-by-ten-inch photo between them. His jaw was as tight as stressed steel.

Lee looked up at him. She looked into his eyes and saw the cost of those pictures. She saw a weight there, an exhausted desolation that seemed to eat away the light. She saw rage and grief and the instinctive wariness of the shy man, and knew that no one else had shared the emotions that fueled Rock O'Connor's fury.

No one else had made it close enough to this insulated man to comfort him. Lee wondered whether anyone even realized how badly he needed comfort.

She didn't think about it. She didn't hesitate. She simply reached up and cupped that rigid, hard face in her hands and she kissed him.

He tightened against her. He tried to pull away. Lee held on, her fingers bent to the rasp of his jaw, her eyes closed, her wrist forgotten for the ache that had flared in her chest.

She heard a rustle, felt a tremor. She smiled when he dropped what he held and held on to her instead. And when he kissed her back, he brought her to her knees.

Chapter 9

"What did you do that for?" he demanded, eyes still closed, forehead resting against hers.

It took Lee a second to answer. She couldn't quite get her voice to work. Crumpled up on the floor like day-old tissue, she couldn't quite catch her breath, much less her thoughts.

So this had been what her body had been warning her about. This had been what she'd been drawn to, afraid of, needing. This heat, this fierce, melting hunger that had exploded in her in the space of one kiss. Her knees were useless and her hands shook. Her chest seemed to have caved right in. Rock held on to her. She held on to him, and neither of them could seem to move from where they'd slumped to the floor.

"I wanted to help," she finally managed, her voice breathless and small, her eyes open to see that Rock was no less affected. He still hadn't opened his eyes or moved away from her. He held on, his hands clamped to her arms, as if terrified of what would happen when he let go. Lee understood. She had the most unholy feeling that if she moved away from him she'd pitch over, her balance lost, her strength forfeited to him.

"What do you mean you wanted to help?" His voice was a rasp that betrayed his struggle for restraint.

She laughed, because the answer seemed so simple, so obvious. At least she tried to. It came out as kind of a strangled gasp. "That little girl," she said. "You were so...so lost, looking at her. I only wanted to make you feel a little less hurt. When Jake looked like that, I used to make him laugh. But I couldn't think of anything funny." She shrugged, brushing against him so she could feel the tensile contours of his chest. So different than last night. Last night he had been comfort and patience and quiet. Tonight he was fire and force and the frayed ends of control.

Tonight he frightened her, because he called up emotions in her just as swift and overwhelming as his.

"No," he murmured against her, his lips inciting brushfires along her skin. "There was nothing to laugh about."

She didn't answer. Didn't know what to say. Tell me, she thought. Tell me what hurts you so badly, what makes you so lonely and hard. Tell me what you scrubbed out of this old house.

"I have to get to the station," he said, not moving.

"Okay," she answered, not moving, either.

His skin was hot and dry where it met hers. His breathing was harsh and his hands trembled. If it had been anything else that had brought Rock to his knees, Lee would have sworn that he suffered from a fever. A high, debilitating fever that produced wild fantasies and wilder needs.

Or was she the one suffering from it? Lee couldn't tell anymore. She was too hot, and her hands shook too badly.

In the end, of course, they both made it to their feet. Lee stood there for a moment, wavering without the reassurance of his touch to cement her together. She wanted to cry. She wanted to lock that heavy front door and never walk out of this house. She wanted answers to her questions, and, standing there in the living room as Rock shoved pictures and reports back into the manila envelope on the kitchen table, she knew that she couldn't get any of that here.

Maybe it was the pain medicine. Maybe it was the fact that her sensitivities were a little heightened by whatever it was that had passed between her and Rock with that kiss. Whatever it was, it was telling her that this was not a good place. No amount of white paint would cover the scars in this house. No laughter was great enough or bright enough to chase away the heaviness that lurked in these corners.

It made her shiver. "Why did you come back?" she asked before she thought about it.

Rock turned on her, his arms full of murder, his eyes still sharp with surprise at what they had done. "Come back?"

She nodded, her eyes on the walls, the stark, empty walls. "To your house. You didn't want to."

She half expected him to deny it. After all, she had a feeling Rock O'Connor didn't share that information with anybody. Instead, he looked, too. And then, he simply walked on in to take her arm and guide her back out the door.

"Some things just need to be faced" was all he said. All he would say.

And so, Lee dropped the subject completely. As she followed Rock back out to the truck, she turned her attention to the information she'd promised him. She answered more questions about her attack, and she talked about her friends and her family and anybody who came to mind she'd met in the last year or so, and she did that all the way back up to Belmont, where the Area One station was. There, she just waited while Rock did whatever it was he'd come to do. She waited and she paged through mug books and she thought how much the white cinderblock walls with their official notices and posters about gun safety and drug programs reminded her of the walls at Rock's house.

He sat her down at his desk, a cluttered, top-heavy affair controlled by paperweights made of everything from geodes to Marine Corps ashtrays to half-filled Chicago Cubs mugs. Lee noticed his handwriting on notes—strong, heavy, with spikes of agitation. She noticed that he kept a spare tie hanging out of the third drawer, and that underneath one stack of papers were several textbooks on advance calculus and non-euclidean geometry.

She looked around at the other desks, some clean, some in even worse shape than Rock's, and realized that this was where she would learn the most about him.

"Don't let him scare you," she heard from behind her.

When she turned it was to come across a skinny, short black man with no hair and laughing brown eyes, dressed in a suit so sharp and stylish it made Rock look like a bagman.

"He's not always this nasty," he said, then grinned wide. "Sometimes he's worse."

Three more detectives wandered by, one of them a woman. Each had the same message, the same teasing grin. Each one opened Rock's top-right drawer and swiped a handful of M&M's he kept in a big coffee tin with a bright orange Danger: Radiation label affixed to the top.

By the time Lee saw Michael Viviano, she'd overdosed on chocolate and laughed with enough cops and stared at enough surly, anonymous pictures that she wanted to go home.

"Don't let him scare you," Michael said.

Lee laughed, opening the drawer so Michael wouldn't have to do it. "I know," she countered. "Sometimes he's worse."

Michael got his M&M's, just like the rest of the crew, and Lee joined him. "It's just that little Havlacjek girl," he said, his eyes losing some of their levity, the candy momentarily forgotten in his hand. "Rock gets a little crazy when a child's involved."

Lee nodded, not knowing what to say. Hurting for Rock all over again. Hurting because he thought he was out there all alone when he faced that kind of horror.

"I don't know why," Michael said, his gaze up to where Rock was conferring with the short black detective. "But this time it's worse."

Lee didn't look up. She didn't react at all, because she knew why it was worse. It was worse because of her. Because she'd interfered with the case that was tearing Rock apart.

She'd only wanted to help. It seemed she'd made matters worse.

"He's been very kind," Lee said, focused on the page of blurred black-and-white photos before her.

Kind. It wasn't the first word that came to mind, especially when Lee's body could so easily call up the memory of his touch, his kiss, the way his hands shook, as if he, too, had been struck down by lightning.

"Well, he may be kind," Michael retorted, suddenly at attention. "But he isn't very observant. If he were, he'd notice that you look like you're about to drop over. I'll get him to take you home."

Lee looked up to argue and found her gaze caught, not by Michael Viviano, but Rock. Standing at the door to one of the other offices, talking to that skinny black detective, one hand on his hip, the other massaging the back of his neck. His eyes so tight they hurt Lee, his posture as taut as pain. And she realized that what he was discussing with that other detective was the little girl. The little girl he saw as a mission.

Instinctively, she saw him as he'd been the night before. Gentle and patient and tender. And she wished with all her heart that there were no more little girls out there who stole Rock O'Connor's smile as this one had.

Blindly she turned the page before her, wanting to at least give some motion to her feelings as Michael headed across to chide his detective. She looked away from them, not able to bear Rock's reaction. She looked right down at the picture of the man who had broken into her apartment.

"You expect that to make me feel better?" Gen demanded an hour later.

Lee didn't bother to stop getting ready for bed. She could hardly stand up anymore. Her arm hurt, her head hurt, and she felt as if she'd been stretched beyond her limit this evening. And, of course, she hadn't called Jake yet.

Who she really wanted to talk to was her sister-in-law, Amanda. Amanda would understand. She'd be able to tell Lee what to do about this man who compelled her with his sensuality, his complexity, his pain. Amanda understood compulsion. Gen only understood medicine, and Jake still didn't want to admit that his little sister could so much as define the word compulsion.

She'd call Amanda. In the morning, when she felt better.

"What is he going to do about it?" Gen demanded, hot on her heels.

"I should never have told you," Lee admitted, slipping on her clean jammies. The purple ones were in the wash bin. Lee had picked them up and smelled Rock on them. Leather and oil and the dark smoke of his own scent. She'd had to close her eyes against the sharp sensations just that provoked. She'd had to turn away from her own sister, because she simply couldn't explain what it was about this man in his battered old truck and his worn-out jeans and his old anger that so enticed her. But then Gen hadn't felt his arms around her when she'd needed them.

Behind her, Gen sighed. "You tell me that somebody's trying to kill you and I'm not supposed to worry?"

"I'm telling you that the police are taking care of it, and that we've already identified the man who broke into the apartment."

"Who is he?"

Lee shrugged. "Somebody who does this for a living, from what I heard. They already put an ATF or whatever out for him."

"APB"

"Right. Now, I'm really tired, Gen."

Gen never moved. "I wish you'd told me sooner. I didn't know what to tell Jake when he called, so he wasn't satisfied. And you know Jake."

Lee whirled around on her sister. "Oh, no, he's not!"

Gen actually looked sorry for her sister. "You didn't really expect him to stay home."

Lee cast a frantic look around the room, as if there was something there with which she could physically hold away her brother. "He can't meet Rock! My God, Gen, do you know what will happen?"

Her sister raised an eyebrow. "He'll knock some sense into you?"

Lee faced her, unarmed, uncertain, unrepentant. "Who does he remind you of?" she demanded, pajama shirt clutched in her hands like a shield.

"Who?" Gen demanded.

"Rock. Who does he remind you of?"

Gen thought a second. "A patient I had last week who tried to clean the infidels from Rush Street with an Uzi. Why?"

But Lee wasn't in the mood for humor. "Jake," she said. "He reminds me of Jake. Don't you want to know why?"

"No, I don't. I want you to be protected. I want you to finish your play and be a raging success, and I want Jake to be able to spend one solid week without feeling as if he has to come bail you out of something."

That brought Lee to a dead halt. She loved Gen with all her heart. She'd do anything for her. But every once in a while, her sister hit too close to home with her accusations, and right now Lee didn't need it.

"This isn't my fault," she reminded her stiffly.

Gen's outrage crumbled like drying sand. "Oh, honey, I know. I'm sorry. I just don't know what to do. Every time I turn around you're back in the hospital, Jake's on the phone buying the next ticket he can from Jackson Hole, and I'm caught here with no way to protect you or ward him off."

"When's he coming?"

"In the morning."

Lee nodded and headed for the phone. "In that case, we'll take care of it right now."

"And exactly what are you going to tell him about this guy?"

"What do you mean?" Lee demanded, receiver already in hand, fingers aimed for buttons. "I'll tell him there's a cop here on the case. All I have to do is convince him that everything is under control and he'll stay home."

"But everything isn't under control," Gen insisted, hands deep in pockets, feet firmly planted. "And you know it."

Lee looked up mid-dial and proceeded to forget the rest of her own number. Gen was serious. And she was serious about more than just the attacks.

Lee settled the phone back on its cradle and faced her sister's worry. "Gen, I'm exhausted, I hurt everywhere, and I've just spent the last hundred or so hours trying to figure out if somebody I know is a criminal."

"And you're falling for the policeman."

Lee surprised herself even more than her sister with the calm truth. "And I'm falling for the policeman. It's just a lot to assimilate on very little sleep and painkillers. I'm doing my best."

"It isn't a good idea," her big sister said, eyes full with every reason she wanted to add.

Lee laughed. "I don't remember saying it was. I can't think of anything I'd rather not do right now than get involved with a policeman who turns into Darth Vader every time a child dies."

"Then you're thinking of getting involved?"

"I'm not thinking of anything past talking Jake out of showing up here tomorrow. Once I do that, we can work on this one step at a time, okay?"

It took Gen a lot of effort, but in the end, she conceded. "Okay."

And Lee was able to finally turn her attention to the phone and the correct area code for Lost Ridge, Wyoming. And when Jake answered, she forced a smile onto her face and into her voice.

"I promise," she told him as if the force of her own conviction could sway his. "Everything's fine. I'm not in any trouble."

"She's in a lot of trouble," the guy from the tac unit told Rock the first thing the next morning.

Rock leaned his elbows on the paperwork he was supposed to be finishing and dropped his head into his hands. He'd sent out the feelers on the case, just to see if anything on it rang bells. He especially wanted to know if anybody had personally tangled with one Sonny Varner, the name that went with the face Lee had picked out of thousands as the man who had torn apart her apartment trying to get to her.

Rock had gotten the message the minute he'd walked in to call Jim Pierson from the tactical units, which did all the special investigations from the State Street bureau.

"Why?" Rock asked. "What do you have to tell me about this guy?"

"Oh, I know Sonny from way back. He started out doing nickel-and-dime stuff, but since his last time in, he's graduated to the big leagues. Anything for the right price, and I mean anything. He's mean and he's good and if he isn't smart, at least he's thorough."

"Thorough?"

"If he didn't find what he wants, he'll be back."

"Wonderful. Any connection to the family?"

"Not anything that set off bells, but I wouldn't put anything past him. He likes to think big, and every so often they have need for outside talent."

Without even thinking about it, Rock drew a slow circle around the third name on the list of suspects he'd started to compile.

"I saw your inquiry on the original hit and run," Jim said. "Your girl have her insurance with Global Trans?"

"Don't think so. Why?"

"Just thought I'd check. We're looking into them for fraud. They're paying off on some pretty questionable accidents lately, several in your area, and the injuries are a lot like your lady's."

Rock checked his files. "I'd be real surprised if she's involved in anything like that, but I'll make sure."

He made the note, even though he didn't want to.

"I'm checking out that theater angle you gave us," Jim said. "Thanks, it's just the kind of stuff we're looking for. Coincidences like that make my palm itch, ya know?"

Rock nodded. "Yeah. I know. Do you have anything on this Holliwell?"

"Not yet. But I can't imagine Mario Gianini's second cousin not finding his way to Mario's very deep pockets for some support." The officer chuckled, obviously enjoying himself. "God, I love this stuff."

Rock hung up the phone a few minutes later wondering whether he was supposed to feel any better or not. He didn't have to wait long to find out. O'Banyon showed up on the other side of his desk, a frown on his heavy features, an interview report in his hand.

"You were right," he said without preamble. "The times don't match on when the girl disappeared. It can't be that guy in Indiana. Now, you want to tell me where you think that damn shoe is?"

And Rock, who didn't think he could feel any worse, told him.

By three in the afternoon, Lee had succeeded in making such a mess of her work that Sierra gave in and let Marlyse run lines with the other cast members while she personally ushered her star and sometime playwright to the back of the theater.

"You're tired, girl. Go home."

Lee wouldn't have minded so much if it had been only that. The truth of the matter was that when she was supposed to be thinking about Mary Tyrone's problems, all she could envision were deep brown eyes. When she looked down at her own hands, the hands in the play that carried the memories of a woman who had sold away her future for security too many years ago to count, all she could think of were long, spatulate fingers rubbing at the back of a taut neck.

She should have been concentrating on Mary's pain. She couldn't feel it through her preoccupation with Rock's pain.

And Sierra was right. Lee was tired. She was more than tired, because even after falling exhausted into bed last night, she hadn't been able to sleep. The dreams that had pursued her all night had left her awake and anxious and impatient.

"I'm sorry," she admitted, slipping her arm back into the sling where it was supposed to have been all along. "I'll do better tomorrow."

Sierra just sighed. "Tomorrow is Sunday. You're not going to do anything."

Sunday. Lee had forgotten. It seemed as if it had been weeks since she'd stood out on Creighton's boat, her face up to the wind and sunshine, her most pressing problem just how to get fictitious characters to behave as she needed them to.

It had only been a matter of days since she'd been introduced to Rock O'Connor, and in that time, he'd successfully pushed her characters to the back of her mind. He'd pushed everything else out of the way, and Lee didn't know what to do about it.

She didn't know what to do about him, because the longer she knew him, the more she knew she needed to get him to laugh. To open up and talk and listen without having to bear that awful weight on his shoulders.

Maybe Amanda would know what to do with this compulsion of Lee's, but Amanda wasn't going to meet Rock, not now that Lee had talked Jake out of showing up. And Lee had the overwhelming feeling that she needed to do something now.

Something positive. Something fun, whether Rock liked it or not.

Well, maybe there was one thing.

"Are the Cubs in town, Sierra?"

Sierra looked at her as if she'd just asked whether she wanted to stage a tribute to Barney, the dinosaur. "The what?"

Lee smiled, already planning. "The Cubs. Baseball, ya know?"

Her director wasn't impressed. "You don't like base-ball."

Lee smiled. "Maybe I just need to see a game with the right person."

"I don't think it'd help if you went with Ryne Sand-berg."

But Lee was already on her way out the door. She had a lot to do before tomorrow.

He'd just come in off the street, where the temperatures had taken a swing up into the nineties. He was hot and wet and furious. They hadn't found the shoe, even with a search warrant and all Rock's conviction. It meant he was back to square one. It meant he had to suffer another round with sobbing parents and uncertain officials. It meant he'd have to find another way to solve the case, but right now he couldn't figure out what. His head hurt and his feet hurt and he figured he smelled like a goat, even in his suit, which he hadn't really gotten out of in the last forty-eight hours while he'd been working on both cases at once.

O'Banyon met him at the door to the detective's bureau with a look of caution. The other detectives avoided him. Rock didn't blame them. He wasn't in a good mood. And then he swung around to dump his stuff on his desk and found her sitting there.

"What's wrong?" he immediately demanded.

She smiled and broke his heart all over again. There was open sky in those eyes. Freedom. There was a purity that made his own eyes ache just at the sight, as if he'd stared too hard at the sun.

"Nothing's wrong," she assured him, getting to her feet. She was in another dress, this one covered in a field of tiny, brightly colored flowers. The thing had thin straps and just kind of fell all the way down to the middle of her calves, where it swung lazily against her when she moved. It should have looked like a burlap bag. Instead, all Rock could think of was that she wasn't wearing a bra under it, and that he could see all that expanse of perfectly tanned shoulder. He almost walked right back out of the office.

"It's five o'clock," she said with that little tilt to her head.

Rock went ahead and unclipped his beeper, unholstered his gun, as if the actions would remind him just who belonged here. "And?"

"And, unless your lieutenant's a liar, you're off duty."

Rock glared at her. Most anybody on the street and not a few police knew not to screw around with that glare. Amaryllis Jane Kendall just smiled all the more brightly, as if he weren't so much a threat as a challenge.

"You need to drive," she admitted, "but I've arranged everything else."

"Everything what?"

She smiled at him, and Rock knew damn well at least five other detectives had stopped in their tracks to watch it.

"My education." And with that, she held up two tickets.

Bleacher tickets.

Rock couldn't come up with a more intelligent answer than, "Baseball?"

She nodded, a kid on a field trip. "I figured you should be the one to teach me about it."

"Not tonight."

"Tonight."

"Lee, I have—"

"You have to take some time off before your lieutenant forces you to. At least that's what he told me."

Rock flushed with frustration. Fine. Now she was enlisting Viviano's help. He felt like a pet goldfish. He turned his glare on the other detectives who had paused in their work and sent them scurrying. Then he deliberately went about putting the beeper back in his drawer.

"I really don't think it's a good idea."

"It's a wonderful idea. I've never eaten a ballpark frank, and you haven't taken any time off work for the last two years."

He sighed, tugging at his tie with impatient hands. "Lee—"

She tilted her head further. Grinned. "Rock—"

And Rock, who had stared down the nastiest mopes in the Midwest, found himself powerless to challenge one set of sky-blue eyes. So he ended up pulling his jeans out of the truck and putting away his files, and he went to the damn ball game. He went expecting to be frustrated and uncomfortable and preoccupied. He found himself so engrossed in Lee that he forgot to be all three.

How could anybody get so excited over a ballpark? Everything set her off: the people, the color, the noise, the music. Even the scoreboard. She laughed and talked and yelled right along with the crowd, and then bent over her scorecard like a kid learning the alphabet.

Rock, who had had season tickets for the last fifteen years, experienced it all again through her eyes and remembered what it had been like when he'd ditched high school so he could sit in the bleachers. He remembered how he'd chanted right along as the right field bleachers insulted the left field bleachers, how the first bite of a hot dog was the best, with the mustard and relish dripping off your chin. He remembered jumping to his feet every time there was a hit, because you just couldn't depend on the Cubs getting another one soon, and he remembered that it was never a real game unless Harry Carey announced it.

He remembered that Wrigley Field was his only asylum in the bad days. It was the only place he was allowed to imagine, to pretend that among all these noisy, laughing strangers, he was safe.

"What's he doing now?" Lee demanded as the catcher stood up and pointed left with his mitted hand.

"Intentional walk," Rock said, seeing the drop of mustard that had fallen onto the front of her dress and wanting to clean it off.

"Why would he do that?" she demanded, sipping noisily at her soda.

Rock's attention wasn't on the play, but on her. Her life, her vitality, her genuine enthusiasm. He wondered how long it would last if it were constantly exposed to him. He wondered how long he was going to last once he had to give it back up again.

When he didn't answer, she turned. For just a moment, her eyes darkened, deepened. Rock knew she understood. He knew she felt the same sudden jab of hunger. He held perfectly still against it, a burning that sucked the air out of his lungs. A knife wound inflicted by pure blue eyes.

"He's walking the batter," she said, running her tongue over her lower lip, as if she were retrieving some taste. "Why?"

Rock couldn't seem to look away from that lip, moist and inviting. Full. Sweeter than life. He could still taste it. He wanted more, and he knew he couldn't have it.

So he looked away. Back at the play where the batter was standing easy, bat on his shoulder, as the pitches floated a good four feet wide of him while the crowd around them booed.

"Because the last two times he's gotten up to bat, he's hit hard, and they have men on base. If he brings one in, we'll tie. If he walks, that doesn't drive in a run."

Lee nodded. Paused. Turned back to the action and booed as heartily as the three guys on her left.

Rock hurt even worse, especially when she laughed at her own actions.

"This is great," she admitted. "Safe outlet for all your aggression. I'm glad you brought me. It means you're going to have to go horseback riding with me, of course."

Rock kept his eyes on the batter, who was tossing the bat aside and trotting to first. "Do I have to cut cows?"

"Not in Schaumburg, you don't."

Rock shook his head. "I don't think so."

Lee laughed again and tilted her head to drain the last of the soda from her cup so that the long, dangly earrings she wore brushed against her throat and skittered like tiny wind chimes.

"Never say no until you've tried it," she advised. "You never know what you'd be missing."

And then, before Rock could safely turn away, she looked right over at him. Eyes dancing with laughter, voice light, meaning hanging on her words like heavy dew on berries.

Rock couldn't breathe. He couldn't concentrate. He didn't even see who stood up to bat next. He completely missed it when whoever it was hit the first pitch for a line triple that cleared the bases. The crowd around them surged to its feet, screaming. Somebody lost their entire carton of popcorn so that it showered over the crowd like exploding fireworks. Like rice at a wedding. Rock didn't notice anything but the challenge, the invitation in those bright, open eyes.

No, he wanted to say. Not now. Not ever. Run as far away from me as you can, little girl. Run where it's safe, where I can't hurt you.

Instead, he turned forward, away from her eyes and her perfectly tanned shoulders and the thrust of her breasts against all those flowers as she heaved in a breath of surprise.

"I still need to talk to you about the case," he said, waving to the vendor for another beer.

It only took her a moment to answer. "We came to enjoy the game," she protested.

"You're still in danger until I find out why somebody keeps going after you."

"Tomorrow."

He took the proffered cup from the guy next to him and passed his money back the same way. "There's a woman named Marlyse something."

"Marlyse White."

He nodded. Waited until he'd emptied half the cup before going on. "Did you know she has a record?"

"I don't want to hear this."

"Seems she tends to get violent if she doesn't get what she wants. What does she want?"

"Nothing," she said, and he knew she was lying.

"I checked on that connection to Holliwell. Mario Gianini has season tickets to the theater."

"So does the mayor."

He finished off his beer, wishing it was colder. Wishing he was drinking it with somebody he wasn't going to hurt.

"What about the party?" he asked.

"I told you," she said, now focusing completely on the game, the scorecard he'd been helping her fill in forgotten in her hand. "It was a party. I didn't notice anything more than I told you."

"There weren't any arguments? No problems?"

"Sure there were problems. It was a fund-raiser. Show me a fund-raiser without problems and I'll show you a miracle."

"What problems?"

"Not enough wine. Too much brass in the band. Senator Peterson showing up with a lady who wasn't his wife, and his wife's best friend showing up right behind him."

"Any arguments you remember?"

"Yeah," she said with a shrug. "But nothing unusual. Just Creighton yelling at me for being gauche. Happens at all the parties. I keep telling him that I'm a playwright from Wyoming. I'm allowed to be gauche. He says I can be colorful as long as I don't compromise his donors." She shrugged again, obviously not terribly upset about the situation.

"Compromised?" Rock asked, interest piqued. "Who did you compromise?"

"Oh, nobody really. Creighton just doesn't like me taking pictures when he hires somebody expensive to do the same . . ."

She turned. Opened her mouth. Came to the same conclusion Rock did at the same moment.

"My camera," she said, startled, eyes so wide Rock thought she'd just let them roll all the way back and faint.

"You took pictures?"

"I took pictures."

Rock didn't have to embarrass himself by singing along with "Take Me Out to the Ball Game" at the seventh-inning stretch, and he didn't have to end up watching the Cubs pull a loss out of near victory. He was already dragging Lee out the gate toward his car and her apartment.

Chapter 10

"Where do you keep it?" Rock asked as they opened the door into Lee's apartment.

"In my saddlebags," she said, running. "On the saddle. The camera's really Gen's. Jake gave it to her for med school graduation, but she never uses it, so I do, and I keep it here . . ."

She slammed open the door to her room, her heart racing as fast as her mouth. She knew this was it. She just knew it. She was excited. Rock was excited. Something she'd taken with the camera, some picture, had been what she'd been threatened over, and once she produced it for him, Rock would take care of the rest. Gen would be off her back, Jake would stay in Wyoming, and Lee could get on with O'Neill, not to mention the final scenes in her own play, which still languished in the computer without her attention. She could get on with finding out exactly what it was about the sergeant and his hard, furrowed face that so fascinated her.

She shoved aside the four dresses and three pants outfits she'd tried on that afternoon and pushed the hall tree out of the way to get to her saddle.

"You don't remember what you might have taken a picture of?" Rock asked again.

Lee shook her head, just as she had when he'd asked before. "I just do it instinctively, at least until somebody yells at me about it."

She crouched down before the saddle that she'd draped over a stack of orange crates and slipped her hand inside the hand-tooled leather bags that hung off the back. She frowned. "Oh, no."

Rock walked right in behind her, close enough she could feel the whisper of air as he moved. "Oh, no, what?"

She straightened. Reached across and checked the other bag, into which she would never have put a camera, because it would have been too hard to reach if she wanted it quickly.

Then she just sat back on her heels. "It's not there. I *always*..."

She felt his disappointment like a cooling in the air. Almost heard his posture slip a little. For herself, she gave way to instinct. "Gen's gonna kill me."

Just those words brought it all back. The walk uptown, the scream, the sudden feeling of flight. The confusion that came and went from the moment she landed on the ground. Crouched there in her own bedroom, she groaned all over again.

"My purse," she said, finally giving in and slumping right down to a sitting position on the hardwood floor. "I think I had it in my purse."

Rock ended up perched on the edge of her bed, as if he couldn't make any fuller contact with the material. He was rubbing at the back of his neck again. "You're sure."

And Lee had to shake her head. "No. I'm not sure of anything from that day. It's kind of...blurry around the edges. It happens when I get concussed. Also, I guess when I get surprised by somebody's front bumper."

Amazingly enough, that was what made Rock smile. "When you get concussed? Just how often does that happen?"

She grinned back, unabashed. "Are you telling me you've never had a concussion in your life?"

His scowl was mighty. "I'm a policeman," he retorted. "It comes with the territory."

"I'm a horsewoman," she countered. "It comes with my territory, too." She didn't add the part about how they'd be perfectly suited for each other, two rather confused people stumbling along with their bouts of dizziness and memory loss.

He was still scowling, but Lee caught a sly gleam of humor in those deep eyes. "Horses, huh?"

"Wonderful animals," she boasted. "Much more loyal and dependable than most people I know."

For that she got an indelicate snort. "So's damn near anything else on the planet. I don't remember seeing a camera of any kind when I found your purse. Do you?"

Lee thought about it and came up empty. She shook her head. Then her eyes lit on something on the other side of the saddle. "Wait! Yeah, maybe..."

She scooted over on her hands and knees and pulled her backpack bag toward her, from where she'd dropped it the day Creighton had brought it back to her.

"We just might be in luck here," she said, yanking on the old zipper. "I usually keep this in the theater. I just haven't had the chance to take it back yet. I had it with me on the boat..."

She overturned it on the floor. Out fell a pair of jeans, a filmy, flowery dress of the type she'd end up wearing for her role, water shoes, sunscreen, a bracelet, three buttons that rolled under the bed and a two piece swimsuit the color of Rock's radiation symbol.

No camera. No extra film.

Lee looked up, frustrated all over again. It made her want to cry. "We missed the end of the game for nothing."

It was then she realized that she'd been bent over in front of Rock. That she didn't have a bra on, and that her dress drooped just enough. That Rock had noticed. All those years of living under Jake's strict rules demanded she straighten immediately. That she pull her dress closer around her. She saw Rock go still and hesitated.

He yanked his gaze away, but Lee saw the sudden sheen of sweat on his forehead. "Not for nothing," Rock assured her, his attention on his hands. "We may not have the pictures, but we might have an idea what they were looking for. Do you remember anything specifically you took a shot of?"

Surprised at how reticent she was at her own action, she finally gave in to caution and sat up straight, curling her feet beneath her on the floor. Her smile was rueful. "Nothing but the senator. But that's because that was when I got yelled at. I also remember taking pictures out on the boat the next day. The skyline looked so spectacular from the water, and it was such a pretty day.... Rock, if the camera was in my purse, why would they try and go after it again?"

Rock thought about it, sitting there on her sea of bright yellow fish, his posture betraying his discomfort, his eyes betraying his distraction. Again Lee thought of a predatory bird, a sharp-eyed osprey caught in the parakeet's cage. Again she fought an instinctive thrill of attraction. After all, this wasn't the time or place to think about things like that—not the time, anyway.

"Maybe because they thought you were too important a witness to leave alone," he said, and she shivered.

Not just from his words, from the sudden, sharp emotion in his eyes. Regret, reproof, frustration.

Attraction.

Lee felt it snake its way toward her again, deadly tendrils of delight. Slow, sensuous streamers of heat she could almost see as they wrapped their way around her. Not so much want, as need. Not nearly as much lust as simple quickfire.

Lee wanted him. She wanted him there on that bright, winsome bed she'd constructed without a thought to who might end up sharing it with her. She wanted him wherever he wanted, wanted his hands in her hair, on her skin, against her mouth. She wanted to feel that fire against her fingertips and then dip her tongue into it to taste like the last flash of a sunset.

She wanted to ease those lines of strain and open those eyes wide with wonder. She wanted to hear him purr and moan and call out her name in the most terrible surprise.

And yet, because she knew better, she sat still. She sat so very still she could have been the prey caught in the sights of that predatory bird. She sat so still she stopped breathing.

It was then she realized that he had stopped breathing, too.

"I have to go, Lee." His voice was a dark rasp, the sound of a match striking steel, a pull on an old, thick door stuck from disuse. His pupils dilated until his eyes were darker than the deep of night, too deep to breach, too dark to understand. His hands, those long, gentle, impatient hands, curled into themselves for control.

It happened that fast, and it frightened her.

"We haven't figured this out," she objected, anyway, her own voice small with wonder.

She curled her own hands, and her nails made small scrabbling sounds on the hardwood.

"We won't," he told her. "Not now."

She wanted to back away. She wanted to fold up in the corner and hide from the waves of heat that swept through her. Her throat stung with it; her breasts felt its weight. She ached. She wanted to move, to stretch out along that cool floor like a cat so that she could massage the need in her nerves.

Rock lurched up off the bed. Lee looked up at him. Outside, there were insects calling in the night. Down the block, somebody was playing reggae, and its beat infected her. Inside this safe, comfortable apartment, Lee had just lost her comfort.

"I have to go," he insisted, not moving.

Not bothering to hide the fact that Lee wasn't the only one who felt the heat this late summer night.

She should have broken eye contact, should have let him free. Instead, she uncurled herself. Slowly. Certainly.

Climbing her way to her feet so that her breasts could brush against the steely edge of his chest. So she could face him with the lightning they had sparked together.

Lee had never had time for broadway musicals. She didn't believe in love at first sight or soulmates or the one woman, one man theory. Suddenly, breathing in the subtle smoky scent of the man before her, she wondered.

"Please," she said.

He didn't move. Kept apart from her by the space of a heartbeat, he held his place, his fingers as tight as talons, his eyes too dark to bear.

Lee reached up, knowing she could bear anything, yet now knowing why. She laid her hand against that hard, furrowed cheek and she sought to tame that predatory bird, to calm his struggle for flight, to show him peace and freedom within her bounds.

"Come here," she whispered, moving closer.

He couldn't even shake his head. "No."

But his hand was already wrapped around the back of her neck. His breath was brushing against her cheek. His eyes, those hot, hard eyes that so compelled her, half closed with desire, and his body arched to close that last millimeter of space.

Lee rose onto her toes, her own gaze locked into his, her own breath caught somewhere in her chest. Her lips open, waiting. Her eyes closed, anticipating. Her heart stumbling against the sudden strength of his.

She lifted her other hand, cupped his strong, stubbled jaw, pulled it close. Pulled him to her, where his hand had already captured her, his fingers sending out showers of need, his grip as harsh as the growl of emotion that rose from his throat.

She tasted that need on him. She tasted surprise and hunger. She fed on the soft comfort of his mouth, on the gentle challenge of his tongue. She met him, mated, mouth to mouth, hand to hand, letting loose the magic. She moaned, deep where her wonder lived, for he incited wonder. She danced, there on her toes, moving against him so that her breasts could sate themselves on the steely feel of him, so her thighs could match the heat in his. She supped on the dark pleasures of his mouth, sang with the delight in his hands.

His hands, oh, his hands. Hungry, hurried, as if he couldn't touch her enough, as if she might simply disappear before he could get his fill of her. Lee met his hands, moving against them, her arms, her waist, her belly, her breasts. She held on, certain she would fall. She challenged, afraid she would never suffer this kind of miracle again.

She never heard the front door open.

"Lee? Is that you?"

The two of them broke apart. Froze. Faced each other for the space of a heartbeat, eyes still wide, hearts still racing, breath ragged as old sails. Lee wished for the breath to laugh, the wisdom for the words that would define what had happened. She had nothing but the pounding in her chest, the slow, melting heat that had been left behind after Rock had broken contact. She had nothing but surprise and the sweet frustration of unmet hunger.

And before she could at least let Rock know, he turned away.

"Lee?"

This time Gen's voice was much more surprised. It had also emanated right from the doorway to Lee's bedroom. Lee turned to her sister and realized that with a big sister's unerring instincts, Gen knew exactly what she'd interrupted. Lee should probably answer Gen's outraged surprise with her own. She couldn't. She still wanted to sing. She wanted to take her sister's hand and send her right back out the front door again so she could find out exactly what would have happened if Gen hadn't interrupted.

All she had left was laughter. So she laughed at the sudden stillness in her sister.

"Bad news, Gen," she said. "I grew up."

Gen wasn't nearly as sanguine about the whole thing. "I...oh, I, uh...excuse me."

"It was all quite innocent, actually," Lee defended Rock, since he still couldn't face her sister, and her sister was watching him as if he had a whip and collar in his hand. "We were at the ball game and I remembered that I'd taken pictures at the party, and we came back to find your camera, and couldn't—"

"You lost my camera?"

Lee did her best not to grin. Gen was so easy to distract. Lee did that by guiding her back out the door into the living room as she talked. "I think it was in my purse. Rock thinks that might be what everybody was after. The pictures."

"Jake gave me that camera," her sister objected, finally giving in to the inevitable and turning her attention away from Lee's bedroom.

"It wasn't my fault," Lee defended herself as she headed the both of them toward the kitchen. Before Gen could think about it, Lee was pouring wine and rhinosoberry into the good jelly glasses. "Besides, you never used it."

"I was going to," her sister answered, shucking the lab coat she'd worn home, which left her in slacks and blouse. "When I got the time."

Lee found it easier to laugh. "Of course you were."

Gen's attention kept drifting back to the rigid silence in Lee's room. Lee wouldn't let her. She asked about work and about Abbie Viviano and whatever she could think of until Rock felt comfortable enough to present himself. She had a feeling that most of the time was spent easing the emotional stresses rather than the more obvious physical one.

"I'll check on that camera," he said suddenly from the living room.

Lee saw what he intended and jumped into action, heading him off just before he made the front door and safe escape.

"Would both of you please grow up?" she demanded. "Rock, have a beer. Gen, sit on the damn couch."

Rock looked as if he would turn to stone. He was evidently trying to glare at Lee. She figured it was some kind of warning. All she could see was that pain, escaping in hard little flashes. She saw the hunger that still lapped at the edges of those dark eyes. She saw that, like her, it hadn't been simple physical need that had exploded back in her bedroom, and she wasn't about to let him retreat now.

"Sit," she insisted, not moving an inch.

She had a feeling he came within about an inch of just picking her up and placing her out of the way so he could escape. He didn't. Not relaxing a millimeter, he turned around. He didn't look any more at ease when he realized that it was Gen holding out the beer to him.

Her peace offering, Lee knew, even though her eyes were still wary with a big sister's reticence.

"So," Gen said, her own glass of wine already depleted by at least half. "Lee finally got into trouble for stealing my camera."

"I didn't steal your camera," Lee objected, heading for the couch once she figured it was safe to relent her post at the door. "I just borrowed it."

"Just like you borrowed all my bras in junior high?"

Lee settled herself onto the couch next to her sister as Jake took up position on the old overstuffed chair by the papier-mâché dragon.

"What'd I tell you?" she said with a grin. "Aren't families great?"

"Abbie Viviano tells me you've been a policeman almost as long as her husband Michael," Gen said.

Lee shook her head in wonder. Never let it be said that families were bound by the constraints of good taste. Gen went right for the kill. Probably because she was feeding all this information right back to Jake. After what happened, Lee would be lucky if he didn't just show up on the doorstep without warning and haul her all the way back to Wyoming underneath his arm like a football.

"Thirteen years," Rock was answering. Gen probably didn't notice the wry cant to his eyebrows, even as he sat in that chair about as comfortably as a wrestler at a ladies' tea. A week ago, Lee wouldn't have picked up on it, either. Gen wasn't putting a thing over on him.

Gen nodded thoughtfully. "You like it?"

Rock shrugged. "I'm good at it."

That got Lee's attention. For a moment, she sipped at the liquid in her glass and contemplated the answers he could have given. The answer she had a feeling Michael Viviano would have given.

"What are the books for?" Lee suddenly asked Rock.

"Books?" Gen asked.

"Piles of 'em," she answered, her attention on Rock, who had suddenly, silently begun to squirm. "Geometry and calculus and history and metaphysics."

Rock shrugged. "College. A cop has to have a degree these days."

"In advanced calculus?" Lee demanded.

"I like calculus."

Lee shot her sister a grin. "And he thinks I'm weird because I like horses."

"Why did you go into police work?" Gen asked.

"Why do you want to know?" Lee countered a bit sharply.

Gen's smile was the soul of innocence. "I don't know. It interests me. Until Michael, I didn't know any police—except for Ed Havers at home, and he became sheriff because his father'd been sheriff and nobody else wanted to do it. From what Abbie says, I think it must be a tough job to do here."

Rock didn't flinch or retreat. He just offered another of those stiff movements of dismissal, as if the answer wasn't as important as anything else. A long taste of beer, as if that could ease the answer through. "It's kind of a neighborhood tradition, where I grew up."

"He lives on Wells," Lee clarified for her sister. "Evidently everybody on the block is a cop."

Gen's smile was patient. But then, Gen had lived in Chicago a lot longer than Lee. She also planned on making it her home. "I know. And it's a tough job, Sergeant?"

This time Rock didn't even move. "It's tough."

Gen nodded, sipped her wine. Lee had just about had enough. Then her sister came up with the coup de grace and brought their little salon to an abrupt close.

"And Michael Viviano is your lieutenant," she said, as if reminding them all.

That did it. With a sigh of impatience, Lee turned to Rock. "My apologies, Rock," she said. "My sister has so little social life that she forgets her manners sometimes." Then she turned to Gen, and for the first time, she was angry. "He's not stupid, honey. He knows you're threatening him. Don't do it again, and here's why. Number one, you don't have any right, no matter how old I am. Number two, just who do you think was kissing whom in there?"

Gen flushed. Rock went rigid with discomfort. Lee waved off the both of them, as if she were the only true adult in the room. "If I don't smack her on the nose every now and then she won't remember that I'm not five and climbing trees anymore."

Even so, Rock didn't last five more minutes before escaping. Lee could hardly blame him. She would have run like hell, too. After dispatching an undisguised look of warning at her sister, she accompanied him down to the car. He walked next to her as if they were heading for the noose at Tyburn.

Lee waited for him to open the door to his truck. She waited for him to get inside and roll down the window on this close, stifling night. She waited, because she knew exactly what he was about to say.

"She's right. It's not a good idea—"

"Good night, Rock," she interrupted. "I'll do my best to find out what pictures I could have taken. I'll lock my doors and not talk to strangers and eat my Wheaties. And I promise I'll never let my sister talk to you like that again."

"Lee—"

Her grin was too bright; she knew that. She didn't care. "Lee, nothing," she insisted, stepping away from the truck as if that could help her escape his dismay. "Go home and get some sleep. I'll talk to you if I find out anything. Thanks for teaching me about baseball. It was great fun."

And before he could call out to her, she deliberately walked back through the door to the house. She walked all the way back up into the apartment and shut the door and faced off with her sister, because she didn't have the courage to face the policeman.

"Gen, I've never had to say this to you," she said to her sister, who sat on the couch, her wine still in hand, obviously not expecting Lee to show up again so quickly. "But honey, you butt into my business one more time without an invitation, and I'll walk out and never come back."

"But Lee," Gen objected, getting to her feet. "Abbie says—"

"I know perfectly well what Abbie says. I know what you say, and I know what Jake says, and I know what Rock says. I don't care. If Rock is a mistake, he's my mistake, and I will make it. I've made mistakes before, and I've paid the consequences all by myself."

"You've only known him a week!"

Lee's smile was as bemused as her thoughts. "Yeah," she admitted. "I have, haven't I?"

Gen stood her ground, her eyes desperate. "He scares me."

Lee nodded. "He scares me, too. There's something deep inside him that hurts him so badly he can hardly bear it."

"Exactly. I've seen men like him before, Lee. He's just going to explode one of these days, and when he does, somebody's going to be hurt."

This time when Lee smiled, it was a soft smile, one that held memories that had changed the face of her family. "So did Jake," she reminded her sister. "And the only one he hurt was himself. I don't want to see that happen to Rock."

"So you're going to be his social worker?"

"I'm going to be his friend, if he'll let me. I don't think he lets many people."

"He was married before, you know."

"I know. But unless he terminated that marriage by burying his wife beneath the front porch, I doubt it's going to make much difference."

"He's going to hurt you," Gen insisted.

Lee faced her with unshakable conviction. "Maybe. But I'll survive it. I don't think he'll survive it if not one person in his life has the guts to help him out."

"Do you really think he'll let you help?"

And that, finally, was the crux of the matter. Lee took a long breath and wished for a good slug of green drink with extra sugar to fortify herself for the truth. "I don't know, Gen. I just don't know."

"I can't let this go on," he said two mornings later when Lee finally got hold of him again.

She sat abruptly on the chair in the front office of the theater and held more tightly to the receiver, as if that would help protect her balance.

"Can't let what go on?" she asked.

"What happened the other night," he said, and she could almost hear him hunch over his desk, so no one else could catch the emotion in his voice. "I'm too busy with these other cases to give yours the attention it needs. I'm too wrapped up in my work and school right now to... to..."

"Consider a relationship."

"It wouldn't be fair. So although I'll take any information and make sure things are coordinated, somebody else will be doing the majority of the footwork on your case."

Lee nodded. "Uh-huh."

"You understand."

"Nope. I don't. But we can discuss it later."

There was the tiniest pause, during which Lee could almost see him close his eyes. "No. We can't. I won't be around your house again. You won't be around mine. Now, I have to go."

Lee thought of that conversation late that same night as she sat down on her couch in the darkened living room and looked outside. It was there, just as it had been the last three nights, tucked into all those BMWs like a coon dog in a poodle show. A battered, worn old truck that undoubtedly smelled like french fries and Neetsfoot oil. Silent, waiting, watching. Lee had seen the patrol cars make their extra sweeps in her neighborhood, just as Rock told her they would. But still that truck sat there, because maybe that wouldn't be enough. It would be there until six-thirty the next morning when Gen walked out of the house to go to work and all good detectives had to leave to get to their shift. And then, at ten the next night, it would appear again.

Lee wondered whether he thought she didn't see it. She wondered what he'd say if she just threw open the front door and walked over to hand him a cup of coffee and a doughnut.

She didn't. She wouldn't. At least not for now. She'd give him a few days to believe she was safe from him. She'd give him the chance to concentrate on that little girl, the one Michael Viviano said caused Rock so much distress.

But only a few days. Otherwise, he might think she actually believed him. And that wouldn't be a good thing at all.

Down on the street, Rock sipped at the cold coffee in the fast food cup and watched the darkened windows on the third floor of the old white-and-green Victorian down the block. He wondered whether she was asleep yet. He could almost see her, curled up on her side, a dryad swimming a winsome sea, her hair catching the moonlight like magic, her lips parted in sleep, her fingers tucked into her pillow. He could imagine finding her there, slipping beneath the waves on her sheet and nestling against the soft curve of her back. He could imagine just sleeping there, safe and whole, within the protection of her spell, her fingers on his face and her eyes bestowing blessings on his shattered soul.

Instead, he sat out in his truck in the dark where he belonged. Instead, he practiced telling himself it was all for the best. Instead, he ached.

He ached hard. Deep, like an old scar that refused to heal. A scar freshly ripped open time and again, and this time the worst. He wanted to lift it to her hands, to her mouth, so she could soothe it. He wanted to open it to the bright, healing light in her eyes.

He couldn't. So he sat here and he died a little more. Just like he would tomorrow and the next night and the next, right until the moment they picked up Sonny Varner trying to sneak back in to finish whatever job he'd been paid to do. Right until the moment Rock personally strangled the life out of whoever it was who had sent a shark like that to hurt her.

He would sit here, and he would wait, and in the morning he would try to prove what had happened to the little girl to the FBI and everybody else who didn't believe him, because even cops sometimes want to believe, and his old, scarred soul would crumble completely, because he knew it was what would set Lee apart from him.

She'd never understand. She wouldn't know that all he wanted was to protect that wonderful eagerness in her eyes. He wanted to seal her up with that family that had so well protected her that she had reached adulthood with an open heart. She wouldn't understand that she would break under the weight of him, and that he couldn't allow that.

So he sat alone and considered how he'd never realized that he'd never had a chance at all. And how if it weren't for that little girl, he might just give up completely.

Chapter 11

"Why didn't you tell me?" Lee demanded.

Creighton threw back his head and blew a cloud of smoke into the sky. "About my family? Darling, what's to tell?"

They were seated outside at a little bistro on Ohio, where the waiters whispered and the wealthy chattered. A square of tables confined by cement planters that spilled with geranium and lobelia, shaded by plum trees and scented with garlic and oregano and bay. It was Creighton's treat for finally getting his first look at the rough draft of *Fire on the Mountain*.

Lee had finished it during the last week with bluegrass on her stereo and a silent truck parked out on her street, and the words had changed. One of the characters, Junior, had become more taciturn. Harder and lonelier, as if he carried around secrets no one else could share. It had been Junior in the end who had saved the land. Junior who had sacrificed everything in the attempt, as if there were no other way.

Lee cried when she wrote the scene, because it seemed as if she couldn't force a happier result. It had taken her two days to gather the courage to have Creighton look at it, because suddenly it hurt worse than it excited, and she didn't know whether that worked.

"The Gianinis," she said, fingering the glass of tap water that had made the waiter curl his delicate nose. Lee didn't drink water with names on it, and the restaurant only served it with names on it. The waiter had acted as if he'd had to go down the block to the McDonald's to get it for her.

"Oh, them," Creighton retorted with an elegant wave of his hand. "I hear the police have been looking into that. Darling, I'd rather talk about your play. I don't think we should limit our thinking to the Chicago pool of actors for this one. One look at that role of Junior, and we could have anyone. Malkovich, Kline, any of the Baldwin brothers..."

"Somebody tried to kill me, Creighton," she said. "Because of that, the police are investigating everyone."

"But I thought you said it was because of that camera of yours. I did tell you it would get you into trouble, didn't I?"

"Well, that's what we think. You aren't getting any money from them, are you?"

"The police?" he retorted, elegant eyebrow arched. "Hardly."

Lee just glared at him. Beside her, the waiter set her salad on the table, warm spinach with balsamic vinegar dressing. Lee looked at it and smiled.

"Now, that's the unhappiest smile I've seen in my young life," Creighton complained. "I thought you liked the food here."

She nodded. "I do. A cop would starve to death, though."

Creighton took a long puff of his cigarette and ground it out in the cut-glass ashtray. "Ah," he said simply, and bent to his own lunch.

Lee looked up with a scowl. "Ah, what?"

He waved a fork in her direction. "Never play poker, my dear. You'd lose."

That didn't make her any happier. "That's what I hear. Are you, Creighton? Getting any money from them?"

He set his fork back down and placed both hands on the coral linen tablecloth, as if that would give his words more strength. "I thought the attempts had stopped."

"They have."

"Then whoever was after you has what they want. Don't you think?"

Lee's heart skipped a beat. "Did they want something of yours?"

"All I have," he said, "is the theater."

She forgot her salad then, the roast garlic and pine nut pasta to follow, the traffic out on the street and the clink of glasses at the bar just inside the open doors. "That's why I'm asking, Creighton. It's all I have, too."

Creighton reached out and took her hand. "Season tickets are not laundered money," he assured her. "And that's the only money any of them have given me. On my honor as a Sicilian on my mother's side. All right?"

Lee could actually feel the breath escaping from where she'd been holding it.

"The police were sniffing around more than a week ago," he said, going back to his terrine. "Why did you wait so long to ask?"

"Because I had to get that play finished."

He just nodded. He didn't realize that Lee hadn't meant it simply as an answer to her deadline. She'd truly needed to finish it, as if someone was looking over her shoulder, pressing down on her with his expectations, his needs, his presence.

She'd needed to exorcise someone she had no intentions of letting out of her life.

"Have you talked to him lately?" Creighton asked.

She'd just about been ready to eat. "Who?"

Creighton chuckled. "Your policeman, of course. I wonder how he'll feel to find himself in a play that's going to be a classic."

Lee was stunned to silence.

"I told you," Creighton said. "Never play poker."

It took Lee almost a full minute to gather the courage to ask her next question. "Should I change it?"

Creighton reacted so strongly to that he almost dropped his fork onto the sidewalk. "Should you what?"

Six separate heads turned at the outrage in his voice. Lee blushed, not yet ready to have this part of her displayed to the public.

"Do you think my... loss of objectivity has hurt the play?" she asked.

Creighton huffed, as if she'd just told him his suit was off the rack. "Didn't you just hear me?" he demanded. "I've already called the people in New York. My dearest Lee, that play is going to be on Broadway within the next two years, I'll guarantee it."

All six heads turned around all over again to find Lee crimson with distress. "I don't want that," she objected.

"I don't care. Some things are just too big to hold."

Lee didn't have an answer to that, so Creighton went back to his food.

"I just have one question," he said.

She nodded.

"Why kill him off?"

That was the hardest question to answer of them all. Lee hadn't really answered it herself. "Because," she admitted, "I think it's in him."

"Tragic hero, huh?"

She thought about it, realized that Creighton more than her sister or brothers would comprehend what Lee had come to understand about Rock. She set her fork back down, considering the deep coral roses in the blown glass vase before her.

"He has more honor and courage than almost any person I've ever known, Creighton. But he doesn't believe it. And because he doesn't believe it, there's going to come a moment when the only way he feels he can save himself is to offer himself up." She looked up, not at all surprised that there were tears in her eyes. "Does that make sense?"

And Creighton, who looked so much like the type of dilettante who would have been more concerned about the

correct presentation of a bisque than the needs of men, held
her hand again. "I don't think he realizes how lucky he is,
does he?"

She wiped her eyes as she laughed. "He doesn't even realize that I've been thinking that much about him."

"In that case, you must change the situation."

"Oh, I will," she said. "I've given him his space this
week while he thinks he needs it. But the time's coming
when he won't have a choice."

"Should I warn Sierra?"

Lee was able to laugh again. "You don't have to tell Sierra anything. She's perfectly aware of how moody I've
been."

"You're about as pleasant as a bear with a hot foot, ya
know that?"

Rock looked up from where he'd been going through interviews with the people in Lee's theater to see his lieutenant standing over his desk. Without waiting for the
question, Rock opened the drawer in his desk.

"Nice to see you, too, Lieu."

Viviano didn't bother with apologies as he reached in for
his handful of candy. "I don't need any more tension in this
workroom, O'Connor."

"Yes, sir."

"I could pull you off the Havlacjek case completely."

"Yes, sir."

Viviano dropped into one of the chairs. "The minute that
case is over, you're going on leave."

Rock looked up, ready to argue. Not knowing what to
say that wouldn't make it worse. How could he tell the
lieutenant that if he had any time off right now, he wasn't
sure he'd make it through to the morning? He couldn't remember the last time he'd slept or what the last thing was
he'd eaten. He remembered Lee's shadow in the window,
though, and the high, keening cry of little Lisa Havlacjek's grandmother when he appeared at her door.

This one was the worst. This one would break him, and
it was because for just that brief moment, he'd tasted the

purity in Amaryllis Jane Kendall and realized he didn't deserve it.

"Sure, Lieu."

Viviano huffed in frustration. "Don't give me that crap, O'Connor. I mean it."

Rock looked back down at the interviews he'd been compiling. "Me, too. The minute I find out who was after Lee Kendall."

"Has anybody else made a try for her house?"

Rock didn't look up. He just kept scribbling notes. "Nope. Not that I know about."

"Then they probably got what they came for."

"Maybe."

"Then it isn't high priority."

"It isn't unless they're just waiting for us to let our guard down so they can come back and make sure Lee doesn't remember anything after all."

For a long few moments, Viviano just sat there. Rock wanted to apologize. He wanted to tell the lieutenant that it wasn't his fault he was like this, that he just needed to close this case. He needed to close the Havlacjek case, and maybe he could see his way past. He wanted to tell him he wouldn't give him any more trouble.

He couldn't.

In the end, Viviano grabbed another handful of M&M's and got back to his feet.

"Last I checked, I was still the Lieutenant," he said. "Which is senior to a sergeant. Which means that when I say you go on leave, you go on leave."

"Okay, Lieu."

This time Viviano just walked away.

"Sugar, you comin' back in or not?" Sierra asked Lee two days later.

Lee looked up from where she was waiting on the phone in the front office. "I'm trying to get hold of Rock."

Sierra plopped herself down on one of the gilded, red velvet chairs that doubled for office furniture and set props. "You gonna tell him what I think?"

"I'm trying. Who knows? Maybe it does mean something after all."

The headlines were on the *Trib* front page before her. Negative Campaign Against Senator Peterson Increases. The story had gone on to say that the senator's opponent, a businessman with a lot of money and little discretion, was accusing Senator Peterson of everything from favoritism to underworld connections. Senator Peterson had been at that party. So had Mario Gianini's wife. At least she was the one on the party list. Nobody could really remember if Mario had been there. Lee could have caught them together, even innocently enough. She could have been accused of snapping incriminating photos against the Senator—who, before he'd entered politics, had gone by the title of Reverend—with his new blond girlfriend.

"You're sure you don't remember anything else I might have snapped by mistake," she asked her friend.

Sierra shook her head. "Girl, you know how I am with faces. The mayor coulda come up and kissed me full on the mouth, and I still wouldn't have recognized him. And there wasn't anybody out on that boat the next day but staff and sea gulls."

Lee still hadn't gotten anybody to take her off hold. "You don't remember any other boats nearby I might have snapped by mistake."

Sierra shrugged. "If there was, only way you're gonna find out is if you get those negatives back. And considerin' where your purse is, that's probably not gonna happen, is it?"

Lee sighed, knowing perfectly well that Sierra was right.

If that was what this was all about. If, in fact, somebody out there was worried about some pictures she might have taken, she'd never know who it was. So, just for safety's sake, just as she had with everyone who had asked about it, she repeated the truth.

"Well, I sure don't remember what it was that has everybody so upset. I doubt I will. Which means, I guess, that they can stop breaking into my apartment any time they want."

"They probably just got any extra film they saw lying around that second time, just in case," Sierra reassured her.

"Probably."

"Are you holding for Sergeant O'Connor?" a voice spoke up from the other end.

Lee came right to attention. "Yes. Is he there?"

"He's not able to come to the phone right now. Can I take a message?"

For a second, Lee didn't know what to do. She could probably give her information to somebody else, but she didn't know who else Rock had asked to help him. In the end, she demurred.

"Uh, will you just tell him that Lee Kendall called and to call me back at Fandango Theater?"

"Okay." She could hear his voice turn away, as if he were making a note. "It might be a while."

"I'll be here awhile," she assured him. "You might also tell him to check out the front page of the *Trib.* He'll understand."

"Okay."

Lee hung up the phone and found herself staring at it, as if she were in need of an answer.

"Expecting him to call back this quickly?" Sierra demanded.

Lee looked up, startled. Frowned. "It's silly," she said. "I just don't feel right."

"You don't feel right how? Don't tell me you're gonna be sick. I don't have enough rehearsal time left till opening night, girl."

Lee smiled, but she knew it lacked conviction. "No. Rock. There was just something about that guy who answered the phone, ya know?"

Regaining her feet, Sierra rolled those expressive eyes of hers. "Now she's tellin' fortunes over the phone. Next thing you'll tell me you're channeling Shakespeare."

There was nothing left to do but follow Sierra in, so Lee did. "As a matter of fact, he wants to talk to you about the way you staged *Twelfth Night* last year."

Sierra hooted with laughter. "Don't be silly. He'd love to see his work done all in pink. Wouldn't you?"

Lee held the door into the theater open for her friend. "We'll talk."

Lee made it through rehearsal. She made it all the way over to the hospital, where she was going to meet Gen. When Abbie Viviano told her the news, though, she gave in and called the station.

She was supposed to meet Gen down in the ER, so she headed in to sit in the doctor's lounge, only to find Abbie there ahead of her making short work of a pizza.

"Mmm," the doctor greeted her. "Pull up a chair and help me here. I eat all this and they're gonna need a dolly to get me in the delivery room."

Lee dug right in.

"When are you going on leave?" she demanded, pulling cheese apart with her fingers. "You look like you're going to tip over now."

Abbie laughed as she wiped grease off her chin. "As a matter of fact, I'm counting down ten more days. Then it's part-time all the way. That's if I come back at all."

Lee looked up in surprise. "You're giving this up?"

Abbie laughed. "I know, it seems impossible. Who wants to live without coffee and popcorn diets, aching backs and the attention of every spitting drunk on the street? I'm going to take my time off with this new fidget, and then I'm going to decide. I'm just not sure I can handle Michael's traumas and mine both."

Lee found herself nodding. "I know what you mean."

Abbie didn't answer right away. When she did, her voice was quiet and sincere. "Gen told me. I'm not sure whether I'm happy for you or sorry for you."

It was Lee's turn to laugh, although the sound was far from happy. "Neither is she."

"But she doesn't know Rock. I meant what I said, Lee. He's a good man."

"I know that."

Abbie nodded. "He's a hard man to know."

This time Lee sighed. "I know that, too."

Neither of them heard the door opening. "Well, there are two of my favorite women."

Lee fought a surge of impatience. She didn't want to talk to Tim right now. She didn't want him interfering when she might actually learn something about Rock. But it wasn't his fault, so she greeted him with a smile.

"Do you ever get time off?" she asked, seeing that he was once again in scrubs.

He walked on in for a cup of coffee. "The streets are full of cars, and the cars keep bumping into one another. It pays for the wine cellar I plan to install. How are things going with you? You've been keeping yourself hidden the last few days."

"I was finishing a play."

Both he and Abbie looked up. "Is it good?" he asked.

Lee shrugged. "It's the best I can do" was all she'd admit.

He nodded, settled himself onto one of the chairs as if he were easing into the seat at the symphony. "Well, it better be," he told her. "I just bought myself season tickets to that theater of yours."

Again he smiled. Again Lee wished she could fall in love with somebody as uncomplicated and bright as he was.

"I think you'll enjoy them," she said.

"You going to stay healthy enough to star in the opener, as advertised?"

Lee went after another piece of pizza. "I think most of the excitement's over," she admitted. "Rock thinks that I was being chased for some pictures I'd taken. We looked, and there's no camera left and no film anywhere, so unless I stuffed it into an ice-cube tray someplace, I imagine my intruder got it. And the way my memory is, unless I see something on a picture, I'm not going to remember what it was. So if any shady characters ask you, tell them I didn't see anything."

His grin was mischievous. "I promise. Well, I'd better get back. I imagine my lady's prepped by now, and I hate to keep an audience waiting."

He opened the door just to let Gen in.

"Hi, Tim. Bye, Tim. Come on, Lee, let's get outta here...."

She almost made it. Then she saw the pizza, which had probably called to her all the way up the seven floors to where she was working pediatric ICU this month.

"Well, maybe just one..."

Abbie shoved the box in her direction and turned her attention back to Lee. "Did you hear the news? It might help."

"News? What news?"

"They have somebody in the Havlacjek case."

For a minute, Lee's breathing stopped completely. "Are they sure?"

"Michael seems to think so. I just talked to him. Rock was doing the interrogation."

Again, Lee felt the flutter of dread, the sudden shift, as if Abbie's words didn't match the sound of the officer's voice she'd heard earlier.

"Did he say who it was?"

Abbie shook her head. "He won't. Not till it's released."

Lee was already looking at the phone. She needed to call. She needed to call now. She was dialing before she even realized it.

"Chicago police, Area One."

"Sergeant O'Connor, please."

"Hold."

Lee heard the clicking and held her breath. Was it good news? Was Rock happy it was over? Would he let her close to him now, so that he didn't have to sit outside in the dark alone while she sat inside watching him from her darkened window night after night?

"Sergeant O'Connor's line."

"Is Rock there, please?"

"Who's calling, please?"

That was when she realized who'd picked up Rock's phone. For a minute, she just felt relief. At least Michael would be able to tell her Rock was okay.

"Michael, hi, it's Lee Kendall. Is Rock around?"

When Michael didn't answer, her heart began to slide. When he did answer, it fell right out.

"Uh, no, Lee, he's not here."

It was his voice. She could hear disaster in it. It must have been what Gen had heard the night they called her to tell her that Lee had fallen down the ravine on Jake's horse. It was a sound no human should hear, because you knew even before they answered that what they would say would hurt you.

"What's wrong?"

Abbie looked up from where she'd picked up a magazine, and Gen came to a halt, pizza in her hand, napkin in her lap.

Michael didn't answer right away. Lee fought the instinctive urge to panic.

"Michael, what happened?"

"Uh, Rock is on disciplinary leave, Lee."

The stuffings came right out of her knees, and she landed on one of the chairs. "Oh, God" was all she could manage at first. She'd known. Somehow she'd known, but it didn't make it any easier. "What happened? I thought he'd solved the Havlacjek case."

"He did. We have someone in custody now."

"But then, what's wrong? That should have helped. That was what he was working so hard on."

Another pause, as if Michael was trying to soften the blow, protect his officer. "He struck someone."

"Who?"

"The suspect."

Lee didn't hear any more. She didn't hear Michael say that he was taking care of things and that Rock was a good enough officer that this wouldn't count too far against him. She didn't hear anything at all.

"How long ago?" she asked.

"About half an hour."

She hung up without remembering to say goodbye. She turned to find both Abbie and her sister on their feet, instinctively closing in for support.

"What?" Gen asked, her eyes melting with concern.

"It's Rock," Lee said, coming back to her feet and turning to the doctor she'd only known a few months. "He's in trouble."

"Can you help?"

"I think so. I need to get there."

"Where?"

"His house. I think he just went to his house. Abbie, I need a car."

Gen tried to interrupt. "Lee, you can't—"

Abbie didn't let her. "The keys are in my purse. Go."

Lee went. She'd never driven in Chicago. Even so, she drove. She battled the traffic all the way down Lake Shore Drive until it dumped into the Eisenhower, and then she battled that until she could reach the Dan Ryan south for the few miles she needed to get to Rock's neighborhood. Lee Kendall, who couldn't remember a name without tags, had a perfect sense of direction. She knew if she could just get to the neighborhood, she'd find the right house.

She did. It wasn't the house, which looked so much like all the others on the block with its concrete porch and chain-link fence and sparse yard. It was the beaten old truck parked halfway into the traffic lane sitting in front of it. Pulling to a stop just behind it, Lee jumped out.

The house was dark. Lee wasn't sure what to do. Bang on the door? Bother a neighbor? Wait? He had to be here. She could feel it, like a faint thrum just beneath her breastbone. It stopped her for a minute out there on the sidewalk where she could hear the television in somebody's house down the block, where she could hear kids yelling in a backyard and a couple of dogs barking, and from the highway with its constant pulse of traffic. There were no sounds, though, from Rock's house, and it made her realize that the sense of certainty was more dread than hope. Fear. She knew Rock was in that house, and it made her want to run.

She climbed the steps, her tennis shoes almost silent on the stained old concrete, and she reached for the door. It was open. She pushed it in, held her breath. She took a look inside to find the living room just as she'd seen it before, the walls empty and the books still piled in haphazard mountains by the easy chair. She couldn't hear a sound.

Please, she thought. Let him be all right. That funny vibration in her chest sharpened and settled, until it interfered with her breathing. Until it drew her hand to it, as if that alone could contain it.

Lee didn't have the nerve to call out, so she just stepped on inside. The house seemed to sigh around her. She shivered and headed for the kitchen.

Nothing. The refrigerator door was listing open, so that the light slid across the bare floor. The table was empty. Lee turned instead to the hallway that led to the back of the house. She stepped carefully, not wanting to surprise him. Hoping he was just asleep.

She knew better. She'd known better since she'd heard the tone of Michael's voice when he'd answered the phone.

Rock wasn't asleep. He was in the farthest bedroom, a room as empty and desolate as the rest of the house. He was sitting on a chair by the window with his back to her, a beer in his hand. On the table at his elbow sat a gun.

"Rock?"

He never moved. Never took his consideration of the view out the window, through which Lee couldn't see much more than a small yard with a tree house in a big oak, and beyond that another house. There was a bed in this room, tumbled and unkempt. A hardwood floor that looked bleached-out and worn. A chest of drawers and a terrible expanse of bare white walls. And the chair, facing the window. Lee took careful steps closer, her heart in her throat.

"Rock, what happened?"

He never turned to acknowledge her. He just laughed, and Lee thought she'd never heard a worse sound. "I've been disciplined."

She edged closer, hurting so badly for the confusion in that voice. "Why? What happened?"

"You know what happened or you wouldn't be here."

"Why did you hit him?"

That earned her a silence as he just sat there. Just sat there as still as death.

"Rock?"

"I knew it," he said, his tone almost conversational. "I always know it. You think they would, too. They're cops, for God's sake."

"Know what?"

"I told them, but they wouldn't listen. This time, they said, it was different. I wanted it to be different, too, ya know. Otherwise I would have seen it sooner."

"What, Rock?" she asked, coming close enough to kneel before his chair. "What did you see?"

It was then she realized that there were tears on his face. Tears. In the dim light, it looked as if they had been what had carved out those furrows in his cheeks, on that hard, solid face that never showed emotions to people who didn't know better. Lee took his hand without thinking and realized that it trembled.

He turned to her, then, and Lee thought she would surely break under that pain.

"It was the parents," he said simply, his eyes as deep and dark as death. "It always is. That little girl's mother and father killed her and then dropped her in that river to confuse us. I knew the minute they went to identify her, because they didn't know what a river would do to her. They didn't know . . . but I did."

Lee reached up and wrapped her arms around him, as if she could protect him from the cold.

"It was the parents," he repeated, as if he needed to convince her.

She kissed his cheek, that furrowed cheek that carried tears. She felt him flinch, almost as if the contact were too great.

"The parents . . ."

She kissed his eyes, closing them against the things he'd seen.

"I tried to kill him."

Then she kissed his lips, silencing the agony she heard. She felt him stiffen in her grasp until she thought surely he

would shatter with the task of holding every pain in the
world to himself. She felt the trembling set in, because even
Rock wasn't that strong. She held on, silent and certain,
knowing there was nothing else that would help. Feeling her
own tears mix with his.

And then the beer can dropped to the floor and he simply folded against her.

She held on, because she knew this was what she wanted.
She knew that this was what he needed. He moaned, and it
sounded like the keening of grief. Lee held on. She cupped
that sharp-edged face into her hands and wouldn't let him
go. He sobbed, a terrible sound, as if the pain of her touch
was too great. Lee understood. She knew she might not be
able to save him after all. But she knew she couldn't leave
without trying. She wasn't deserting him, when he still had
no one to comfort him.

"Come here," she whispered, her forehead against his,
her hands at his jaw.

His own hands had come up, had caught her around the
back. His hands shook suddenly, and his eyes closed.
"No," he said.

Lee shook him herself. She waited for those eyes to open.
"Yes," she said, and took him by the hand. And this time,
she didn't let go until he followed, and he followed her to
bed.

Chapter 12

Ever since that moment in her bedroom, Lee had known that when she and Rock made love, it would be fierce. It would be wind and light and sweet, melting heat. She hadn't realized that it would also be so quiet. That Rock would tremble like a young boy, that she would lead the way, because he was too lost to do it for her.

She hadn't realized that when they did make love, it would mean much more than just attraction and affection and joy. It would mean healing and comfort and wisdom. It would mean a communion Lee had never known in her life, with all her friends, with all her family, with all the wonders of her imagination.

But that was because with all her celebrated imagination, all her experience and her friends and her family, she had never imagined Francis Xavier Aloysius O'Connor.

His bed was as spare and sterile as the rest of his house. Lee would have wanted to make love on undulating green-and-gold waves. She would have wanted music and laughter. She knew, though, that tears were a more precious thing.

She stood by the bed with him, never taking her hands away, never letting him free. She reached up with her fingers and accepted his grief and fury, and with her eyes she gave him her heart. It was all it took. Rock pulled her to him, and she knew it was right.

Lee had been loved. She had never been needed. Rock needed her. He told her with his hands, with his mouth, with the harsh groans that swelled from his chest. He praised her and thanked her and begged her, and Lee begged back.

It would be later when she would remember what his body felt like. She would lie in the dark in her own room and catalog the scars that made up the man, the hard, unyielding planes of chest and arm and thigh. With quiet smiles and softer memories she would remember how his hair tickled her as she first laid her cheek against his naked chest, and how it felt to finally let her hands loose on his sweat-dampened skin. She would remember these things and let them be the cement of certainty.

But she didn't notice those things then. She saw only the awful grief in Rock's eyes. She felt only the need in his hands. She knew only that the swirl of attraction that had almost pulled them both under on a night when there had been nothing at stake seared her with its heat as Rock's hands slid up her bare waist. It sapped her strength as he bent her head back with the force of his kiss. It ignited the very room when he moaned her name as if that were the only thing that could possibly pull him from the depths.

She knew these things and let herself sink so fast beneath the tide of hunger that she would only remember later how gentle this man was, even as he swept her into his arms and away from the world.

She tumbled with him to the bed, clothing pulled and shoved and discarded in a pile. She lost herself in his hands, in his mouth that sought solace from hers. She melted into the tide of need his hands incited and his mouth quenched, and she lost herself to him, until there was nothing to separate them at all.

They wrapped into each other as if afraid of becoming lost. They sang and whispered and moaned, their bodies slick with hunger and hot with waiting. They tasted and touched and lavished, need fueling desire and desire exploding into a torrent of fire that swept them away, until Rock cried out Lee's name and she knew he would tumble over the hard edge of ecstasy into her arms.

The light was leaving as Lee nestled her head against Rock's shoulder and waited for her heart to calm. Air stirred against her damp skin and raised gooseflesh. Rock's heart met her pace and exceeded it, the sound as reassuring as the feel of his hand in her hair.

Somewhere in the back of her traditional mind, she knew she should pull up the sheet. She should explain or apologize or ask. Instead, she watched and listened and waited, knowing that for the first time since she'd known him, Rock O'Connor was still. Quiescent, at least for a moment. Comfortable before the guilt and guessing and regret set in. She didn't want to face that just yet, because her body was still telling her how much of a waste remorse would be.

Lee wasn't the kind of person to second-guess her actions. She knew she wouldn't need to now. But she also knew Rock would feel compelled, and once he did, this perfect moment of comfort and communion would begin to dissolve like the rainbow at the edge of a soap bubble.

Maybe he felt it, too, because for a long time, he simply held her, his arms around her, his hand tangled in her hair, his body quiet. Lee did her best to hang on to the hope that it would be enough, and let herself watch that lean, spare body that had been hidden away beneath all those rumpled suits. A body that had been worked hard and abused even more. A body that fit hers so well she found herself distracted by thoughts of more.

"Why did you do that?" Rock finally whispered, kissing the top of her head.

Lee closed her eyes, just for a moment, praying for the right answer. "Because I wanted to."

"Not to make me feel better?"

She sought something to focus on, but there was just bare white wall. Just the sense that Rock punished himself with this house. She laid her hand out flat against his chest so that her fingers were splayed across his ribs, as if she could hold him to her, where it was safe and good.

"To make us both feel better," she acknowledged, gauging her answer by the sound of his heart against her ear.

"I'm sorry," he said, his heart giving him away. "I shouldn't have . . . I had no right."

Lee didn't move. She didn't challenge him eye to eye, because she knew his were still too raw and honest to allow her close. So she held on to him with calm hands and did her challenging with calm words.

"You weren't the one who made the invitation," she said.

"I should have thrown your cute little butt outta here for your own good."

"I wouldn't have gone."

Lee kept her hand to Rock, but she let her attention drift. She realized now that she hadn't seen the real view from this bed. She hadn't seen how Rock had positioned both bed and chair to find that view no matter what time of day or night.

The window. The tree house made with a small boy's hands. The open sky that looked so promising beyond these terrible walls.

She guessed she'd known the minute she'd seen it. Now she understood. Just like Jake, Rock kept his secrets in his old room where a simple chair had been placed before a window like a penitent's kneeler before an altar of hope. He had hidden the truth back in this small room that must have been his all those long years he'd grown up in this house. All the years that had ended up fueling his terrible crusade.

Rock wasn't such a mystery now. He had simply never let any of his friends see this place that defined him.

"It must have been awful," she said in response to her own imagination, which gave sound and motion to the empty, echoing rooms.

Rock misunderstood her. "I did all right until that bastard blamed his daughter for what happened. That was when I hit him."

No, Lee wanted to say. I want to hear the other story. The one that really matters, that made all those little girls such a penance for you.

She raised herself up on an elbow and gently challenged the flash of fury in eyes that shouldn't have held such heat. She lifted her hand to that furrowed cheek. "I'm sorry," she said simply, and he went perfectly still.

He knew. He saw the truth in her eyes, saw that he wasn't hiding anything from her. Lee could feel it in the way his body tightened, as if expecting a physical blow. She heard it in the sudden pause in his breathing. She saw it in his eyes, those eyes that said so much more than anyone realized.

"How'd you know?" he asked.

She smiled for him, her hand still at his cheek, her voice quiet with import. "Your window," she said. "I bet that tree house out there could be quite a refuge. Who was it, your mom or your dad?"

He shrugged, so tight, so controlled, as if allowing the real truth free would be too much to bear. Lee understood. Even as she asked him what had happened, she didn't want to know. She didn't want to hurt that much.

"Depended on who was drinking more," he acknowledged. "My dad hit harder, but my mom had a hell of a backswing with a hairbrush."

She couldn't think of what to say. There had to be something for this brave, strong man who had allowed himself nothing but retribution over the years. It explained so much. He hadn't been able to defend himself against his parents, so he defended the other children. He tried, again and again, to believe that parents simply wouldn't do that to their children. And when he was proven wrong, he died all over again.

Lee couldn't think of anything to say, so she stroked his cheek. She couldn't think of a gift that would take away the isolation of a boy's childhood, so she shared herself with the adult. She traced those gentle lips with her finger and then met them with her mouth.

Rock's hand tightened against the back of her head. His breath caught, there where Lee placed her other hand. His mouth, that clever, strong, sexy mouth Lee so loved to taste, welcomed her. There wasn't anything Lee could say, but she didn't need to, because she said it with her hands and her lips and her body. And Rock, so long alone in this sterile, empty room, wanted to answer.

She tasted the hunger still in him. She tasted old fear and new fury. She tasted a need she'd never known and a yearning that made her weak, because it was a yearning for her.

She knew it was too much, even before he pushed her away.

"Lee—"

She opened her eyes to see the warring emotions in his eyes. "No," he said. "This isn't—"

She simply placed her hand over his mouth. "Do you want to make love with me?" she asked.

He pulled her hand away. "It's not—"

"A good idea," she said. "I know. Gen would say exactly the same thing. She'd say that I'm probably getting too close to you, too used to you, and she might be right. But right now I need you and you need me, and I can't think of a better thing to do about it."

He held on tight. "You deserve more than me."

That made her want to punch him. She went very still. "Francis Xavier Aloysius O'Connor," she chastised him. "I deserve everything I want. How do you know you're not what I always wanted?"

He wasn't laughing. "Am I?"

She tilted her head to the side, smiled. "Actually, no. I'd never anticipated you. I was going to settle for Tommy Halpern."

Rock didn't move, didn't let her move. He kept rubbing at her shoulders with his thumbs, as if wearing the texture of her into his memory. "Don't you understand?" he demanded. "This happened for the wrong reasons."

"The wrong reasons?" she countered. "And just what are those? Were you trying to hurt me?"

"No, of course not."

"Were you trying to take advantage of me?"

"Lee, I—"

"You hurt. Well, I hurt, too. I hurt for that little girl and I hurt for the little boy who had nothing but an old tree house to protect him from the people who were supposed to be his protection. I hurt for me, because I care about the man that little boy has become, and he won't let me close. Make love with me, Rock. Make something good here in this lonely place."

The strain on his beautiful face was terrible. "I have nothing to give you," he protested, and all Lee wanted to do was winnow her fingers through that dark hair that tumbled over the pillow beneath.

She smiled again for him, sating herself at least on the feel of his jaw against her fingers.

"What more could you give me than you?" she asked. "I sure don't want anything more."

"You deserve more."

She faced him then without artifice or deceit. She gave him, with her eyes and her words and her hands, the most elemental truth she knew. The most vital. "I'm a simple girl, Rock. I need simple things. Believe me when I tell you that you give me every one of those things, and more. Things I never knew I wanted. Please—" She lifted that hand, traced the edges of his mouth with her finger, saw the heat build in his eyes. "Make love to me now."

She felt his body respond. She felt her own answer, the need for him spreading through her like the first rays of the sun as it topped the land. She felt it creep up from her toes, settle in her hips and belly, reach for her breasts where they rested against his chest. It made her want to move, and so she moved, just a little. Just enough so that she saw the weight of arousal half close his eyes.

"I don't want to hurt you," he said, and he was pleading.

Lee wanted to cry. She wanted him to understand that he was hurting her already. He'd hurt her so badly she'd been crying for a week over the pages of a play that should have had nothing to do with him. She wanted him to know that he would always hurt her, but that a hurt like that was sometimes what told you you were alive, because you couldn't hurt like that if you didn't also love.

Instead, she could only find words that seemed flip, maybe even arrogant. She could only pretend that neither of them was as committed as they both knew they were.

"I may look like Peter Pan," she told him, trying so hard to tell the truth with her eyes. "But I grew up a long time ago. I'm just asking for now."

Rock reached up and cupped her face to him in those hard, strong hands. He held her very still for just a second, and she knew that if she wanted to back out, this was her last chance. She didn't.

He groaned with the force of his own need. "I never said you looked like Peter Pan."

And then, before she could object or ask or agree, Lee found herself on her back on those crisp, plain sheets that weren't so lonely anymore. She found herself captured, committed. She found herself singing with the sudden exultation of passion.

Rock never let go of her. He held her in his hands, in his gentle, eager hands. He praised her with them, quieted her with them, swept her along with them onto a tide of wonder. Lee couldn't hold still. She couldn't stay away, claiming her own discoveries. Inciting moans and chuckles and gasps of surprise as she took him for her own, stamped him with her handprint and her tongue print and the heat of her lips. She writhed beneath him, danced, sighed, sang, as his fingers found her waiting, as his mouth made her wanting. He kissed her and he claimed her and he nestled against her breasts and brought them to aching, sharp attention with his mouth and his tongue and his teeth. He called her name, over and over again, with wonder and with hunger and with delight, and he branded her with his touch so there would never be another touch. He caressed her with his smile, so that no one would ever again smile. He urged her body to respond with such fury that she wept and pleaded, and then he cherished her with his concern when he made her wait just long enough for her own protection. Just as he had before, even when he'd needed her so much. When they had both needed each other.

And then, his deep, sweet brown eyes keeping claim of her as he returned, he entered her, and she wrapped herself up in him, knowing he was home.

She smelled the musk of his excitement. She tasted the salt of spent tears and couldn't tell who had given them. She sated her hands on the rasp of his skin and pulled him closer, even closer with her hands and her hips and her legs, until they were too intertwined to part. Until his lips were against her throat and his hands were at her hips and he filled her with the sweet hot sensation of shattering.

Her eyes flew open. Her head fell back. Her body arched in instinctive rhythm, and he answered. She opened her mouth to cry out as the tide coursed through her. She couldn't even seem to manage sound as she scrabbled at his back and pulled him even deeper. She moaned and keened like the wind in the high plains that swept to the mountains, and then she heard the same song rise in his throat as he followed.

It was only much later, when the darkness protected them and the air cooled them, that reality once again intruded.

"Oh, dear," Lee murmured where she lay curled into him.

"Oh, dear?"

"Abbie's car."

That got his attention. "What about it?"

"I have to get it back to her. I imagine she has to go home soon."

For a second, he lay where he was, his fingers in her hair and at her hip, his breathing calm, his eyes closed.

"She knows you're here?"

There was nothing to do but admit the truth. "She and Gen both."

For some reason, that actually got him to laugh. It was a revelation, a deep rumbling Lee could feel against her cheek that made her smile. "I bet your sister's thrilled to death."

Lee wanted to look at that laugh, just to make sure. She kept her place. "She doesn't have any say in the matter. Besides, she knows perfectly well how I feel about you."

She got another pause for that statement. She waited, her heart stuttering with dread. He shied so easily, a wild thing caught in a corner. She didn't want to trap him, she wanted to set him free. Sometimes, though, it was tough to tell the difference until he could see the sky.

"You don't even know me," he finally said.

Lee thought about that for a minute. "Well, I know you like the Cubs and that you haven't learned to love horses yet. I know you're a cop and that you're friends with some other cops, and that you're divorced. You didn't bury your first wife under the porch, did you?"

"What?"

"Never mind. I know you like beer and M&M's and calculus. That's more than my mother knew about my father when she married him."

"Marriage?"

She shrugged, more as an excuse to nestle closer than as a statement. "You'll want to know about me, of course. I'm an award-winning horsewoman, I have two brothers and a sister, one sister-in-law who is an award-winning author, a niece, a nephew and an undecided, a home in Wyoming and an apartment in Chicago. I don't like beer, but I know you're going to love the mountains. It's the most beautiful place on earth."

"More beautiful than Wrigley Field?"

"Well, all right, it doesn't have ivy-covered walls. But does Wrigley Field have eagles?"

"The Cardinals come there sometimes."

"All right, we'll commute. What else do you want to know?"

"I want to know why you have Abbie Viviano's car."

"Because we were worried about you. Abbie really likes you, ya know."

"Lee, this isn't going to work."

Lee didn't move. Didn't give an inch of ground, because that was the only way she knew to deal with things that frightened her, and the tone of Rock's voice frightened her.

"You don't like eagles?" she asked.

She could feel the frustration build in him. It shimmered off him, collected in his muscles until he wasn't a comfortable companion anymore. Still Lee didn't move.

"We just don't see the world in the same way," he said, and she could tell that he wanted to say so much more.

She rested her hand against his heart to keep him close. Still she didn't chance disillusionment by looking up at his eyes. "Tell me how you see the world," she suggested.

"No." He wrapped her close, nuzzled his mouth against her head. "It would change everything."

Lee closed her eyes against the sharp terror. She held on to him as tightly as he held on to her. "It wouldn't. I promise."

"You saved me, Amaryllis," he whispered against her, and she began to cry. "Let me just have that for now."

"No, I didn't. You would have made it just fine. You just needed somebody to remind you that not everyone out there is thoughtless and cruel."

He laughed, but his laugh this time was sore and lonely. "That," he said, as if he were saying goodbye, "is why I don't deserve you. Because you don't realize how rare you are."

That brought her up and around, fire in her eyes. "I don't want to hear this don't deserve stuff again," she demanded.

He didn't answer her. Instead he caught her to him. He kissed her, a long, slow meeting of mouth and tongue and soft murmurs that told her everything he didn't have the words for.

It didn't stop her tears, so he brushed them away for her. "Don't cry, Amaryllis. Please don't ever cry, or I won't make it."

"The only way you can make me cry is to send me away," she said.

Again he didn't answer. Not with words. But Lee saw the truth take the light from his eyes and she wanted to argue. She wanted to pound on him and scream and rage. But Lee Kendall had grown up around stubborn men, and she knew that for now she had to give him back that space in which he could think. She had to back away now before he was forced to push her.

She smiled for him and dropped one last kiss and told him what he thought he wanted to hear.

"I should get the car back, anyway."

"I'll follow you to the hospital and then drop you at your apartment."

She looked long and hard, needing the truth now. "You're all right?"

He lifted a hand to her, and the hand was gentle. "I promise. I won't hit another suspect as long as I live."

"But are you all right?"

He considered the question a moment and seemed surprised by the answer. "Yes," he admitted with a smile that actually reached his eyes. "I'm all right. Now let's get you home."

Abbie Viviano didn't seem to know quite what to do with the sight of Rock following Lee into the doctor's lounge. She smiled, and then she frowned and then she stepped forward.

"We didn't mean to gang up on you," she offered in hesitant apology.

She seemed even more surprised when Rock not only smiled, but dropped a kiss on the top of her head. "You're a courageous woman, Abbie Viviano," he told her. "You let this madwoman loose with your Volvo in rush-hour traffic."

Abbie managed a weak grin. "It seemed a good idea at the time."

Rock grinned back and damn near brought Abbie to her knees. "Do yourself a favor. Never watch her drive. You won't know how close you came to losing that thing."

If Lee weren't seriously relieved by Rock's attitude, she would have been less than amused by his teasing. But all she could think of was the gun on that nightstand. The desperation that had so deadened those beautiful eyes. The hoarse cry of discovery as he had allowed himself to share the freedom of intimacy.

"Well, do *me* a favor," Abbie said, "and call off Michael. He's at the triage desk phoning somebody to check on you two."

Lee exchanged surreptitious glances with Rock as he swung back out of the room. Evidently not surreptitious enough.

"My God," Abbie breathed in wonder. "You did it."

"I beg your pardon?"

"You brought him back. You can't imagine how scared Michael's been. He was sure Rock was all set to go home and eat his gun."

Lee slumped into the chair she'd jumped out of so many hours ago. "I think he might have, Ab. He scared me, too."

"But he's okay now."

Lee looked up at the doctor and recognized the narcotic of hope. "This time. Just how many of these cases is he supposed to go through before somebody realizes how much they hurt him?"

"They hurt everybody."

Lee shook her head. "Not like Rock. They're killing him, Abbie, and he won't admit it."

Abbie found her own chair and sat. "But he won't let anybody else take them."

Lee nodded, suddenly so tired she could hardly see. "I know."

"He got the people who did this, though," Abbie insisted. "That has to count for something."

Lee thought about that empty room and wondered. Then she thought of how they'd filled it with the music of life, and she hoped. Her sister-in-law Amanda had a rule about life. One step at a time. One day at a time. Well, Lee could manage that. If Amanda could save Jake with nothing but determination and laughter, Lee could do no less with her taciturn detective. He certainly deserved no less.

"It gives us time, anyway," Lee admitted more to herself than Abbie.

And when Rock opened the door again, Michael right behind him, she believed it. He was gruff and growling, but that was because his lieutenant was giving him grief about making sure Abbie's car was safe. Lee could see a spark deep in those dark eyes, a faint flicker of humor that betrayed him. She could hear the tentative animation in his voice, where hours earlier there had been nothing but desolation.

And so she hoped. She began, like any woman, to plan. To anticipate ambushes and slow, certain seductions. She began to smile to herself and delude herself that it would take only persistence and commitment, two qualities for which she was prized.

"Just for once," Michael said as he and Abbie ushered the two of them back out the door, "consider this as a vacation. Relax."

And to Lee's astonishment, Rock nodded. "Maybe I will," he said, walking close to her, close enough to surreptitiously brush hands. "Maybe I will."

And then, twenty minutes later, Rock pulled to a stop in front of the house and it all changed again.

Lee leaned forward in the passenger's seat of Rock's truck, because she didn't believe what she saw.

"No...oh, no..."

She had the door open before Rock had the truck to a stop.

"Lee, wait!" he yelled, slamming on the brakes and throwing open his own door.

But Lee was already on the run, screaming in fear and fury, running for the doorway to the beautiful little green-

and-white Victorian house that was belching out black, terrible smoke.

"Gen!" she screamed, and screamed again, because the smoke was pouring out of the shattered third-floor window.

Chapter 13

"Genny, where are you?" Lee yelled, and then choked on the smoke.

She was crawling, feeling her way across the floor in a black nightmare of heat and smoke. Somewhere she heard Rock calling to her and she knew his voice was frantic. It didn't matter. Genny was in here somewhere, and she wouldn't answer, and the smoke was deadly.

"Genevieve Anastasia Kendall, damn it, answer me!"

Sirens. She could hear them somewhere, keening in the late night like a banshee at an Irish funeral. She bumped into the coffee table with her shoulder and took a left. Toward Gen's bedroom.

"Lee, damn it, where are you?" Rock called, closer. At the door maybe.

"Get Mrs. Moffitt out!" Lee yelled back, coughing and spitting at the soot that clogged her throat. Her eyes were burning and her lungs were struggling.

A doorway. She crept through, feeling her way with a free hand, terrified she was going to be surprised by a flash of fire. More terrified she wasn't going to find Gen in time.

"Please," she prayed, her heart hammering, her eyes swimming. "Please let her be all right."

She bumped into the bed. Ran desperate hands along it to find the sheets bunched up. Empty. She sobbed in frustration. Where was she? Where had she tried to get to?

The window. Of course.

Lee vaulted the bed. She heard a funny whooshing sound behind her but didn't notice. There was something on the floor. A bundle huddled against the wall by the window. A too-still, too-silent bundle.

She reached for it and knew already it was her sister. It didn't occur to Lee that she might be too small to haul Gen out. She didn't stop to think that she might wait for the help that was even now screeching to a stop three stories below the window, lights shuddering in the night out beyond the oily black smoke. Lee grabbed her sister under the arms and began to yank her out.

Her lungs were going to burst. Her head was swimming. For the first time, Lee felt the heat in the room beyond her and turned to find that where there had only been black before, there was orange. Deadly, licking orange. The flames had broken free.

Lee sobbed, pulled, scooted. Gen's head lolled against her chest. Lee could just see the pale globe of her face, her slack mouth and closed eyes. She couldn't tell if her sister was even breathing and she pulled harder, the effort making her stumble with the dizziness and strain.

She couldn't breathe. She couldn't see or think. She couldn't stop. She got Gen through the doorway when she stumbled into a thick wall.

"You little idiot!"

She hadn't even seen him. Suddenly, he was just there, a towering black shadow that simply took over. She let him.

"Get her out, Rock!" she panted, giving her sister away.

It wasn't enough. Rock swung Gen up over his shoulder like a rag doll and grabbed Lee under the arm. He pulled them both right back through the shuddering, shifting living room just as booted, helmeted figures thundered up the stairs.

* * *

Rock batted Lee's hand away and replaced the oxygen
mask over her face. She wouldn't have it. Soot-blackened,
her eyes red and running, her chest heaving with the exer-
tion of breathing, she fought to get to her sister, who lay so
still in the grass where the paramedics had found the three
of them.

"Come on, Gen," she urged, patting her sister's face as
the paramedic tried to get a line in the woman's arm.
"You're the doctor, not me. What do we do here?"

Rock couldn't breathe. He'd swallowed some smoke, but
that wasn't it. He'd almost lost her. He'd stumbled through
those rooms like a mad man, terrified that she'd take a
wrong turn and get separated from him, get disoriented.

God, he just couldn't take much more of this. Rock
O'Connor, who had spent the last thirty years of his life
working to chain his emotions closed, had seen them laid
open, stripped bare and tossed over like a trailer in a tor-
nado. He wasn't ready for this. He wasn't capable.

He'd talked himself into believing he was so comfortably numb. So carefully and assiduously deadened, figuring that except for rage no emotion was worth the trouble
of keeping around. And then Amaryllis Jane Kendall had
come along and yanked him right out of his stupor.

She'd known. She'd taken one look at his house, at that
haphazard, crumbling old tree fort in the backyard where
he'd once pretended he was free, and she'd known. And
still she'd given him what no other person had ever given
him in his life. She'd given herself. Totally, without reser-
vation or demand or expectation. A simple gift of sharing
and healing that had hauled him right back from the brink,
an instinctive generosity that he could still feel at the edges
of his fingers and deeper in his soul than anything he'd ever
known.

And suddenly, where once he hadn't even cared what
happened to him in this nasty, useless old world, he cared
very much what happened to her. He cared that she was
hurting and terrified and guilty. He'd thought he couldn't
hurt anymore, after all this time. He'd been wrong. He'd

never hurt so much in his life as he did this moment, watching her flutter uselessly around her sister.

He wanted to help. He wanted to be able to give her what she'd given him, and God, he didn't know how. He didn't know what to do to make her feel better, and that alone hurt more than all the pain he'd ever known.

"Lee, it's okay," he assured her, handing back the oxygen.

She just pushed him away. "No, it's not. It's my fault. I should have been here. I should have . . ."

Coughing so hard she was doubled over, she patted at her sister again, getting in the way of the paramedics, who were busy pumping fluids and oxygen into the still form on the ground.

She should have been there. Instead, she'd been with Rock. He wanted to walk away, before she had a chance to apologize for the truth, because, of course, she would. Instead, he grabbed her by the shoulders and pulled her away so the team could work.

She flailed at him, her eyes wild. Rock held on, because that was all he knew to do.

"She'll be okay," he insisted, knowing nothing about it.

"She'll be okay," one of the paramedics echoed, as if asked. "You got her out in time."

Tears had tracked through the grime on Lee's face. They pooled in her eyes and slid into the corners of her mouth. Rock wanted to kiss them away. He couldn't. He couldn't give her anything but a too-late, too-small gift.

"I did manage to get this out," he offered, reaching into his jacket pocket. "I'm sorry, Lee. I tried to get more."

She reached for his gift and then turned those huge blue eyes on him. "The Christmas picture," she whispered.

He'd gotten it on his second run into the apartment as the room had melted around him. A lone sentinel against the destruction that had consumed all the bright whimsy in those rooms. They were lucky. Nobody had been killed. But Rock felt almost as if those monsters and chimes and bright chintz pillows had been losses he'd suffered instead.

"I can't . . . I . . ."

He pulled her against him, furious he couldn't do more. "I'm sorry. God, I'm so sorry. You finally lost your pictures."

Oddly enough, she laughed. "I have Gen," she said against his shirt. "I have Gen, and I have you . . . the hell with the pictures."

And then, finally, she broke down sobbing, and Rock was left with nothing to give her but the patience of his arms.

Around them, the world was peopled in grim, sooty faces. Excited voices, running figures. Somewhere glass shattered, and Rock could hear the roof give way. The fire blossomed into the night sending sparks showering toward neighboring houses. On the lawn, Mrs. Moffitt, whom he'd pulled from the first floor, held hands with the young couple who'd stumbled out of the second floor as Rock had vaulted up those stairs two at a time. Neighbors waited around in various stages of undress, and a camera crew was pulling up. Rock ignored it all, except for that fire that licked out those windows like a tongue savoring the taste of crisp wood.

"You're a cop?" one of the firemen asked, stopping by them.

Rock didn't ease his grip on Lee. "Yeah."

The fireman nodded, rubbed at a raw spot on the back of his neck as another team ran by with a hose. "What do you think?"

"I think I smelled kerosene. What do you think?"

The fireman considered him for a minute with tired eyes and nodded. "Yeah. I thought accelerant, too. Got a reason?"

Rock nodded. "I'll tell you all about it as soon as I get these two ladies taken care of."

"They haven't stopped," he heard muffled against his chest. Then Lee pulled back, the oxygen mask dangling useless from her neck again. "Oh, God, Rock. They haven't stopped. What are we gonna do?"

Rock gave into the impulse to lift a hand and gently brush his knuckles against that distraught face. "We're gonna get Gen to the hospital and feeling better. And then we're getting you as far away from here as possible so I can figure out what's going on.''

"Wyoming?" Michael demanded an hour later. "Why the hell Wyoming?"

"Who the hell could find anybody in Wyoming?" Rock retorted.

They were standing in the work lane of Memorial, foam cups in hand, bleary-eyed and drained, the both of them. Gen Kendall was on her way up to intensive care, and Lee was on the phone with her brother the rancher. Rock saw the fresh tears and wanted to hold her. He didn't know how.

Michael was watching her, too. He frowned and rubbed at his eyes, which were suspiciously alert for three in the morning. "What does she say about it?"

Rock downed the rest of his coffee as if that were a statement in and of itself. "She's not going to have a choice."

Michael gave a contemplative nod. "Fine. Go with her."

That brought Rock to a dead stop. "What?"

Michael faced him then, and Rock knew that his boss wasn't kidding. "Go with her. Make sure she's safe."

"Go to Wyoming?" Rock made it sound as if Michael had sentenced him to Menard State Prison.

Michael only smiled. "You're on disciplinary leave, remember? I can either give you a good recommendation or a bad recommendation. You know what the difference can mean."

Rock stood there in the center of the hall, poleaxed. "Why would you do that to me?" he demanded.

"Because you need the time off," Michael said evenly. "And you're not going to get it if you stay here."

"But Lieu—"

"The mountains are supposed to be good for you. Fresh air and eagles and all that stuff."

"Rocks and dirt and cowsh—"

"I'm serious, Rock." He didn't need to say it to make Rock a believer. Even so, Rock had to argue.

"Somebody set fire to that house tonight, Lieu. It means this case is still wide open."

"And there are several perfectly good detectives available to work on it while you get Miss Kendall settled with her family and take a few days off."

By now Rock was growling. He didn't want a few days off. He didn't need the fresh air and the expectations of Lee's family. He didn't want time to deal with the emotions and memories she'd succeeded in setting free.

Rock was still reeling from it, from the feel of her hands against his chest, from her liquid eyes and magic, healing hands. God, he wanted so much suddenly, and he knew better. He wanted her, and he couldn't have her, no matter what either of them thought.

And here the lieutenant was forcing him to face everything that meant.

"I could quit right now," he threatened, knowing just how much weight his words would carry.

Viviano just laughed. "Yeah, and I could sign up for traffic control. Live with it, O'Connor. I'm ordering you to go have a good time."

"Even if it kills me."

"Even if it kills you."

"I can't go to Wyoming," Lee protested, just as Rock knew she would. "Gen's still in intensive care."

"You can't stay here," he countered as evenly as he could. His head throbbed. His throat ached. He couldn't think of anything but how, for just a brief moment tonight, he'd felt whole. He'd lost himself in her. God, how he wanted to go back to her apartment. He wanted to take her to that bed of hers with its fishes and waves and make her laugh and moan and cry out, but that bed was gone. The fishes and the waves and the saddle and the hot, dangerous red chemises were all lost to a fire set by a desperate arsonist.

"But I wasn't even home," she protested. "Maybe they weren't really after me. Maybe they just thought I still had what they wanted and took care of it."

Rock shook his head. "It doesn't matter, Lee. *You're* in danger. The lieutenant agrees with me. A flight leaves at noon, and you're going to be on it."

Lee looked up at him with those great, tear-swollen eyes. She'd finally had the chance to shower off once the emergency department staff was assured her carbon monoxide levels were down and her lungs were clear. They'd supplied her with a scrub suit and shampoo, but she still smelled like a day-old barbecue and looked like a disaster survivor. Rock had never seen her look so beautiful.

He tucked a strand of hair behind her ear. "She'll be okay. Abbie told you herself. Gen just needs rest and fluids, and then she's going home with Abbie."

"Why can't I just go home with you?" Lee asked in a small, miserable voice.

Rock disciplined himself against his real reaction. He gave her logic, when all he felt was shame. "That's not a place for you, Lee. Please. I'll fly out there with you myself."

As if it had been his idea. He felt like a rank fake when her eyes lit up. "Really? You could meet my brother, Jake. I think you'd like each other."

Rock managed a laugh for that. "Your brother is not going to like me, honey. But he is going to watch out for you, which is all that matters. Now, do you have anything you need to take with you?"

She laughed, too, but the sound was forlorn. "I think the term 'clothes on my back' pretty much covers it. I did have my credit card and my temporary driver's license with me. Oh, and my backpack is at the theater. It has some jeans and stuff in it for emergencies. We need to stop there anyway and let them . . . let them know. . . ."

She was giving him that look that made him want to just pick her up and run from whatever was going to hurt her. The tears welled, but she brushed these aside. "The play."

"The one you were writing?" he countered, suddenly feeling worse. "Don't you have a—"

"Not that play," she assured him, trying to smile as if it was really all right after all. "I gave that one to Creighton already."

"You finished it?"

She nodded. Rock had a terrible feeling she wanted to say something more, but she didn't. She just looked off into space—someplace, he thought, where her expectations waited, and her eyes grew soft with regret.

"No," she said. "I'm going to have to tell Sierra I can't open in *Long Day's Journey* next week."

Rock didn't care what anybody thought. He didn't care what consequences he'd end up having to suffer. Right then, the only thing to be done was to ease that look of loss. Without another word, there in the busy work lane where people had to step around them and there was no privacy, he pulled her back into his arms where he wanted her to be. He tucked that almost-white blond hair beneath his chin and closed his eyes and protected her, just for the moment, from what he was about to do to her. And just for that moment, she let him. She wrapped her arms around him and laid her cheek against his chest and rested.

And Rock, who had never learned to be selfish, was selfish. He felt glad that she'd let him be the one to buffer the disappointment. He stood in the middle of a busy, noisy hallway with lighting as soft as a police lineup, and he listened only to her. He felt only her. He bent his head over hers and wrapped his arms close around her lithe, quick body and wanted only her. He felt her shudder with loss and knew just how she felt.

"Do you know what my brother would do to you if he knew what we were up to?" Lee demanded an hour or so later on a giggle.

Rock tossed the key onto the desk and set his overnight bag down inside the doorway before edging it closed again. "We're not 'up to' anything."

Lee turned on him with false energy and very real determination. "We're having an assignation," she insisted, her eyes just a little too bright. "I've never had an assignation."

Rock scowled at her in a way that betrayed him. "I don't even know what an assignation is," he said, and she knew he was lying.

He checked out the window and the sterile white tile bathroom and the closet alcove and then returned to the bedroom with its demure brace of double beds and its television bolted to the wall and its forgettable pastel watercolors over the bed. Lee waited for him to finish, knowing it was important to him. Not really believing herself that anyone would have the energy or interest at almost dawn to follow them from Memorial to Rock's, where he'd lent her a pair of jeans and a T-shirt, and then to the motel Rock and his boss had picked for them to crash in before heading out in the morning.

Rock had refused to simply stay at his place like she'd wanted. Lee understood why. She was actually glad he'd turned down the idea, because she wanted to begin taking him away from what that house represented. She wanted to teach him that a bolt hole built with desperation and secondhand lumber wasn't the only place a person could dream, and that dreams of rescue weren't the only ones a person was allowed.

He had saved her. He'd saved Gen, and then he'd risked his life to pull one of the pictures out, because he knew what they meant to her. And he really didn't understand how special that was.

"Anybody lurking in the shower?" she asked.

He locked the front door and only then shrugged out of the jacket that had been hiding the gun at his hip. "Not a soul," he said. "Why?"

Lee waited for him to turn to her and then rewarded him with a slow, meaningful smile. "Because I can still smell ashes and soot on me. I'm going to take a nice shower, and then I just thought I might seduce a certain policeman."

That brought him to a dead halt, not four feet away. Lee saw the reaction in his eyes before he could control it. She saw the flash of yearning, the slow creep of hunger. She saw the darkening of those very dark eyes and knew that whatever he said, he wanted it, too.

"Lee, come on," he protested, his hands caught halfway toward where he'd been about to unfasten the top button of the crisp white shirt he'd changed into at his house. "It's been a real long night. We're both exhausted, we have a plane to catch in a few hours, and we have to go by the theater before then to get that bag of clothes. It's just not a good idea...."

His jaw. Lee watched how it worked, as if he could gnaw away his desire. She watched the way he hooked his hands on his belt as if that would be a safe place for them to be. She saw how his mouth tightened, as if that could keep him from kissing her.

She saw these and knew just what his common sense was costing him. So she sauntered right up and stretched against the length of that taut, unyielding body to give him a big kiss right on that grim-looking mouth.

"I know," she said and smiled. A big smile. A telling smile. The smile women had used to seduce men since long before Delilah had sauntered up to Samson with the shears. "But I find myself strangely attracted to you all the same, Sergeant. And I believe with all my heart that no matter what else is going on, it might not be a bad idea to take a little time for ourselves."

This time he just glared. Placed sensible hands on her shoulders and turned her for the bathroom. "Tough. Take your shower and then go to bed. Alone."

She was already in the bathroom before she allowed herself to smile. Poor Rock. He really didn't know what to do with a determined woman. Well, she had an idea he was about to find out.

She thought about it as she stepped under the assault of a very hot shower. She thought about it as she soaped up and savored the bottomless hot water tank and somebody else's soap and shampoo. She thought about it as she finally gave in to the exhaustion and frustration and fear and allowed herself a few selfish tears for the mementos and memories she'd lost, the dreams that had come away from this night, soot-stained and stale. For the sister she'd almost seen sacrificed to a seemingly capricious crime.

What could she have seen? Lee wondered yet again. Why would anybody be so intent on stopping her from revealing what she didn't know that they'd indiscriminately sacrifice her sister for it?

It didn't matter anymore. Nothing mattered. Lee was too sore and tired and battered to care who was doing this. She just wanted it to stop. She wanted her life back, her sister safe and her career carefully on track. She wanted a few days alone with that contrary, frustrating man out in the bedroom without traumas or terrors to interrupt them.

Her chest hurt so badly, an ache like a sore tooth. But Lee knew it wasn't from the smoke or the struggle to get Gen out of the apartment. It was from everything. It was from knowing that not more than fifteen feet away stalked a man in a million, and she had the terrible feeling that in all this mess, he'd slip right out of her hands.

So she did what she'd always done in situations like this. She lifted her head, took a deep breath, and charged ahead, no matter what.

She did it this time by stepping out of the shower and wrapping a towel around her still-damp body. Then, with only one more telling breath for courage, she stepped on out into the bedroom.

He was sitting in the chair by the window watching CNN. The gray light from the TV flickered across his features to betray the strain, the parallel creases that had deepened between his eyes, the too-taut cant of his jaw, the rigid posture. Lee knew he heard the door open to his right, but he refused to turn.

She shook her head. "You're so damn honorable."

That did get his attention. He smiled, still watching the set. "No I'm not. That's why I'm not looking. Now, get into bed before I change my mind."

Lee walked over to stand in front of his chair. Rock kept his focus where it was, as if he could still see the flickering mayhem through her.

"Lee—"

She smiled. "Rock—"

She could see him tighten up, could see the instinctive withdrawal, the struggle for control. She saw it in the way his hands curled into themselves, the way he straightened just a little in the chair, the way his nostrils flared and his eyes dilated. She could still smell the fire on him, and somehow it enticed her. She could see the weariness in his eyes, the aftermath of too many new emotions in too short a time, and it compelled her. She could hear the rasp of his breathing as he tried to do what was right, and it challenged her, because he didn't know what was right. He didn't realize that what she needed was what he was too honorable to give. So she had to take it.

Without another word, she hooked a thumb into the edge of the towel. His head snapped up and his eyes widened. If he'd been a deer, Lee would have sworn he would have just bounded off, tail up to warn of danger. As it was, he was a cop, so he swore.

"Don't you dare—"

She dared. She let the towel fall loose so that he could see the water that still glistened on her body in the half light. She let the towel puddle to the floor at her feet so that he had no choice but to look at her. She stood before him, naked and needing, and she finally got him to look up at her to realize it.

"You don't want this," he warned her, his voice as harsh as his breathing.

Lee just tilted her head to the side a little until she saw his defenses begin to crumble. "You keep telling me what I want. How 'bout I tell you?"

"Lee, don't—"

She didn't say another word. Not one. She stood there before him, the air-conditioning chilling her wet skin until her nipples tightened into hard little buds, her heart thundering in her chest, her breath caught behind the terrible need this man inflicted in her. She couldn't ask him. She wanted him to see. To see and understand and react. She wanted him to make love to her without her having to beg for it, because that was the way it should be this time.

He saw. He understood. He moaned with the terrible struggle over old disbelief and new hope. He reached out with a tentative hand and simply laid it against her thigh. He lifted his gaze to her, and Lee knew that no matter what, this man loved her. Without words, without promises, without exception. She knew he would give her himself tonight, when he had never given himself to anyone before. Not really. She saw that in his eyes, in his dark, dark eyes and in the terrible hope that had begun to flicker to light in their depths.

"Oh, my Lee," he said to her, his voice little more than a whisper. "What are you trying to do to me?"

She tried smiling again, even past the sudden glissando of shivers he set up. "I'm trying to seduce you, you jerk. Can't you just give in and enjoy it?"

Finally, freely, heartily, as if she'd just shattered his last reserve, he laughed. He tilted his head back, looked her in the eye, and laughed with the delight of it all. And Lee, who had been falling in love, tumbled all the way. Lee, who had battled a terrible attraction to this man, shuddered with hunger.

"My poor Lee," he mourned, not moving, his eyes as warm as soft chocolate. "You've been through so much...."

He laid his other hand on her other thigh. Just that. It set her to trembling. Every nerve ending in her body begged its chance. Her own hands refused to answer, as if the fresh, thick heat in those deep brown eyes weighted them down where they were.

"...So very much. Would it be so horrible if I just made you feel better?"

Very slowly, he slid his hands around the outside of her thighs until he cupped her before him. He still looked up, his face inches from her, his chest struggling for air.

"Would it?"

She fought for a breath. She did her best to reign in sanity that had never seemed so lost in her life. "I don't think so," she managed, her voice husky with the flare of desire. "I don't think so at all."

"Ah, God," he moaned, all pretense of humor lost in that moment of honesty. "What am I gonna do with you?"

She didn't answer. She just met his hot gaze and waited for his decision. She waited, her breasts heavy and sweet before him, her skin beaded with moisture, her legs trembling with the pleasure of his touch.

He closed his eyes again and nuzzled her breast with his cheek. The sensation of day-old beard against her too-sensitive skin sent shrieks of need through her. Her breath caught. Her heart stumbled. He lifted a hand away from her, caught her breast in his hand. Lifted it to him, so he could take it in his mouth and pleasure it.

That was when Lee finally gave in and let her hand stray to him. She dug her fingers into his hair, his thick dark hair that felt like heavy satin in her hands. She pulled him closer, begged him with her touch to torment her with his lips and tongue and teeth. She moaned, her head back, as lightning splintered in her and settled low.

"I want...to touch...you," she gasped, not close enough, not nearly close enough. Needing the hard edges of his body against hers. Needing the heat that would turn them both slick with sweat. Needing him in her, deep in her where she didn't have to share him or lose him or promise him she didn't want any more than this.

"Not...just yet," he answered on a soft growl, his mouth against the soft underside of her breast, his hand seeking the juncture of her thighs. She gave it to him, opened just enough that he could find her there waiting, ready. Hot and sweet and wet for him. His fingers tasted her and she tautened in his hands, surprised by the shaft of pleasure he released. Hungry now beyond words, beyond needs or hopes or dreams. Hungry for those hands to be set loose, for that mouth to claim her, every curve and dip and secret place she'd hidden away for so long.

She arched against him, seeking contact, pulling him against her so that finally that unyielding jaw found its pillow in the soft contour of her belly. She bent over him, folded him to her, sating herself on the abrasion of a stubbly chin, the calluses of a work-roughened hand, the slick sweetness of a soft mouth hidden away behind denial and isolation. And then, with a swiftness that left her spinning, he had her in his arms, carrying her over to one of those plain double beds, and he settled her onto it with enough tenderness to make a girl cry. He eased his own body over hers, cushioning her against the cold air, against the darkness outside, against the turmoil they'd faced, and he came to her with the gentlest of hands and the hungriest of mouths.

"Now," she begged, liquid and languid and restless as a summer wind. "I want to touch you."

He smiled, really smiled, to the depths of his eyes, and Lee knew joy. "This still isn't a good idea," he warned, brushing the hair off her hot forehead with tender fingers.

"You're right," she retorted, already working the rest of his buttons. "It's a terrible idea."

He bent to sip the water that had collected in the hollow of her throat. "What are you going to tell your brother?"

She yanked the shirt out of his pants and fumbled with the belt. "That I'm a wanton woman, and he'd better live with it."

He sought her again with his hands and took his fill of her breasts. "A wanton woman, huh? That has possibilities."

She'd finally gotten the belt undone, the zipper undone, and she slid her hand inside to find him. She folded her palm against the rigid length of him, hot, so hot even through the cotton, and she smiled. She smiled and she stretched and she laughed with the delicious pleasure of him. "Oh yeah," she said. "Definite possibilities."

They didn't talk at all after that.

"You haven't said anything," he said late that afternoon.

Lee looked up from where she was shredding the airline magazine in her hands. "What am I going to tell him?" she asked.

Rock took hold of those restless hands and calmed them. "About what?" he asked. "This morning?"

She laughed, and Rock thought he heard something fragile splinter in her. "I figure I'll fill Jake in about that in about ten years or so. If he can handle it by then. No, I let Gen down. I almost let her get killed."

Rock held on more tightly, demanding her attention. Clad in one of those filmy, flowery dresses she wore when she rehearsed her role as Mary Tyrone, she looked like a waif. Lost, uncertain. She turned those wide, soft blue eyes on him, and he did his best to smile for her. "No," he said in a tone that brooked no argument. "I almost got her killed. That's for me to settle with your brother."

Her answering smile was tremulous at best, even through the tears that seemed to swell the color of her eyes. "Did I tell you how brave you are?"

Rock scowled. "I'm not sure I want to hear that before I meet your brother."

"You'll love him," she insisted, turning instinctively toward the window of the small commuter plane that was even now circling the airport at Jackson Hole. "He'll love you."

"Uh-huh."

In the end, Rock wasn't sure just who was more nervous about the people who waited at the end of this particular plane ride. Rock sure as hell knew he didn't want to have to explain to some cowboy with a hunting rifle how he'd enjoyed his sister's attentions, not once but several times. How, given half the chance, he'd do it again. How, in the end, he'd have to leave her alone so she could get on with the life she'd carved out for herself.

He was even less sure when he followed Lee off the plane to see the cluster of people waving at the window. A couple of kids jumping up and down, a small woman with brown hair and a suspiciously big midsection, and the brother. Obviously the brother. Tall, solid as granite, jeans and flannel all the way, with spurs on his beaten-up boots and a battered old Stetson of some kind pulled down over his eyes. Rock recognized the attitude right away. Cops did the same thing with their caps when they wanted to intimidate somebody. It worked just as well with a cowboy hat.

Well, he at least understood the brother. He wasn't at all sure they'd get along.

"Jake!" Lee shrieked, already on the run.

Rock followed behind, carrying both bags so she could be free to throw herself in the big man's arms. She did, too, full tilt enough that a lesser man would have been knocked back a good ten feet. This guy took it without flinching, his hat not even getting knocked off as Lee wrapped herself up in him and babbled.

The woman, the sister-in-law Lee had talked about, stood alongside smiling, and the kids tumbled around like anxious puppies. Rock saw it, a real Rockwell painting, and felt the twist of something old and hurtful in his gut. He was jealous. All those afternoons alone in his tree house he'd spent watching the neighborhood. He'd seen Mrs. O'Reilly march her brood to morning mass like a family of chattering little quail, cuffing and hugging her brood with equal energy. He'd watched the Byrnes, whose father was a fire chief, play ball in the backyard. He'd watched the Kellys farther down the block as they'd fought and made up and stuck together whenever anybody else threatened so much as a second cousin.

He'd sat alone, every damn day of his life, begging one of those families to see him there alone and take him home. To laugh with him and play ball and hug him after they'd yelled at him for doing something dangerous. He'd waited and he'd wished and, in the end, he'd always walked back into that house alone.

And now, all over again, he was watching from the periphery, wishing for something that simply wasn't his to have. He stood there in an airport at the edge of the mountains and knew that he'd just locked himself right back into that prison with the white walls and the empty rooms. As

soon as he got Lee settled, he was leaving, because there was
only so much of this he could take. He'd been right. Lee
was going to hurt him. Only this time, he wasn't going to
recover.

Chapter 14

"Don't you think it's about time to introduce your friend?" Jake asked dryly.

Lee wiped the fresh tears away, startled at her own oversight. "Oh, Rock, I'm sorry," she apologized, turning to include him. "Sergeant—" She deliberately hesitated just to see what Rock would do with the sly hint that she'd let his real name slip. He just watched, hooded and observant, as if they'd never met before. Careful. Lee almost sighed with the disappointment. "—Rock O'Connor," she said, "I'd like you to meet my brother Jake."

The two men shook hands, eye to eye and both as rigid as righteousness. Again Lee thought of predatory birds. Two of them, hawk-nosed and silent and aggressive as hell, sizing each other up before the contest.

Thank God for Amanda, who laughed with delight at the show. "One of you can let go now," she allowed. "You both win."

Lee chuckled. "And my sister-in-law, Amanda Marlow Kendall..."

Rock had that look of awe most people did who met Amanda. Lee had the feeling that if he'd been wearing a hat, he would have doffed it.

"I've read your work," he said, accepting her hand for a quick shake and surprising Lee with the news. "It's a pleasure to meet you."

Amanda, never one to ignore a good-looking man, even when she was five months pregnant, glowed. "Thank you, Sergeant. I know Jake was just about to say how glad we are you were there to help Lee and Gen out."

Rock shrugged and Jake grunted, leaving the meaning up to anyone's opinion.

"Are you really a cop?" Mick asked, stepping forward.

Rock seemed a little nonplussed by the boy's question. "Yeah."

"You got a gun?"

"Mick," both Amanda and Jake admonished him at the same time.

"My name's Melissa," Lee's niece greeted Rock.

Rock immediately hunkered down to meet the little girl at eye level. "It's nice to meet you, Melissa," he offered with a genuine smile.

Melissa giggled and blushed and gave him her hand. Lee saw Jake and Amanda exchange glances, and knew it would be all right.

"See?" she said to her brother as they followed everyone out of the airport into the parking lot where the Jeep waited. "He can't be all bad." She motioned to the two kids, who were circling Rock like satellites, peppering him with unending questions he answered patiently and honestly. "If he were, the kids wouldn't like him. Kids have great instincts, ya know."

Jake just snorted again, his arm around Lee's shoulder. "Not those two. Give 'em a chance to talk, and they'd walk off with Charlie Manson."

Lee just laughed. "It's good to be home."

Jake gave her a squeeze. "It's about time. Where'd the dress come from? After that phone call, I thought you'd show up wearing scrub suits from the hospital."

"My bag at the theater," she acknowledged, running an instinctive hand over the flowered cotton material of the dress. "We stopped off to get it and to let Creighton know I won't be opening next week."

She got another squeeze, a half shrug that betrayed the emotions Jake didn't allow in a public place. "I'm really sorry about that, squirt."

Lee squeezed back and forced herself to sound nonchalant past the fresh ache. "I know, Jake. Thanks. I talked to Gen before we left. She's just as nasty as ever."

He nodded. "Zeke's on his way to Chicago to keep an eye on her. We figured it'd help to keep you under control."

"We?" she demanded. "We who?"

He didn't so much as crack a smile. "Your wonderful policeman over there and I."

Lee pulled to a halt, bringing Jake with her. "You decided all this without talking to me?"

Jake looked way down at her, his eyes shaded beneath the brim of his hat, just the way they always had been when he was making a parental decision. "You woulda just argued about it."

Lee glared at her brother for a minute. She saw Amanda standing over his shoulder waiting. She heard the kids telling Rock how to find the Jeep. She whirled on her heel, neatly dislodging herself from her brother's hold, and stalked after her "wonderful policeman."

"Francis Aloysius Xavier O'Connor!"

It was, in the end, revenge enough.

After Lee waded through greetings from the ranch staff, accepting kisses and hugs and questioning looks at her companion, she headed in to change out of the impractical dress. Maybe she was being foolish, but she pulled out Rock's jeans to wear, which didn't fit her nearly as well as her old pair in the bag, but which somehow made her feel more secure. Rock noticed right away. Back in that nondescript hotel in Chicago, that would have pleased her. For some reason, here, it only made her more restless.

She should have felt so much better. Comforted, settled. She was back on the ranch, where life really began and ended for her. Here she could balance everything else in her life against the quiet majesty of the sky. Here the mountains energized her and the wind soothed her. The horses were her best friends, running to the fences to greet her when she got close, and the people were her strength. She was home.

For the first time in her life, though, home wasn't enough. The mountains weren't spectacular enough, the wildflowers didn't seem to dip and sway in quite the same dance. The smells and sights and sounds that were so special to her didn't work their same magic.

She realized why when she watched Rock. He was polite. He was attentive and patient and laughed out loud when Mick and Melissa harassed him. He bore introductions to all the staff who had raised Lee as one of their own with surprising patience, and then joined the tour when Jake had his final rounds of the different barns after dinner.

He was a gentleman. He was a restless, impatient gentleman who was too polite to betray his discomfort, and that was what kept Lee up all night.

She'd wanted him to feel it. She'd prayed that somehow the peace of this place would seep into his heart like a tonic and salve that sore soul of his. She'd wanted the magic to work for him, just as it worked for her. Instead, it propelled him out into the night, where he paced along the fences in the waning moonlight, and it woke him earlier than anyone else on a working ranch, so that he was standing at the front window watching the mountains when the sky blushed its way toward morning.

Lee didn't know what to do. Only hours before they had been exhausted and quiet, safe in each other's arms where nobody could reach them. Now, in the one safe place in the world, Rock had backed away again.

It was afternoon before Lee finally found him alone. She knew she shouldn't push it this soon, but it meant too much to her. It meant everything. She walked up next to him, where he'd finally lit at the long fence to the lower pasture, and rested her foot on the lower rung of the fence.

"You don't like it here."

Rock didn't even bother to look over from where he watched the foals gamboling in the high sun. It was a beautiful day, all sky and wind and trembling grass. The mountains were crisp and alive, sturdy sentinels that broke the backs of storms and trapped the colors of sunset. Overhead a red-tailed hawk wheeled into the sun, and on the other side of the stream, Clovis, her brother's second in command, was herding some yearlings in for a vet's visit.

"I don't belong here," Rock said simply.

Lee looked over to see that the wind had scoured his cheeks with a ruddy glow. His hair was so glossy and thick she fought the urge to test it again with her fingers. He leaned against the fence as if he'd always stood just that way, his forearms resting on the top, his jeans as worn and tattered as anybody's on the ranch, his T-shirt molding him to perfection.

He looked healthy and handsome. What he didn't look was happy.

"Why?" Lee asked.

He smiled out to the scenery, but it wasn't a pleased smile. "This could almost convince you that Chicago wasn't back there waiting."

Lee gave into impulse and took her own look around. She saw miles of fencing, red outbuildings tucked into the folds of the ground, the main house of wood and stone where she'd learned to walk on hardwood floors and practiced the piano in the living room.

"Then let it," she said.

He turned to her then, and Lee thought her heart would break. "No wonder you write about such good people," he said with some wonder, his hand cupping her cheek. "That's where you grew up. I have no business bringing what I do to this. It would only ruin it all."

Lee saw the bleak light in those earth-brown eyes, and for the first time felt afraid. "What are you talking about? You think I can't understand?"

"I think you shouldn't have to." He stroked her cheek, a gesture of leaving, of capturing a sensation before it was given away.

Oddly enough, that made Lee laugh. "You're a little too late, Rock."

He turned away, rested his arms on the top rung of the fence, gazed out into nothing. "I doubt it."

For a minute Lee just stood there, struggling to come to grips with what he was saying. Unfamiliar with the fine art of fatalism. Lee firmly believed that anything was possible. She was proof. They all were in her family. But then, she'd been taught that early. Rock certainly hadn't.

"Why don't you give me a chance?" she asked, keeping a careful distance so that her needs didn't get mixed up with her sense.

Rock didn't look around. "Because it's too late. I'm thirty-three, Lee. I've given away everything but my job, and you see what my job does to a person. How long do you want to put up with that?"

"You really think so?"

He faced her then, and she saw all the shadows back in those beautiful eyes. "I really think so."

"Why is it too late?" she demanded. "Because you're too old? Because you don't have anything else you want to do?"

"Yes."

She nodded, not realizing that she'd balled up her hands on her hips, an instinctive defensive posture. Except the person she was defending was the one arguing with her. She just had to get him to realize that. "Why are you a cop, Rock?"

He shrugged. "That's what you do where I live."

"Is it what you wanted to do?"

"It doesn't matter."

"Of course it does."

"No." His eyes flashed now, hard as agates. Flat and impenetrable and angry. "It doesn't. I'm good at what I do. I have seniority."

"And you have those kids."

"Yes!"

"Those kids who are killing you."

"Who else do you think should do it, Lee? I solve those cases. I get the job done."

Her heart had begun to hammer. She heard it now, the subtext of desperation. Instinctive answers honed over years of practice to protect the emptiness at the core of the argument.

"But what did you *want* to do?" she demanded.

That stopped him. "Be a cop," he insisted, and she didn't believe him.

"No you didn't. What did you want to do, Rock? Back in high school when you thought you could do anything? When it all still seemed possible?"

"Nothing ever seemed possible," he said. "I got out as fast as I could, and I found a job I could do well. It was more than I could have ever hoped for."

"But if you hoped," she insisted. "What would you hope for?"

She'd tried. She saw her failure the minute he shook his head. His eyes were steely and cold, his jaw so taut it should have shattered like frozen steel. "I don't hope," he told her. "That's how I get by."

He turned to walk away from her, but she couldn't let him go. Not yet.

"You really don't think you deserve that?" she demanded. "You have no right to be happy?"

He stopped, his back to her, his head up a little, as if he were considering the layout of the ranch that spread out over the high, sloping meadow. "You never grew up in my house, Lee. You don't know."

"I know that a person is limited only by what they let limit them."

He whipped around on her, and she expected him to be angry. Instead, there was a wry, soft light in his eyes. A regret rather than a rage. "Let's see if I have this right," he said. "'The past is the present, isn't it? It's the future, too. We all try to lie out of that, but life won't let us.'" An eyebrow crooked. His smile was sad. "Recognize it?"

Lee thought she'd crumble on the spot. "I thought you didn't like theater," she retorted in a small voice.

"I thought I'd see what O'Neill had to say in that play you've been working so hard on. I realized he was pretty smart."

"Those characters gave away their futures. Why should you have to?"

He shook his head. "You still don't get it. It's already been done. I can't go back anymore. I've invested too much in what I am to be anything else. Just like that sad old lady you play."

Again, he turned away. Again Lee fought.

"How old do you think my brother Jake was when he learned to read?" she demanded to his back.

His step faltered with her question. He looked back. "What?"

"Thirty-five." Lee shrugged, praying she was taking the right chances. "I just thought you'd like to know, since you were talking about it being too late. He was illiterate. That was because you see a different ranch here than the one I grew up in. My mother was always sick, and my daddy...well, daddy just didn't have the cow sense to run a ranch. This place was scrub and dying cattle and skinny, hungry kids without much more than the town's pity. So Jake took over. He was twelve, and I was a baby, and no-body thinks I can remember, but I can. I can remember the wind whining through the bedroom walls and my mama crying herself to sleep because she couldn't get out of bed even to tend to me, and I remember Jake always tired from working. Jake took it all on, and he was good at it. He was so good at it that nobody realized that it was killing him. Then Amanda came along, and funny thing, she saw it right away. I just thought I'd let you know. The thing Jake wanted most in his life was to read, and he thought it was too late. Maybe there's something you want, Rock, but unless you go after it, you're never going to have it."

"I don't want it!" he insisted, frustrated and fright-ened. "Not while kids are dying and I can do something about it."

"You've served your sentence," she protested. "You've paid your parents back."

"No I haven't." He stalked up to her, so fast and so hard that she backed against the fence, for the first time unnerved by the fires in those eyes. "Not by a long shot."

"So you're just going to give up?" she demanded.

"You just can't see it," he said. "You have no idea what goes on in the streets. You don't know what I've been up against. And it's all I can bring you, Lee. Frustration and rage and dirt. Is that what you want?"

That almost made her laugh. "You forget honor and courage and integrity. My God, Rock. After everything you've been through, everything you've seen, you're still trying. You still go out on the street and hope that you can make a difference. Is that such a terrible thing to bring me? Am I wrong to think we could share it all together?"

One last time, as if just the power of his gaze could quell her, he faced her down. "Find someone who has options, Lee. I don't."

"Teach," she said, not knowing at all where the impulse came from.

His laugh was so bitter and quick she knew she'd hit it on the head. "Teach what?"

She shrugged. "Anything. Think about it. You can share all those passions you have, and maybe, just maybe, you can intercept one of those kids before somebody has to call out a homicide team."

This time he didn't even answer. He just walked away, and Lee thought there would be nothing left of him at all. She'd attacked him and goaded him and pleaded with him. She'd been left alone out in the high white sun of Wyoming, the wind tugging at her hair as if calling her to come join it, the trees shooshing her and the horses kicking up mud in simple exuberance.

And in the place she loved the most in the world, Lee Kendall felt lost.

"Damn you, Rock O'Connor!" she yelled after him, even knowing that wouldn't help. "I love you!"

It didn't.

* * *

"What should I do?" she asked her sister-in-law
Amanda as the two of them sat in the kitchen and drank
coffee. Amanda drank coffee. Lee stared into her cup and
wished she could stop crying.

Amanda rubbed at her belly as if wishing for an answer.
"You love him?"

Lee sighed, fighting tears all over again. "Oh, yeah," she
admitted. "As stupid as it sounds. I've gotten him to laugh
once, seen him really enjoy himself for about an hour at a
time, and I know damn well he borrowed the Jeep to go
into Jackson to get back on the police computer so he
doesn't get withdrawal. And I love him."

Amanda's answering smile was knowing. "Sounds a lot
like your brother."

"Don't tell either of them that."

"Do you think he's worth saving?"

Lee didn't even have to think about it. "Yes. There's a
good, gentle, caring man down there someplace beneath all
that cynicism."

"Then give him everything you've got. Wear him down.
Make him see the light."

"And if it doesn't work?"

"Walk away."

Lee stared at her sister-in-law as if she'd just lost her
mind. "What?"

Amanda shrugged. "Honey, there's no bonus in heaven
for a woman who keeps dragging around after a man who
can't get past his self-destructive tendencies. He either gets
the message or he doesn't. If he doesn't, you have to make
a clean break and do just what he suggested. Find someone else. Or find no one else."

"You would have done that to Jake?"

"Eventually. Yes."

Lee shook her head, not ready for that answer yet. "He'll
see the light," she stated with grim determination. "Or I'll
kill him." The decision made, she launched herself to her
feet. "In the meantime, damn it, I've been looking forward to coming home for the last eighteen months. I'm

going to take a horse up onto the high meadow. Wanna come?''

Amanda shook her head. "Thanks, no. But have fun."

That did get Lee to laugh. Have fun. She was running away. That wasn't any fun at all.

He'd never run away from anything in his life. So why was he suddenly running away from Lee? Rock sat like a stone behind the wheel of the Jeep and looked out over the valley of Jackson Hole and beyond to the sharp-toothed horizon of the Tetons. It was a spectacular view. It was a beautiful day, all clean and fresh and brilliant as a new dream. The kind of day poets rhapsodized about and moviemakers put on film. Rock barely noticed any of it.

He sat alone in a borrowed Jeep on his way to the nearest police station like a kid running home after he'd found out he wasn't tall enough to make the team.

He'd just told Lee he wanted nothing to do with her, when what he really wanted was to lose himself in her and never find his way back out again. He wanted peace and hope and the narcotic of her bright-eyed smile. The problem was, he'd told her the truth. It was too late. He didn't know how to want those things anymore. He didn't know how to feel as if he deserved them. He deserved hard work and obsession and isolation. He even considered himself lucky most days because he'd made it as far as he had. A quiet, clean house he could actually face without flinching. A pile of books about the world he'd never get to enjoy. A good supply of beer to dull the edges of panic when he thought about what he'd be doing in thirty years or so.

He'd known all along he didn't deserve her. He'd been force-fed the truth on that damn ranch, where every person down to the kid who broke horses for a living greeted him with that silent assessment that told him what they'd do to him if he ever hurt their Lee. They knew what she deserved. She deserved a man to share her dreams, to cushion her disappointments and bolster her spirits. She deserved a man who could keep a foot in both worlds, just the way she did. She deserved happiness and passion and

bright-eyed children. What she did not deserve was a
burned-out cop whose only prospect was a pension after
twenty-five years and an obsession he couldn't seem to
cure.

She said he had a chance. That was because she didn't
know any better. No matter what she'd seen, she'd never
been taught it. She'd never been convinced with fists and
feet and foul language that she didn't deserve anything.

She'd always been the bright star in a perfect universe,
and she should be able to stay that way. She should be able
to shoot as high as she could, because all those silent,
watchful people on that ranch were right. She deserved
what he couldn't give her.

Reaching over, Rock flipped on the ignition and put the
Jeep into gear. It was time to get on down to town. He
needed the reassurance of familiar faces, familiar lingo,
shared war stories. He needed to know he belonged. Because no matter what he wanted, he didn't belong up on
that ranch that housed all those laughing, happy people.

Lee did just what Amanda suggested. She tried to wear
Rock down. She tried patience and coercion and accom-
modation. She tried humor and pathos, and she tried to let
the mountains work their magic. In the end, it didn't seem
to be enough. Rock stayed away as much as he could, and
when he was there, he let the kids take his attention. And
even though Jake grudgingly admitted that he wouldn't
exactly kick the policeman out of his house, the tension
didn't ease appreciably.

And so it was that four days later, with the news that Gen
was out of the hospital and driving Zeke nuts looking for a
new apartment while the old one was being renovated and
that things were finally beginning to break on the case in
Chicago, Rock finally escaped once and for all.

"Don't give me that 'I'm leaving you because I love you'
garbage," Lee warned, tears threatening as she waited to see
him off at the airport.

Rock's smile was bittersweet as he brushed a lock of hair
back from Lee's face with the gentlest of hands. "I'm

leaving you because I love you," he told her, and she knew he meant it.

"You really do love me?"

"It'd be a lot easier if I didn't."

"Just say it," she insisted. "Once, right now. Please."

Ignoring the noise and shuffle of the place, he pulled her to him, wrapped her in sure arms and bent his head over hers. "I love you," he said simply.

She'd always thought those words would make her feel better. They didn't. Not when the voice carrying them also carried the weight of their loss. "Then don't go."

Around them, the airport bustled with foot traffic. The intercom announced an incoming flight from Salt Lake City, and the line for Rock's flight out snaked behind him. Suddenly Lee felt as if it were her last chance to save him. He let her go, and she almost cried out with the sense of loss.

"You'll be safe here on the ranch," he said. "Stay here until we find something."

"It could take forever," she protested. "I don't have forever."

She earned a smile for that one. "You'd make a lousy cop," he informed her, running that same finger down her nose. "Stay put. The lieutenant says we have a lead on your breaking-and-entering friend. I'm going back to talk to him personally. That should tear things wide open. I promise. I'll get you back to Chicago as soon as I can."

She tried one last time. "Don't go."

He didn't even smile this time. He just kissed her good-bye, a soft lingering kiss meant for memories when the two of them had nothing else. It finally loosed the tears, and Lee didn't bother to wipe them away. He was slipping through her fingers and there was nothing she could do about it.

"You never did ride a horse," she protested, her voice nothing more than a strangled whisper.

He shrugged and let go. "Maybe next time." And then he turned to leave, and she knew there would be no next time.

* * *

Lee walked out of the terminal before the plane left and she refused to look back. All the way home she wiped her eyes and sang along with whatever was on the radio and promised herself that she'd never be such an idiot again, knowing perfectly well that she'd be an idiot again the minute she set foot in Chicago.

Amanda was right. There came a moment when a woman had to understand that saving a man simply wasn't worth it. Lee just wasn't sure she'd reached that moment yet, and already she was planning on how exactly to wage her campaign.

She planned it all the way home and during the time she shoved a few extra clothes into that ubiquitous little backpack and while she saddled up her little roan filly, and while she said a temporary goodbye to her family, as if she really were heading off to the other end of the world. Where she was really headed was up to the high meadow and the cabin that still stood from the time the first Kendalls had settled the valley.

The cabin had always been there for them all, a refuge from whatever was bothering them, an oasis of calm in a sometimes noisy family. Jake had kept it that way, even in the days when he'd been a boy trying to scrape a living off the ranch. Lately Amanda had added heating for the winter and computer support, perfect for a writer, like herself, who wished to escape to the solitude of the empty mountains for inspiration. Lee added pictures and music, since with Jake's family taking up more and more of the main house, she spent a lot of time up there.

Jake protested, but Amanda held him still as Lee swung into the saddle. Amanda knew what Lee needed. Lee just wished Lee knew. She did know, though, that she couldn't stay at the ranch, where she'd hoped for so much, so she turned Apple Annie up toward the north mountains and the meadow with its little one-room house, where maybe she could sit out on the old porch and listen to the old voices in the wind.

* * *

For the next few days, she did her best to listen to those old voices that usually settled her. She sat out on the porch in the early morning to watch the wildlife nudge up to the stream. She wandered the meadow and the high aspen wood, and she sat down to her computer at night with a fire crackling in the hearthstone fireplace to try and let the words loose that had clotted up against her chest. She tried to pretend that everything would be okay if she wanted it to be. For the first time in her life, she wasn't sure. She wasn't sure at all.

For the first time in her life, she made her plans of recovery as she wiped away the tears anticipating loss.

On the fifth morning, Lee woke up feeling puffy and listless and empty. She knew darn well she should get herself outside to exercise off the doldrums, but she simply couldn't seem to do it. For once, even the high meadow wasn't helping. Still dressed in Amanda's flannel nightgown, she just sat watching out the window as the meadow came to life. It didn't touch her. Nothing seemed to touch her.

Nothing except the chill of early morning.

If she'd had more energy, Lee probably never would have made the discovery. She would have pulled on her boots just like she always did and walked back outside. She might have ridden Annie farther up into the hills to pick berries or chase shadows. She might have turned back down to the ranch to sample some of Maria's homemade biscuits.

She didn't have the energy, though. She just wanted to sit there, maybe in front of a fire, with her hands warm and her feet warm and her world wrapped in silence. So instead of her boots and her jeans, she reached for the slip-on shoes she kept in her theater backpack for emergencies. And that was when things changed all over again.

When she couldn't get her left shoe on the first time, Lee really didn't waste time on it. She was just too sleepy and too cranky and too sorry. So she pulled on the right one instead. Then she went back to the left one, as if that would have made all the difference.

Again her toe hit something hard. She sat there in the cabin staring at the stupid shoe as if it would tell her something important. Then she picked it up and shook it, figuring that would teach it a lesson.

It didn't. What it did do was loosen something inside. Something that rolled out on the floor. Something black and cylindrical and familiar.

"Oh, my God…" she breathed, staring at the thing that bounced across the floor as if it had just talked to her.

A roll of film.

A roll of film she must have stuffed into her shoe on the boat and forgotten. A roll that had obviously become wedged so tightly that when she'd shaken the bag, it hadn't fallen out.

The answer to her problems.

The first real chance that everything that had happened would come to an end.

For a long moment, Lee just stood there, frozen, the implications tumbling through her head like loaded dice. Did she really want to know who was on the film? What if it was nothing, and they had to start all over again in another direction? What if it answered all the questions they had, ended the case, and she couldn't think of any other thing to keep Rock close?

What if nothing changed at all?

It didn't matter. She had to know. She had to do something.

In the end, she yanked on her boots after all, threw on the rest of her clothes and saddled Apple Annie for the ride down to the main house and a car. First she was going to take that film into a one-hour place in Jackson and see exactly what was on it. Then she was going to call Rock. Or maybe she wouldn't call him. Maybe she'd bring the film to him in person just so she could see the look on his face.

It didn't occur to Lee as she swung up onto Annie's back and turned her for the house at a gallop that her lassitude had disappeared.

Chapter 15

Rock knew he wasn't getting anything accomplished. He couldn't concentrate. He'd walked back into Viviano's office three days earlier pleading for something to do, and now he couldn't do it.

"Lovely tan, dear," one of the detectives cooed on the way by.

"Get stuffed," Rock retorted instinctively.

It was what he'd come home for. Camaraderie, a little friendly abuse, a feeling of belonging. Rock didn't feel anything but empty.

She'd been right. It had been a magical place. He'd never been to the mountains before, didn't know that the air could smell so good or the light be so strong and clear. He didn't know people could be so honestly, simply good.

It was why he'd come home. It had made him hope. She made him hope, and he was past that. It made him want her, and he knew just how good that would have been for her.

"You ready to go in and talk to him?" O'Banyon asked.

Sonny Varner. They'd hauled him in the evening before while he was busy with his girlfriend. Rock and O'Banyon had spent the last four hours talking, cajoling, threatening and listening. Now, the DA had come in with a decent deal. It was time to really talk.

Rock finished the stale coffee in his cup and headed back into interrogation. His head hurt. He was tired already, and he'd only been back to work for three days. Just like he'd known all along, the time off hadn't made him feel better. It had made him dread all the years that were piling up before him.

"So, Sonny, you have something to tell us?" Rock asked, closing the door on the battered old room where the perp sat sucking down his hundredth or so cigarette.

Rock hated cigarettes. He hadn't realized it until now.

Until last week when he'd stood out in that open air listening to the echo of stillness.

"The DA ain't hosin' me, is he?" Sonny asked. "I really only get a small B and E instead of attempted murder?"

All beady eyes and greasy hair, this one was a poster child for bad hygiene. Rock eased back into his chair and did his best not to groan at the aches he'd already accumulated during the night.

"He ain't," he assured his guest.

At least he hadn't killed him yet. But that was because the Lieu was watching him with an eagle eye. Rock wanted this guy dead sure. He wasn't going to screw it up by pushing his face through the one-way mirror, just because he'd scared Lee like that. Because he'd chased her through her house and probably returned to set the place on fire.

Well, he wasn't going to screw it up unless Sonny didn't serve up.

Sonny served up. Rock knew it the minute he saw that feral little smile betray the sad condition of Sonny's teeth.

"Okay then," their prime suspect said, leaning forward to stub out one cigarette and pick up another. "How's this for news? Did you know there was a poor guy murdered the same day your girl went under the tires for the first time?"

"Which you did."

A shrug of acquiescence. "Neither here nor there. She took a picture she shouldn't have, and I was hired to make sure nobody found it. It would have been enough to take my man down, you know what I mean. And you know, I only attempted. He did the big time. Now that man, I got his name, you want it."

"He murdered this unfortunate guy?" O'Banyon asked.

"Yeah. Seems the police were too interested in him for my man's own good. Seein' as how this poor unfortunate guy has a mouth like a PA system, he thought he should just...prevent problems. Now, you want his name or not? I think you're gonna be real surprised."

Rock was surprised. He was so surprised, he stalked right out of the room and put out an APB. And then he called the ranch in Wyoming to make sure Lee knew, too, only to find that evidently ranchers took some time away, too. Only ranchers evidently didn't have answering machines.

For some reason, that made him nervous. It made him even more nervous when an hour later his suspect still hadn't been found.

"Wyoming has police," Viviano reminded him.

Rock faced his lieutenant with every ounce of control he had. He could barely stand still. He was too far away. Too far. And they were standing in the Lieu's office like Rock was asking for an extra holiday or something.

"Come on, Lieu. I pulled a couple of favors with the feds. I can catch a ride in thirty minutes that would put me there in under four hours. I need to get there, just in case. She doesn't know yet."

Viviano didn't react. Rock did his best to wait out his boss. He knew he was being irrational. The Lieu was right. Rock would probably be in the air when the man showed up at the station, thousand-dollar-an-hour lawyer in tow, to turn himself in. If he'd somehow caught wind that the police had Sonny, he was probably moving as fast as his money let him in the exact opposite direction from anybody who could come between him and his freedom. It would make more sense to notify Lee's local authorities and let them get hold of her. Let one of them accompany her back so she could ID Sonny and put a nice, clean wrapper on the case.

Rock didn't care about sense. His gut was gnawing at him. His good sense was being overridden by his need to move.

He needed, suddenly, to see her. To know she was okay. To guard her himself so he knew she was safe out there in her mountains where the bad guys didn't come.

He had to keep her away from those streets she thought she knew, because she didn't know like he did what they'd end up doing to her.

"Get outta here," the Lieu growled, leaning back in his chair.

"O'Banyon's making the Wyoming calls!" Rock yelled to his boss on his way out. "If you hear from her, tell her to stay put!"

"Just make sure she's okay!"

Lee tried to call Rock from the ranch house on the way out to develop the pictures, but he was tied up. So she called Gen, just to cover her bases. In case anybody asked.

"I tried to get you," she'd say with perfect sincerity. "I even left a message with my sister." That way he couldn't argue too much when she showed up at his office with the photos in her hand.

Not that they were all that much to crow about. Maybe Rock would see something she didn't. When she stopped by the empty ranch house on her way back for a glass of Kool-Aid and a note to Jake, she took the time for her fifteenth or sixteenth look at the pictures.

Sailboats. She saw a lot of sailboats. A few had tacked close enough for her to make out faces on the shots, but she didn't know who she should be looking for, so they all seemed like blurred strangers. She'd taken a few of the do-ings on the boat, but that wasn't anything she didn't expect. Creighton toasting success and Creighton at the wheel and Creighton below in front of open cabinets fixing lunch.

Lee almost found herself grinning. If nothing else, maybe she could use them to make Rock jealous. Creighton did look damn good in white duck trousers and an open blue shirt. He also had an awfully well-stocked galley on his very expensive boat. She could make out full bags of something inside the open cabinet doors.

But that would wait. She needed to figure out what else there was she wasn't seeing.

She had three pictures of the skyline from the water. Lee allowed herself to admire them just for a moment—she really had caught the sharp peaks of the buildings against the sharper blue of the sky and the soft billow of a lone strand of clouds—before setting those aside. Unless the city of Chicago was angry at her for unauthorized picture-taking, she couldn't see what importance those could have.

The only two left were of Gen and the crew at Memorial that morning. Lee had snapped a couple of shots at the ER triage station where they'd been sharing a little birthday cake for one of the nurses. No surprises there. Gen, Abbie grimacing over the chocolate she was going to have to work back off, Tim walking down the hall, nurses and doctors and nothing else.

No surprises. No answers.

Lee finished off her glass of punch and considered again what she should do. She really was stuck out here in the middle of the mountains with the one piece of evidence Rock seemed to need. She had no idea what it was he might find pertinent in it, and she couldn't seem to get hold of him to find out.

Well, she thought, if Muhammad won't come to the mountain.

The thought had barely cleared the starting block before Lee was on her feet. It only made sense, after all. Rock needed the pictures, and she needed to see Rock. Therefore, the only course of action open to consideration was the one she'd been surreptitiously talking herself into all morning. The one she'd made arrangements for on the way back to the ranch. She was flying to Chicago.

The only problem was, her credit card was sitting up at the cabin, and if she wanted to pay for the ticket she'd reserved, she was going to have to charge it.

Lee took another quick look around, as if that would change things. The hands were out preparing to bring the horses down from the high meadows. Jake and Amanda and the kids were due back from the horse auction at Casper later that afternoon. If Rock called, he wouldn't get an answer, and if he didn't get an answer, maybe he'd call Gen, who knew all about the pictures.

Lee checked her watch. Just about two o'clock. She could still catch a flight out and maybe make it to Chicago tonight. With any luck, she could see this whole thing wrapped up in a few days, which meant she might still have a chance at maybe part of the run of *Long Day's Journey*.

Lee smiled. Poor Marlyse. Just when she thought she had a free run at it. Poor Rock. Just when he thought he was safely away from her.

It took Lee no more than a few minutes to scribble the pertinent facts down for Jake and Amanda. She didn't want them to worry, after all. She just didn't want them to stop her. Then, feeling hopeful for the first time since she'd first set eyes on Rock O'Connor, she bolted for the door.

She was already up on Annie when she thought she heard the phone ring. Instead of turning back to answer it, she kicked the filly in the flanks and pointed her toward the high meadow. If she answered the phone right now, somebody'd just talk some sense into her. And today, she didn't want sense. She wanted to be in Chicago.

Rock called on the flight to Denver. He called from Stapleton International and again an hour out of Jackson Hole. Still nobody at the ranch. The sheriff had been by once, but hadn't found anybody there. The APB in Chicago had turned up zilch except for the fact that several checking and savings accounts had been cleared out, and the odds were that their man had taken his money and run. Rock was praying for that one.

"Oh, by the way," O'Banyon said after filling him in on the rest. "The sister called. Said you should call her back."

"The sister?"

"Yeah. The doc. Said it was important."

"And you didn't call her?"

"I just found the note."

Rock called, praying that the news was good. At least neutral. It wasn't.

"She called this morning about ten or so," Gen told him. "She said she tried to get you, but you were busy."

"To tell me she'd found the film."

"She was on her way in to get it developed. I told her not to, but you know Lee."

"And you said he was there when she called?"

"Well, yeah. He just stopped by to see how I was doing. To make sure Lee was all right. Are you positive it's him?"

"We're positive. Does he know where Lee is?"

There was a pause now. A new note of dread that crept into the brisk, positive voice. "I think I might have mentioned the ranch. He knows where it is. We're always talking about it."

Rock felt the first flush of relief. "Well, I doubt he could have beaten me here. I took the first flight out."

Another pause, the kind he was beginning to hate. "He has his own plane."

For a minute, Rock couldn't speak. He couldn't even think. Lee had called while he'd been in interrogation. And when she hadn't gotten Rock, she'd inadvertently ended up notifying a man who could have flown directly to Jackson.

"Excuse me, officer," the stewardess interrupted gently. "You need to fasten your seat belt."

Rock nodded blindly. "Keep calling the ranch," he told Gen. "Try and get her. Tell her to stay put. Not to let anybody in but me."

"She might be up at the cabin," Gen protested.

Rock fought an urge to jump to his feet. He was trapped. Too far away to help, too late to prevent what was going on.

"Call her," he insisted and then hung up.

He used the phone again to set up his plans. Action, precaution, coordination. Positive motion that usually gave him at least a sense of control in a perilous situation. This time it didn't help. No matter what he orchestrated, Rock could feel her alone out there with no one to help her, happily oblivious to the danger that approached.

And he was too far away to help.

Oh God, he prayed, eyes closed, heart hammering. She doesn't deserve this. Let me get there. Just let me get to her, and I won't ask anything more in this life.

Just let her be sitting at the kitchen table when I show up, drinking Kool-Aid with the local sheriff and laughing about how much I overreact.

For once, just for once, let my gut be wrong.

Fifty miles away, Lee pulled Annie to a stop at the front porch of the cabin and swung down to tie her up. Lee's mind was on details. Notes she had to leave to appease the angry older brother gods, connections she had to make. Police she had to placate.

She didn't care. Suddenly, for the first time in what seemed like years, she felt like smiling. She was going to see Rock, and there wasn't a darned thing he could do about it.

She was so preoccupied that she got a boot up on the porch before she saw the note taped to the door. Lee grinned. Must be from that new deputy over at Lost Ridge. He was the only one in the county who didn't call her Lee.

"Ms. Kendall," it read in looping scrawl. "Please get back to main house. Urgent."

He could have waited up here for her to get back, she thought. If he'd come in and out the road, she'd make it back down to the ranchhouse before he did. But then, he didn't know where she was. He probably figured he'd wait where there was a phone and an indoor toilet. It must mean that Gen had finally gotten hold of Rock for her. Good. Lee might even let the deputy escort her back to the airport so she could return to Chicago. That was if he wouldn't mind explaining this all to Jake later.

She didn't bother to take the note down. Instead she reached for the door. Before she could do even that, it swung open on its own.

"I see you got your message."

And Lee, whose first instinct was to smile in greeting, realized that she wasn't going to Chicago after all. She'd been right about those pictures. Something in them was dangerous. So dangerous that the man standing in the doorway had come a thousand miles to find a cabin in the middle of the mountains just to get them back.

"What are you doing here?" she asked, anyway.

The gun in Tim LaPierre's hand was all the answer Lee needed.

Chapter 16

"What the hell is going on?" the voice boomed from the back door. "Where the hell is Lee?"

Rock looked up from the topography maps spread out on the kitchen table and faced Lee's older brother, who was shouldering his way through law enforcement officials like Moses hitting the edge of the Red Sea.

Jake Kendall was the last thing Rock wanted to deal with right now. Even so, he owed the man that much. Especially since it had been Rock who'd let Tim LaPierre this close to Lee in the first place.

"We've been trying to get hold of her," he said, straightening to face the rancher. "I think she'd up at the cabin you keep. A helicopter spotted a horse up there."

Jake planted himself in front of Rock like a mountain of challenge. Rock didn't give an inch.

"And?" the man demanded, only his eyes giving him away. Rock knew he was holding his temper with nothing more then awesome control. He saw the fear glitter in the other man's eyes and understood it.

Rock motioned to the other men in the room. "And we're going to get her."

"From what? We haven't had a range war in years."

"From the man I brought her out here to hide from. Dr. Timothy LaPierre. He killed a man who was helping him in a scheme to defraud insurance companies, and we think Lee accidentally got proof. At least, she ruined his alibi by getting a picture of him at the hospital at the time of the victim's death. Nobody else remembers seeing him there, so Lee is carrying all the evidence."

The brother's voice was even quieter, the tic at his jaw more obvious. Rock noticed he hadn't even bothered to take off his hat, and that he couldn't see his eyes again.

"So you think he has her up at the cabin?"

"We also spotted a green four-by-four tucked into the woods behind the house. Any other reason for it to be there?"

No answer, which meant just what Rock had feared all along. Out of the corner of his eye, he saw Amanda Kendall reach the edge of the room, her eyes wide and eloquent. Rock didn't know what to say to her, either.

"How do you know she's still alive?" the brother asked in that deadly quiet voice of his.

Rock took a slow breath and faced Lee's brother with the truth. "We don't."

Rock saw it coming and didn't flinch. Jake Kendall reared back with every ounce of anger in him and threw a punch the size of Detroit. One minute Rock was standing there facing him, the next he was sprawled in the kitchen floor with a jaw that grated and a head that was spinning sideways. The room erupted with drawn guns and officials grabbing the rancher from behind.

"Knock it off," Rock growled, giving his head a good shake to clear it. "I deserved that."

Climbing back to his feet, he steadied himself against the island in the middle of the room where the gleaming copper pots that hung from the ceiling still swayed from the disturbed air. As guns were reholstered and Jake shook off his guard, Amanda worked her way through the crowd. She didn't say a word, just walked over to the refrigerator that took up the corner and opened up the ice compartment.

Rock turned his attention back to Jake. "Help us get her out."

Jake took one look around at all the uniforms and firepower and shook his head. "No way. You wouldn't get within four miles of the place. He'd spot you like a crow in a cornfield."

"Then what do we do?"

Jake stared down Rock, as if that would make a difference. "I go alone."

"I really never wanted to hurt you," Tim was saying as he secured another knot with the precision of a ... well, a surgeon.

Lee giggled without meaning to.

Tim stopped and looked up. "You think that's funny?"

She closed her eyes, shook her head. This was not turning out to be the kind of day she'd been planning at all. "No," she said. "It's a ... breathing technique I learned in theater. To calm me."

Tim nodded as if that made perfect sense. Giving the knots one last tug at the cast, he retrieved the shiny little semiautomatic handgun he'd brandished and headed back for the remains of the fire he'd set with the film.

"I did my best to keep you separate from everything," he said, taking the poker in hands he'd protected with surgical gloves.

"Separate?" Lee demanded. "You hit me with a car. You had somebody break in and then burn down my house. What do you call involved, Tim?"

"You weren't supposed to be home," he insisted. "Neither of you. I told him that. I just wanted the evidence destroyed. I didn't want you hurt ... especially after I got to know you." His smile, even now, was compelling. Lee couldn't imagine what kind of rationalization he had to practice to keep himself going. "My God, do you realize how upset I was when I realized that it was Sonny who'd hurt your wrist again? I almost fired him that night."

"And the hit and run?"

He shrugged. "Sonny's one of the best fall-down artists around. He would never have really hurt you. All we were really after was your purse." He flashed another rueful smile, a little boy excusing the mud on his best clothes. "We were just in the business to make money. Not to hurt anybody."

Lee closed her eyes a second and battled for some sanity. Sonny really wouldn't have hurt her. Sonny had wanted to kill her. She'd heard it in his voice that night.

"If I could only get you to stay here and keep quiet until I'm safely away," he said, "I'd just leave you be."

For some reason Lee knew he really thought he meant it.

"Why did you kill him?" she asked.

"Barney?" Tim looked up, considered the answer with the same kind of clinical detachment he had the night they'd talked about wines. "The police had come around to talk to him. His penchant for using nothing but late-model Fords in the accidents, I guess. It tipped them off. He was getting too nervous. I think he was going to turn state's evidence against me, and by then we were into multimillion-dollar fraud."

Lee watched the elegant way Tim moved. She watched those brilliant, gentle physician's hands and realized that Rock was right. She didn't know anything. She didn't want to know anything, not if it meant she should suspect everyone around her. Not if it meant she had to realize that most real criminals wore friendly smiles and misguided talent.

"But why?" she asked, anyway.

He looked up at her from where he was stirring the last of the ashes, just to make sure nobody could reconstruct the negatives later. "To protect myself," he said.

If she just listened to him, it all made perfect sense. Perfect, terrible sense. He wasn't insane or angry or conniving. He was practical. He was, after all, a surgeon, trained to consider all possible courses of action and then, simply, act. And now he was acting out of a sense of simple preservation.

"How far are we going?" Lee asked, resettling herself in the hardback chair so her hands weren't pulled so tightly behind her.

"I'm not sure," he admitted, giving the ashes one final poke and then turning his attention back to her. "Where would you like to go?"

Lee did her best to stay in control. Using the real breathing techniques, she slowed her bounding heart rate just a little. Her fingers were aching with the pressure of trying to get both arms behind her back, and her brain was racing with questions, suppositions and imagination.

Terrible imagination. Because no matter what Rock said, she understood too well sometimes what people were capable of. She knew damn well that no matter what Tim felt for her, he would end up convincing himself that Lee would be too great a liability to be carted around. She'd last as long as the threat of law enforcement elevated her worth as a hostage. After that...

After that, Lee simply didn't think about. She thought instead about how to calm herself down. How to focus herself, as if this were an acting exercise. How to get herself out of this alive before somebody else got involved.

At least Rock wasn't here. She might be able to keep her head long enough to get away. She'd never do it if she knew Rock was involved. She'd be too afraid of what he'd do to protect her.

He was in Chicago, though. It was all right.

"You have the plane," she said to him. "Wherever you want."

Stay alive, she thought. Stay thinking. Figure out a way to give yourself enough time to escape.

Tim actually considered her suggestion. "Does Brazil sound okay to you? There isn't any extradition there."

"Brazil sounds great."

She wasn't going to get within five thousand miles of Brazil, and she knew it.

Calm, stay calm. Think.

Lee looked around for ideas and came up with nothing. Her hands were tied behind her back, Tim had a gun, and there was somebody riding up the meadow.

She took a second look out the window just to be sure and almost gasped out loud.

Jake.

Oh, God, what was he doing here? She had to warn him. She had to get him away so he'd be safe. Lee took a look at Tim, who was making a final check of things in the cabin, that deadly little gun still in his hand, and she decided the only defense was an offense of some kind. Any kind at all.

"Oh, God," she promptly gasped. "It's Jake."

Tim whirled around to see that Lee was looking out the front window and followed suit. He saw the very same thing Lee did, a horse approaching in a slow, easy canter along the stream, the rider tall and straight and hidden beneath the low brim of his battered old hat.

"My brother," Lee explained, already on her feet to get a better look. Trying to figure out what was wrong with what she saw. "He must have had one of the hands tape that note on the door. Damn it, anyway."

"He knows," Tim insisted, turning his attention on her, his eyes suddenly restless with surprise. "He wouldn't be here if he didn't."

Lee shook her head, almost eye to eye with the surgeon, her heart racing and her hands sweating. "He'd be riding flat out if he thought there was a problem. He's just up checking stock, figured he'd drop by and ask why I didn't come down. I've been helping his stockman with a mare who's having trouble. Jake takes his horses seriously, ya know? Drives me nuts."

She took another look out the window and realized with a start that her instincts had been right. Something was funny. Jake wasn't on Buck, his stallion. He wasn't riding any of his regular string, and that wasn't like him.

He was riding a bay. A big bay with a blaze down its nose.

He was on Pokey.

Good God, she thought, trying her damnedest to be surreptitious. What the hell was Jake doing? Pokey was the oldest horse they owned, a quiet mare kept around just for greenhorns. Jake had never in his entire life lowered himself to riding an animal that slow and patient.

Not only that, but he looked as if he'd been stuck on that horse with a glue gun. Lee had never seen Jake look so stiff and uncomfortable in a saddle, not even the time he'd broken his ribs from a bad bronc. Jake worked a horse better than any man had a right to. And right now he was riding like he'd never been on a horse in his—

"Oh, my God—"

Tim looked around again just in time to catch the dreadful realization in Lee's expression.

"What?"

She turned away from the window. Did her best to pull herself together enough to bluff through this, even though her heart had just dropped right to her feet. She'd been afraid before. She'd just exploded straight to blind panic.

It wasn't Jake out there. It was Rock. Rock, riding a horse he'd never been on before, up a valley he didn't know, toward a cabin he'd never seen. Rock, come to save her.

Rock, come to get himself killed. Oh, God, she had to do something.

"Please," she said, needing no talent to act so desperate. "I'll do anything you ask. I'll go anywhere, swear to anything, carry anything. Just let me talk him into going home."

Tim hesitated and turned to take another look.

Lee refused to let him. "Please!" she begged, her voice strident enough that Tim turned back to her without noticing that he might actually recognize the approaching rider. Keep that hat low, Lee begged silently. Stay on the damn horse. Just don't let this man know you know less about horses than I do about double plays. "He's my brother. You know what he means to me, Tim. It's not going to cost you anything, I promise. I'll just yell at him, like he's interrupting something, and tell him I'll be down tomorrow when my work's done. He understands that. Amanda does that to him all the time when she's on a hot deadline for a book.''

She was babbling now; she knew it. But Rock was getting close, and Lee didn't know what to do about it. She didn't know what he was planning, except that the last time she'd seen him he'd carried a terrible shade of fatalism in those deadly dark brown eyes. Please, God, she prayed, and could think of no more. Please . . .

''Go on,'' Tim said, and Lee's breath escaped in a painful gasp.

''My hands . . .''

He undid the knots, as precisely as he'd tied them. Lee did her best to control the sudden trembling.

''Stay right here,'' she begged and turned to him a final time. ''I'll get him to go away.''

And taking another calming breath, she pulled open the door and stepped out onto the stage.

He could make a good horseman one of these days, Lee couldn't help but think. He looked great up there, even though she'd finally caught that look of incipient panic a new rider always had when he was about to have to rein in his horse for the first time. Stepping off the porch, she held up her hand, and Pokey, just like she always did, turned for her and slowed to an easy walk.

''I'm a big girl, Jake,'' Lee said loudly enough that Tim could hear her. ''I don't need you to check on me every ten minutes of the day.''

Rock lowered his head so there was only shadow beneath the brim of the hat. Pokey, ever the oversized puppy, nuzzled the side of Lee's neck and whuffled in greeting. The sun was balanced atop the mountains at the far end of the meadow and the shadows had stretched into long geometrics. A long V of geese sailed across an azure sky at the edge of sunset. The meadow had never looked quite so lovely. At any other moment of her life, Lee would have been moved almost to tears by the perfection of it all. Rock up here in the meadow with her, the world settling into another spectacular dusk that would nestle them like lovers into night.

Lee looked up at the man she loved even more than the high meadow of her childhood, and she was terrified for him. She couldn't get her heart to slow down enough or her hand to unclench from around the bridle. She wanted to say so much, but there wasn't time. There simply weren't the words. She wanted to just smack Pokey in the ribs and send her off so Rock would be safe, but she knew better. One way or another, Rock had set the finale into motion, and Lee couldn't do anything but play it out.

"You okay?" Rock finally asked, his voice low enough that from inside Tim would just hear the rumble.

Lee did her best to smile. "See? I told you I'd get you to ride a horse in the mountains."

"He's watching?"

"You're absolutely right, Jake," she answered, voice carefully calculated to reach the back rows. "I am busy. I tell you that every time you come up to make sure I'm okay. I'm okay. Now, go on down or Amanda's going to throw out your dinner."

Get someplace safe before he realizes who you are, Lee begged silently with her eyes.

Rock didn't move. Didn't raise his head so she could see what was at the bottom of those eyes. Didn't betray his feelings or his anxieties. He just sat atop that horse as if he'd been welded there, a tribute to honor and strength and endurance.

"Keep talking," he said. "There are men approaching from the road. We need to get them into place."

Which meant he was the diversion. Maybe the sacrificial goat. Lee didn't care. She had to be careful. She had to keep him safe. Stroking Pokey's nose, she made a show of heaving a sigh of frustration, then lifted a hand to shield her eyes so she could look way across the stream into the woods. "Nope," she said. "I haven't seen any today at all. I haven't been paying attention, though. You know how I am when I write."

Rock made it a point to follow her example, pointing in some vague direction with a glove-encased hand. Leather gloves. Work gloves. Gloves Lee knew smelled sharp with sweat and use. Different than those slick, unreal things Tim was wearing. Lee wanted Rock to touch her with those gloves, those work-encased hands of his. She wanted just one more chance to hold him to her, and she was so terrified she'd never get it.

"He's got a handgun," she said under her breath as Rock talked about elk or buffalo or something. Typical Chicagoan. Didn't know that the buffalo weren't here anymore. "A semiautomatic."

"Well, I have sharpshooters," Rock retorted easily.

"Get out of range, Rock," she begged, holding Pokey so tightly the horse pulled her head back in protest.

Rock resettled in the saddle, reached down across Pokey's withers to touch Lee's hand. Just that. A touch. It was enough to bring up the tears from where she'd been so rigidly corralling them.

"I love you," she told him, finally finding those eyes beneath the shadow of Jake's hat. "I mean it. Now, get out of here."

"I love you, too," he answered, and smiled. A wonderful smile. A smile born of his heart and his dreams and his longings.

Which was how he seduced her into forgetting what he was really there for. Lee was ready to let Pokey go. To push her and her rider away to safety, knowing that Tim still watched her. Rock never gave her the chance.

"Move toward the back of the horse, Lee."

She blinked.

"Do it," he snapped. "Now."

She began to move. She stopped, turned to him. "No."

She raised her hand to slap Pokey into motion.

"Move out of the way, Lee."

"Get out—"

She never finished her sentence. Suddenly, Rock was swinging out of the saddle, and Lee knew just what he was going to do.

"No!" she cried out with every terrible instinct in her.

She didn't have to look back to know that Tim had reacted. She saw it in Rock's gaze. She felt it in the sudden
stiffening of his posture as he reached the ground in front
of her. She knew it the minute Rock grabbed her by the
shoulders and swung her around so that he would be in between her and the gun in that cabin.

"No!" she screamed, pushing just as hard as he pulled,
trying to look over her shoulder at Tim. "Don't!"

"Lee, damn it . . . !" Rock snarled.

They were caught in a deadly dance, Rock trying so hard
to insinuate himself between her and danger, Lee refusing.
Alongside, Pokey danced away, snorting in irritation.

Lee lost her balance. Rock caught her, swung her safely
around just as she caught sight of the door opening to the
cabin. Just as she felt Rock stiffen and grunt against her.
Just as she heard the flat crack of a gun echo across the
valley.

"Rock!"

He didn't answer. He was falling, carrying her with him.
Straight down, flat onto the ground, knocking the wind out
of her. Still holding on, so that his weight fell full on her,
so that his hat tumbled off over her head as he fell and his
head hit the dirt just over her shoulder and he lay still.

Lee heard the explosion of movement from the woods
beyond and knew it was too late. Rock had done what he'd
come to do. He'd saved her with his own life. But Lee knew
she was the one dying out there on that bright, warm summer afternoon in the mountains.

Chapter 17

"I didn't want to do this," Tim protested, his attention on Lee, his gun still pointed in shaking hands.

Lee heard the thudding of running feet. She heard Jake's voice, raw and furious, at the back of the house. She smelled dust and sweat and smoke, and none of it meant anything.

"Rock, please," she pleaded, pulling her hands free of him, trying to move him off her. Trying to find life in him, any life.

He was so still. So heavy and motionless atop her, his eyes closed, his head slack against her shoulder. She was trapped by him, even as she saw Tim step out onto the porch. As she saw the men running around the corner of the house with guns drawn.

Jake was there, and the sheriff and all the hands. She didn't care. All she saw was Tim, all she felt was the weight of Rock's body.

"You tell them that," Tim demanded, stepping closer. "It wasn't my fault."

That did it. Something terrible snapped in Lee and she lost her sense of self-preservation. She lost her compassion and her sanity, all apiece, and she turned on him.

"You did this!" she screamed, her gaze impaling him there as he stepped from the porch, her hands and legs pushing her free so she could get at Tim. So she could get at Rock's gun and kill Tim herself. "You sick bastard, you've killed him!"

"Put the gun down, Dr. LaPierre," someone said.

Lee didn't hear him. She was trying to reach Rock's outstretched hand and the gun still in it. She wanted that gun. She wanted Tim to understand what he'd done with his capricious cowardice.

She wanted to kill him.

"Damn it," she heard in her ear. "Hold still. I'm protecting you."

Lee froze. She wanted to look. God, she wanted to look, but Tim was closer now, standing so the deputies couldn't quite get a good shot without possibly hitting the two on the ground.

"Oh . . . God . . ." she moaned, half relieved, half dreading that she hadn't really heard anything at all.

"Now, son, you want to put down that gun," the sheriff suggested, "before things get worse. Lee, you just hold still, honey. Everything's going to be okay."

Lee saw the consequences flash across Tim's expression. She saw him cast for options and knew just what his next move was going to be even before he took another step. She saw the lawmen circle, and knew that she had to break the deadlock.

"Trust me," she muttered, and yanked the gun out of Rock's hand, praying he didn't move. He was safe as long as he kept playing dead. He'd think her safe as long as he lay sprawled across her so a gunshot couldn't hurt her.

So she pointed the gun she'd taken right at Tim's forehead, and she let the tears come. She let Rock be dead again to her, and that was all it took to be convincing.

"I'm not going with you," she said, her voice flat and empty. "So you might as well shoot me. I don't care anymore. But I think you do. And if you shoot, I will, and they will, and you'll end up being shipped back to Chicago in a tea strainer.''

She thought she felt Rock shuddering against her. He'd better not be laughing. She was having trouble enough breathing and threatening and trying her best to maintain some control at the same time.

And she was doing it flat on her back with two hundred pounds of dead weight across her chest.

''Well?''

Tim didn't say a word. He just took another look over to where the ring of men was closing in, all with rifles and shotguns pointed right at him. He looked down at Lee and saw the determination in her eyes even as she lay on the ground beneath the deadweight of the man who'd come to save her. He saw the inevitability of the situation and, finally, simply shrugged.

The sheriff walked up to relieve him of the gun, and Lee let Rock's fall back to the ground. ''You can move now,'' she said to the man lying across her. ''I can't breathe.''

He moved. He rolled over and just lay on the ground on his back. For a minute, Lee could do no more than stare up at the bright, sharp blue sky. Then she sat up and punched Rock on the chest.

''You jerk!'' she sniffed, completely done in. ''I thought you were dead!''

''So did I,'' he assured her, his eyes closed as if he were just lounging on the grass. ''The next time somebody throws himself in front of you to protect you, could you at least have the courtesy to let him?''

After everything that had happened, that was what brought the real tears. It had all come much too close to the outcome of her play, the one in which the man who'd ended up sounding so much like Rock O'Connor lay dead, sacrificed to a man's need for self-worth. Lee punched at Rock again and sobbed. ''Don't you *ever* do that again...I thought...I didn't...''

That got his eyes open. Lee saw the regret there, the guilt and relief all at once, and it made her cry harder. ''I didn't mean to scare you," he protested gently, lifting a hand to brush against her cheek.

She caught his hand and held on to it, the full impact of what had happened swamping her. "You're such a stupid jerk," she accused, still sobbing. "I was so afraid you were going to do something . . . stupid . . ."

"Like get myself killed."

"Yes!"

"If you're yelling, I guess it means you're okay," Jake offered from where he'd come to a halt no more than a few feet away.

Lee looked way up from where she was still sitting to see the brand-new creases on her brother's features. A new set of Lee Worry Wrinkles. She climbed to her feet and gave her big brother a hug.

"I'm sorry, Jake. I didn't mean to cause trouble."

She knew she was forgiven even before Jake hugged her back.

"You kept your head, squirt," Jake told her, tousling her hair with a hand that was shaking more than he'd ever admit. "I'm proud of you."

Over on the porch somebody was snapping handcuffs onto the elegant wrists of Dr. Timothy LaPierre. A few feet the other way Pokey had lost interest in the goings-on and focused on a nice little patch of clover. By her right foreleg, Rock was still lounging on his back in the grass.

"I'm not careful, Viviano'll give her my job," he mused.

Lee scowled down at him. "You going to join us now?" she asked.

He pointed with his left hand toward the bright sky. "There's a hawk up there."

The sheriff ambled up, his shotgun draped over his shoulder. "You okay, son? You want me to look at that?" he asked.

Lee looked up at him in confusion. He was watching Rock.

Rock was just lying there watching the clouds in the sky. "I'd rather not move just yet, if it's all the same to you."

Something about the way he said that sent fresh chills down Lee's back. "Rock?"

"Yes, Lee."

"Look at what?"

Both the sheriff and Jake turned to her in some surprise. "You couldn't see from where you were," the sheriff offered. "He caught him one in the shoulder when he was tusslin' with you, girl."

Lee whipped around on Rock as if she'd just caught him naked with the wrong woman. "You mean you *were* shot?"

Rock didn't seem particularly upset. Probably because Lee was going to be upset enough for the both of them. "I'm not dead," he countered. "Doesn't that count for something?"

"You were *shot*?" Lee demanded, incredulous that everyone was just standing around doing nothing. That she hadn't even realized it. "Why are you just lying there?"

"Because it hurts to move." He was grinning now. Really grinning, as if he were having the best time of his life.

"You're not funny at all."

"I'm very funny. Didn't you see me on that horse?"

The sheriff nodded assent and pulled out his cigarettes. "Well, you let me know. We got a helicopter on the way. Pay all that money for high-tech emergency transport, might as well use it."

"Hey," Lee protested as they all turned to other business. "You're not going to just . . ."

She was stopped dead in her tracks by a hand taking hold of hers. "Sit down."

"What?"

"Sit down. I'm fine. I told you. It just hurts a little. Ya know, I was just thinking that the last time I got shot, all I could see were trash bins and wine bottles. I could get used to this."

Lee couldn't think of anything else to do but sit down, so she did. She laughed, even with the tears still coursing down her cheeks.

"I should hit you again," she said on a half sob. "You are not fine."

Even Rock laughed at that. "Honey, you don't know how fine I am. I'm lying out here watching the sun go down in the mountains after playing Wyatt Earp on a horse, I got the bad guy, and I get a free trip in a helicopter. What more could a man want?"

Lee took hold of his hand again. She reached up and brushed his hair back off his forehead and stroked his cheek. She ignored all her neighbors and friends who milled aimlessly around now that the action was over, and she ignored her big brother who was standing off to the side a little in an attempt to afford Lee some privacy. Lee had eyes only for the handsome man with the sweet brown eyes who was smiling at her.

"A pretty girl?" she asked.

"A beautiful woman," he corrected her.

She smiled, holding on tight. "And her family."

"And her family."

"And all her friends."

For just a second, he hesitated. Lee saw something in his eyes she couldn't calibrate. She thought, though, it was hope. "Are you sure?" he asked quietly.

She laughed out loud, turning heads and making her neighbors smile with the sound. "I don't think you understand, Sergeant. You saved my life today. That counts for automatic membership to the whole tribe. Family, ranch, town, state. We're like that in Wyoming."

"You are, huh?"

"Yeah. We are."

He held on more tightly to her hand, and Lee thought of all those hours a little boy spent alone in the trees watching a world he couldn't have. She thought of the man who had just been invited down.

"Teaching, huh?" he asked.

And Lee knew it was going to be all right. She could hear the whine of an approaching helicopter. Jake stood just behind her, and at the other end of the clearing men were beginning to meander back to where they'd hidden their cars. It was all over. It was really over.

"I think you'd make a great teacher," she said, the tears welling again. "You have so much to give."

"Only what you've given me," he answered, and brought his hand up to pull her down for a kiss.

A long kiss. The kind of kiss that had her brother muttering and several of the ranch hands applauding. The kind of kiss that left Lee flushed and Rock just a little out of breath. The kind of kiss Lee had been waiting for all her life.

"You sure a famous playwright can live with a teacher?" he asked.

"Are you sure a famous teacher can live with a playwright?"

He thought about it for a minute. Reassessed his future through her eyes. Lee could see it in his. Saw the hope catch and flare where it had never resided before, and she knew that if she gave him only one thing in her life, this was the best gift she could give him.

"It does occur to me," he said as the helicopter chased the hawk from the sky and stirred up the grass beneath, "that it's nice to prevent something for a change instead of just cleaning it up."

"Just think," she said, leaning close so he could hear her. "Together we wouldn't just prevent things. We'd create them."

Rock pulled her close. "Create, huh?"

Lee smiled. "Oh, yes, Sergeant. I told you. I'm a simple girl. I have simple needs. I can't think of anything in this whole wide world I could need with a man like you by my side. Except, maybe, somebody else to share it with."

He grinned, the tentative exhilaration in his eyes more enticing to Lee than any riches the world could ever give her. "We could take them to Cubs games."

"And rodeos."

"Planetariums."

"Theaters."

"Museums."

"Home."

She caught him again. Saw that catch of instinct. Saw it shift and brighten in the realization that she meant the mountains. That she had meant it as his home now, too. She saw his eyes glisten with an emotion the old Rock O'Connor would never have allowed. "Just think what we could give them, Lee."

She smiled at her policeman, who still didn't understand his own worth. Well, she had plenty of time to teach him. And she couldn't think of anything else she'd rather do.

"There is one thing," she cautioned, "we will not give them."

For a second, Rock hesitated.

Lee fought hard, but she maintained her serious composure. "What we will not give them, Francis Xavier Aloysius O'Connor," she said, "are any of our Christian names."

When the paramedics arrived with boxes of emergency equipment and the litter meant to cart off a seriously injured man, they were a little upset to find that man laughing so hard. They were even more upset that it took them a good ten minutes to get him to unwind himself from the pretty blond woman who was kissing him. But what really upset them was the fact that when they suggested breaking things up, no fewer than six of the men still standing out in the field raised guns on them.

And the weirdest part of all was the cute blond yelling up at the big guy with the .30-30 and a scowl the size of the Tetons. "There, see? He did it again and you saw it! He laughed. Gen owes me ten!"

* * * * *

Rugged and lean...and the best-looking,
sweetest-talking men to be found in the
entire Lone Star state!

*Diana
Palmer*

LONG, TALL TEXANS

In July 1994, Silhouette is very proud to bring you
Diana Palmer's first three LONG, TALL TEXANS.
CALHOUN, JUSTIN and TYLER—the three cowboys
who started the legend. Now they're back by popular
demand in one classic volume—and they're ready to
lasso your heart! Beautifully repackaged for this
special event, this collection is sure to be a
longtime keepsake!

"Diana Palmer makes a reader want to find a Texan
of her own to love!"   —*Affaire de Coeur*

**LONG, TALL TEXANS—the first three—
reunited in this special roundup!**

**Available in July,
wherever Silhouette books are sold.**

Silhouette®

Take 4 bestselling love stories FREE

Plus get a FREE surprise gift!

Special Limited-time Offer

Mail to Silhouette Reader Service™

> 3010 Walden Avenue
> P.O. Box 1867
> Buffalo, N.Y. 14269-1867

YES! Please send me 4 free Silhouette Intimate Moments® novels and my free surprise gift. Then send me 6 brand-new novels every month, which I will receive months before they appear in bookstores. Bill me at the low price of $2.89 each plus 25¢ delivery and applicable sales tax, if any.* That's the complete price and—compared to the cover prices of $3.50 each—quite a bargain! I understand that accepting the books and gift places me under no obligation ever to buy any books. I can always return a shipment and cancel at any time. Even if I never buy another book from Silhouette, the 4 free books and the surprise gift are mine to keep forever.

245 BPA ANRR

Name	(PLEASE PRINT)	
Address	Apt. No.	
City	State	Zip

This offer is limited to one order per household and not valid to present Silhouette Intimate Moments® subscribers. *Terms and prices are subject to change without notice.
Sales tax applicable in N.Y.

UMOM-94R   ©1990 Harlequin Enterprises Limited

CAN YOU STAND THE HEAT?

You're in for a serious heat wave with Silhouette's latest selection of sizzling summer reading. This sensuous collection of three short stories provides the perfect vacation escape! And what better authors to relax with than

ANNETTE BROADRICK
JACKIE MERRITT
JUSTINE DAVIS

And that's not all....

With the purchase of *Silhouette Summer Sizzlers '94*, you can send in for a FREE Summer Sizzlers beach bag!

SUMMER JUST GOT HOTTER— WITH SILHOUETTE BOOKS!

HE'S AN

AMERICAN HERO

Men of mettle. Men of integrity. Real men who know the real meaning of love. Each month, Intimate Moments salutes these true American Heroes.

For July: THAT SAME OLD FEELING,
by Judith Duncan.
Chase McCall had come home a new man. Yet old lover Devon Manyfeathers soon stirred familiar feelings—and renewed desire.

For August: MICHAEL'S GIFT,
by Marilyn Pappano.
Michael Bennett knew his visions prophesied certain death. Yet he would move the high heavens to change beautiful Valery Navarre's fate.

For September: DEFENDER,
by Kathleen Eagle.
Gideon Defender had reformed his bad-boy ways to become a leader among his people. Yet one habit—loving Raina McKenny—had never died, especially after Gideon learned she'd returned home.

AMERICAN HEROES: Men who give all they've got for their country, their work—the women they love.

Only from

SILHOUETTE *Shadows*

Join award-winning author Rachel Lee as

explores the dark side of love....

Rachel Lee will tingle your senses in August when she visits the dark side of love in her latest Conard County title, **THUNDER MOUNTAIN, SS #37.**

For years, Gray Cloud had guarded his beloved Thunder Mountain, protecting its secrets and mystical powers from human exploitation. Then came Mercy Kendrick.... But someone—or something—wanted her dead. Alone with the tempestuous forces of nature, Mercy turned to Gray Cloud, only to find a storm of a very different kind raging in his eyes. Look for their terrifying tale, only from Silhouette Shadows.

ROMANTIC TRADITIONS

Barbara Faith heats up ROMANTIC TRADITIONS in July with DESERT MAN, IM #578, featuring the forever-sultry sheikh plot line.

Josie McCall knew better than to get involved with Sheikh Kumar Ben Ari. Worlds apart in thought and custom, both suspected their love was destined for failure. Then a tribal war began, and Josie faced the grim possibility of losing her desert lover—for good.

October 1994 will feature Justine Davis's LEFT AT THE ALTAR, her timely take on the classic story line of the same name. And remember, **ROMANTIC TRADITIONS** will continue to bring you the best-loved plot lines from your most-cherished authors, so don't miss any of them—only in ♥ **INTIMATE MOMENTS®**

Silhouette®

INTIMATE MOMENTS®

™ *Silhouette*®

WIDE OPEN SPACES

Return to Southern Alberta's rustic ranch land as Judith Duncan's Wide Open Spaces miniseries continues in July with THAT SAME OLD FEELING, IM#577.

Chase McCall had come home a new man. Yet painful memories—and an old but familiar lover— awaited his return. Devon Manyfeathers had refused him once, but one look into her soulful brown eyes had Chance focusing on forever.

And there will be more McCalls to meet in future months, as they learn love's lessons in the wide open spaces of Western Canada.